Murder Is Revealing

A Write Club Mystery

Michelle Corbier

MJM Creations LLC

701 Green Valley Road, Suite 100, #325

Greensboro, NC 27408

For more information contact:

www.MichelleCorbier.com

All rights reserved. No part of this book may be reproduced or transmitted in any form or by any means, electronic or mechanical, including photocopying, recording, or any information storage and retrieval system, without permission in writing from the publisher.

This is a work of fiction. Names, characters, places, brands, media, and incidents are either the product of the author's imagination or are used fictitiously.

Cover and interior design by Ebook Launch Covers.

Murder is Revealing

Copyright © 2022 by Michelle Corbier

978-1-7375252-0-2 Murder Is Revealing, paperback

978-1-7375252-1-9 Murder Is Revealing, hardback

978-1-7375252-2-6 Murder Is Revealing, eBook

978-1-7375252-3-3 Murder Is Revealing, audiobook

For Jean-Michel, all my love.

iii

Acknowledgements

This book came to fruition through the assistance of many people. Special thanks to my mom, Lula, who started my interest in mysteries; Corina, Maria, Mary, and Stacie for reading preliminary manuscripts, listening to my gripes and encouraging me through the process; and my critique group members, Frank and Pat.

Epigraph

"I'm confident, in fact, that back regulators will pay close attention to the kinds of loans that are being made, and make sure that underwriting is being done right. But I do think this is mostly a localized problem, and not something that's going to affect the national economy." – Ben Bernanke, July 2005

Prologue

First, she noticed the eyes. Open empty globes stared up at the ceiling in the small office. She hurried over to the body. A scent of expensive perfume hung in the air. In front of a large wooden desk, Candace lay crumpled on the linoleum floor. Her body twisted and her right hand extended away from her torso.

She had dreamt of this moment, fantasized about it. But now, seeing Candace splayed across the floor.... Without thinking she knelt down. Her shaking hand reached out toward the blue silk blouse. She froze. Her gaze hovered over a spot where blood oozed onto the fabric. As she stared at the spot, Candace's eyelids fluttered.

Startled, she fell backward onto her buttocks, bumped up against a chair next to the desk. On her hands and knees, she leaned forward, scrutinized the face. Candace's unseeing eyes never deviated, remaining fixated on the ceiling. The image disturbed her. She drew down the eyelids, careful not to touch any blood.

Cheap metal cabinets hugged the walls on both sides of the room. She scanned the space, considered whether to search for her documents or depart. Eerily silent, the walls seemed to press down upon her. She heard the air conditioner kick on. Cold pricked her skin, goosebumps erupted along her arms. She struggled to remain calm. Seconds ticked by.

Candace wasn't supposed to be there. She couldn't ransack the office with a dead body present, even if the deceased had been someone she loathed. She wondered if anyone heard the shot, unsure she decided to leave. When she stood back up, the room seemed to simultaneously expand and contract. Sweat trickled down her back, her heart raced. Anxious, her hand instinctively reached for the revolver inside her purse. Instead of engendering confidence, the cool steely weapon frightened her.

She backed out of the room, observed the areas where she stepped. Without thinking, her hand reached forward to shut the door. *Fingerprints.* She jerked her hand away and ran, leaving the office door ajar.

Taking the stairs, she arrived on the first floor and hid behind a large plastic tree. A handful of people were walking through the lobby. At the entrance, a woman stood next to the automatic doors.

In the opposite direction, she spotted a red neon exit sign shining like a beacon. With her head down, careful not to be seen, she paced herself and crossed the lobby. She escaped from the rear of the building.

Humid summer air smacked against her face. The sudden warmth made her sweat even more. Before the door closed behind her, she raced across a small patch of pine trees separating the office complex from an adjacent shopping center. Her gait slowed as she intermingled with shoppers. On the other side of the parking lot, she located her vehicle.

Once inside, she locked the door, wiped sweat from her forehead and leaned back against the headrest. Bile refluxed in the back of her throat leaving a bitter taste in her mouth. She craved water.

She counted backward from ten as her heart rate slowed. Her gaze swept the area, she checked her surroundings, listened for police sirens. The thought uppermost in her mind—where to ditch the gun.

Chapter 1

"I'm confident that bank regulators will pay close
attention to the kinds of loans that are being made,
making sure that underwriting is being done right. I
do think this is mainly a localized problem and not
something that's going to affect the national economy." – Ben Bernanke, 2005

June 2007

Situated off Lawndale Drive, her office more resembled a tiny
craftsman home than a medical building. Myaisha purchased it years
ago when she first opened her internal medicine-pediatrics practice.
This evening, only three cars remained parked in the asphalt parking
lot out front. Her staff parked in the back.

In exam room one, reading over the form again, she noticed a section labeled genitalia.

"Hal," she said, "this form requires a testicular exam."

She cracked open the door and called for her medical assistant. "Dina, I need a chaperone."

Boggle eyed, Hal squirmed on the exam table clutching the cloth gown around his body. His voice quivered. "Do I have to do this?" he asked.

After she closed the door, she walked over to the glove box and wrangled her hands into disposable gloves. Re-reading the form, she noted the deadline for the document read next week.

"No, Hal. It's up to you. I can write on the form you deferred the genital exam, and you can discuss it with your recruiter." She watched him contemplate his options. He must have expected a simply cursory examination. Unfortunately for him, the military demanded a complete examination, lab work, and vaccinations. She read the consternation cross his face as his eyebrows knitted.

He cleared his throat. "That's okay, Dr. Douglas."

The visit continued as she questioned his about his sexual history, ordered tests for sexually transmitted diseases and a tuberculosis test in the EHR, electronic health record. She was educating him about how to use condoms as her medical assistant entered the room wearing a surgical face mask and gloves.

With a brief glance at her assistant, she explained what she required. She made a mental note to speak with Dina later about using the surgical masks with the face shields. She believed her medical assistant had undiagnosed obsessive compulsive disorder. A face mask and gloves were a daily part of their occupation, but Dina took it to the extreme—she wore them even when she greeted patients at the front desk or answered phones. She put those thoughts aside and completed the examination.

After removing her gloves and washing her hands, she said, "Bye, Hal. Good luck."

In the hallway, she heard her staff cleaning the exam rooms. The lobby was empty. Hal had been her last patient of the day. She retired to her modest office located in the back of the building.

Behind her desk, she slipped her feet out of her Birkenstocks. Draped her lab coat over the back of the chair and reached over to a side table. She turned on an electric tea kettle and started charting on her patients.

No reason to rush home. Josiah, her only child, started college last fall. He probably wouldn't come home for summer vacation. He barely made it back for spring break, she recalled. The last time they spoke, he mentioned a possible summer internship in Raleigh. Other than Boomer, her black Labrador, no one expected her home. Since she installed an automatic doggy door, even he didn't need her home right away.

She extended her arms in a yoga pose, and stretched her back. The tension in her neck eased. From the corner of her eyes, she glimpsed the photo of her deceased husband. If Sammy were alive, she would be planning dinner. Five years ago, a stroke killed him and upended her life. With her thoughts on Sammy, her fingers caressed the cool silver frame. It had always been her favorite picture of him, taken before their engagement. In the photo, he sported a large grin and an afro, a basketball balanced on his hip. Tears glistened in her eyes. She tasted the salty tears as she swiveled back toward her computer and returned to her charting.

Dina poked her head through the open door and knocked on the adjoining wall.

"Come in," she said, eyes glued to the computer.

Dina adjusted the mask on her face, and said, "Everyone's gone. I scheduled two new patient visits for tomorrow. Do you need anything else?"

Her tea kettle whistled. She dropped a tea bag into a cup and poured in boiling water. "No, I'm good. Thank you. Oh, by the way, stop wearing those surgical face masks with the splash guard."

"But, doctor—"

"I know, Dina, you're worried about infections. You can wear the regular disposable masks. The others cost too much for you to wear every day. See you tomorrow."

"Yes, Dr. Douglas. See yah tomorrow. Don't forget to lock up."

Scents of vanilla and honey filled the room. She sipped her tea and charted. Noises from her staff closing up the office drifted through her door. An appointment reminder popped up on her computer monitor. Her writing group met in two hours. She didn't want to be late. Tonight would be their first time at the new location.

Since their group formed, they never had a permanent meeting place. They gathered in each other's homes, in libraries, or the park. Finally, they would have a consistent place. Her college friend, Candace Knight, negotiated the donation of a permanent meeting place. Surprising given she never knew her friend had any interest in writing.

Myaisha found solace in writing. An avid reader, she dreamed of creating stories from her favorite genres, mysteries and thrillers. She even entered writing contests in college. After Sammy died, writing helped her cope with her grief. Their writers group provided her with a social and emotional outlet.

Given her monetary contribution, Candace would more than likely attend the meeting tonight. Myaisha would make sure to thank her. With a quick glance at the clock again, she considered her task folder. Patient calls. Medication refills. Disability forms. Everything competed for her attention. She realized she had to hurry.

Chapter 2

Kevin hopped onto the sidewalk, a baseball cap low over his eyes shielding the bright sunlight. A man exited the Bradley Building and held the door open for him. Refreshed by the cool air, he muttered thanks as he entered the office complex. He walked over to the building directory. His eyes quickly bypassed the notices for medical and dental offices and located the name he sought. Gold cursive letters spelled out the name Candace Knight.

Stairs offered the anonymity he desired. A heavy gray door led to a stairway smelling of damp and cigarettes. He exited the stairwell onto the third floor. An office door displayed even larger gold lettering. He cracked his knuckles, fought the temptation to rip the stenciling off the wooden door and toss the letters into the trash. Seeing her name on bold display made him angry all over again.

He came to speak with Candace about getting out of his mortgage. He hoped she would agree to assist him, or else. Up to this point, he hadn't worked out the 'or else' part of his plan.

He yanked open the door and stomped up to the lobby window. His hands slapped down on the countertop harder than he intended. A pen bounced off the surface and onto the floor.

The receptionist's eyes enlarged, and she sat up straighter in her chair. "May I help you?" she asked.

He gave only a fleeting glance at her makeup and long, polished nails. The spidery wrinkles at the corners of her eyes conflicted with her youthful dress. "My name is Kevin Washington. I need to speak with Mrs. Knight," he said.

"Do you have an appointment?"

He had called several times in the past week to discuss his concerns. Using her syrupy drawl, Candace had tried to put him off with a complicated explanation about refinancing his home mortgage. The information left him even more confused and he insisted on speaking with her in person. She had gotten him into this mess, she damn well better get him out of it.

He pushed his cap farther back on his bald head and cracked his knuckles. "She's expecting me. I told her I was comin' over."

Even as he spoke, his eyes skimmed the office. He heard traffic from the road outside. Several leather chairs, some flower art work on the walls, and a magazine rack filled the space—nothing of interest to him. From the corner of his eye, he saw the receptionist pick up the phone. She covered the mouth piece with her cupped hand as she spoke into the receiver. Her head nodded as she listened, an occasional sly glance crept his way.

His fist banged on the countertop. "Forget it. I'll help myself. I know the way."

He hurried to the door beside the reception window and found it locked. His burly shoulder pressed against the obstacle. He was mad—desperate. The increase in his mortgage payments had him up all night worrying. The hollow particle board door creaked under his weight, and continued pressure caused the door to break. Without delay, he headed toward the room in back.

The receptionist called after him. "Sir. Sir, you can't go back there. Stop."

She was no match for his long strides. Her voice faded into the background.

He heard someone talking inside the room. From a crack in the doorway he saw a woman seated at a large desk on the telephone. He pushed the door aside, slammed it against the opposite wall. A scowled creased his forehead as he scowled down at Candace Knight.

Kevin's entry caught Candace by surprise. She was speaking on the phone with her assistant, LaDonna, when she heard a crash. Before he flung her door open, she instructed LaDonna to call the police. Now, she hung up the phone and stood facing him.

She said, "Mr. Washington—"

Over the large wooden desk, he leaned forward, glared into her face and cut her off. A bent hairy finger pointed at her. "Don't even try it. I want out of this mortgage. You knew what you were doing selling me a house I couldn't afford."

Her manicured hands smoothed out her suit jacket. She displayed a contrite grin. "Kevin, why don't you sit down. We can discuss this like adults."

His hands waved wildly in her face. "There is nothing to discuss. I want out of this mortgage. I told you what I could afford."

"Kevin, if you cannot conduct yourself appropriately, then I will have to ask you to leave."

Spittle flew out his mouth as he spoke. "I'm not going anywhere 'til you tell me how to get out of this mess. I told you what I needed for my mortgage. You sold me this house to collect a big fat fee."

She buttoned her jacket and lifted her chin. "You are a grown man. I didn't make you do anything you didn't want to do. If you neglected to read the contract you signed, then that is your problem."

"You were supposed to get me a 30 year VA loan. I didn't tell you I wanted an adjustable rate mortgage. In another year, I won't even be able to afford my payments."

"We discussed this at the closing. Now, if you would like my assistance I suggest you sit down and compose yourself. Otherwise—"

Before she could complete her sentence, he rushed around the side of the desk. He snatched up her arm and twisted it.

His calloused hands felt like sandpaper. She smelled the musk of the outdoors on him. Her eyes grew wide, her mouth hung open as she gaped at him.

Two police officers entered with LaDonna in tow before she could react. She looked beyond her attacker, saw the officer in front place his right hand on his weapon. His left hand extended toward Kevin. A second officer stood beside LaDonna.

The first officer said, "Sir, I'm gonna need you to step away from the lady."

Kevin's head snapped toward the door.

Both police officers had entered the room, crowding its small interior. Candace considered the likelihood of her client getting shot in her office. Her one thought, how the bad publicity would impact her business and the stains on the linoleum.

Kevin gazed at where he grasped her arm and released it. Then he stepped away from her with his palms raised.

The first officer directed Kevin down onto his knees. Circling from behind, the second officer approached with his handcuffs out. They cuffed him and led him away.

Candace rubbed her arm and straightened her sleeve.

LaDonna rushed to her side. "Are you alright?"

"I'm fine."

LaDonna spoke in hurried sentences, helped her retrieve the papers spilled onto the floor. "I can't believe he pushed his way in here like that. He broke the door to the lobby."

She ignored LaDonna's comments, thought about how Kevin could have seriously hurt her. She needed to be more careful—take precautions. "I'm fine," she said. "I got this. Go call maintenance to fix the door."

"But—"

A police officer returned, interrupting LaDonna's protestations. The officer inquired about what occurred.

Over LaDonna's objections—instead of detailing what happened—she told the officer she didn't want to file a complaint. She regained her seat and disclosed to the officer Kevin Washington had been a client. Retired military, he suffered from post-traumatic stress disorder, she stated. She explained she simply wanted him removed from the premises.

After he collected their statements, the officer departed. LaDonna followed him out.

Settled back into her chair, Candace pulled out a small hand mirror and checked her appearance—short brown hair with blond highlights. She adjusted her bangs and touched up her lipstick. Then she powdered blush over her high sharp cheekbones and green contacts touched off her appearance. She needed to look her best.

The writers meeting tonight would launch her next business venture. She checked the time. She spritzed the air with a few squirts of her perfume—she could still smell Kevin's musty odor.

After powering down her computer, she removed her purse from the side drawer. Before she left, she made sure to load her gun. For good measure, she dropped in an extra magazine.

Maybe she should employ a personal security service. No time for that now. She rushed out the office. She had something important to take care of before the meeting.

Chapter 3

Nicknamed the 'Gate City' in 1891 when the railroad linked it in the south to Charlotte and north to Goldsboro, Greensboro was spelled Greensborough until 1895. Spring weather retained its hold over North Carolina. Summer waited, if impatiently, for its time.

Candace surveyed the area. The mud smelled rank, similar to cow manure. She contemplated her leather boots, wary of the sludge puddles. With her arms crossed over her chest, she reclined against the side of her cheery red Cadillac convertible and waited. She didn't intend to show up late for the writers meeting tonight.

Located half an hour outside Greensboro, the abandoned railway station served as a perfect place for an inconspicuous rendezvous. Ominous ash gray clouds loomed above, a momentary break in the rain which threatened a downpour at any moment. Moist air added a heaviness to the atmosphere.

Traffic noise from Highway 68 muffled the sound of his car engine. She watched his minivan leave the road and bump along the potholes. He was late. Breezes swayed the tree tops. She shivered, wrapped her arms tighter around her chest.

Parking several yards away, he exited his car and sauntered in her direction.

She noticed how hard he looked. Short pepper gray hair, balding on top, he was a middle aged man with a protuberant abdomen hanging over his belt. He looked pathetic—nothing like she remembered. She had admired him for his business acumen. His appetite for risk mirrored her own. At the time they met, Charles Marshall had become one of the most successful bankers in Charlotte and worked for one of the largest banks in the country.

She sought out his advice when she decided to pursue a real estate business in Greensboro. With his assistance she acquired her realtors license and obtained her first rental listings. For many years they worked well together. Voted the top real estate agent in the county for the past three years, the Greensboro association of business owners named her woman of the year two years ago. She owned multiple franchises and last year launched a medical supply business. Now, looking at this practical stranger, she failed to see the man whose personal ambitions rivaled her own.

She smelled rain in the air. Unfolding her arms, she pushed off the convertible with her boot and met him halfway between their vehicles. Eager to conclude their business and get to the writers meeting.

Across the swampy expanse separating them, she asked, "Why did you call me?"

Charles stopped about two feet away from her and snickered. "Not even a hello for an old friend?"

"We were never friends."

"What were we?

"Business partners. That's all."

A gust of wind blew leaves off the tall pines and rustled her hair across her face. She pulled her knee length leather jacket tight around her body.

He glanced up at the sky with a grimace. A large raindrop plopped in the center of his face and dripped down his full brown cracked lips. Nimbus clouds blocked the setting sun. He rubbed his stubble chin. "Fine. Let's get down to business. You owe me, and I intend to collect."

"I owe you nothing. If you were too stupid to hedge your bets, then that's your problem. How long did you think the housing market boom would last? I told you to unload your properties last year."

"No one knew the market would collapse. Besides, this is about more than just myself. If my bank gets audited, they'll discover the loans we arranged for your clients."

"We? I came to you as a customer. If you made bad loans, the bank will come after you." She pointed her chin in his direction.

A long ashy finger flew in her direction. "You knew exactly what we were doing."

A lopsided smile crept over her face. "People have been shorting the housing market for years. Smart people knew how to make money. I acted in the best interests of my clients. *They* were my responsibility. *Your* responsibility was to the bank."

"You won't get away with this." His lips quivered. "If I go down, I'm taking you with me."

"I don't think so. My name isn't on any of the paperwork—just yours and my clients." Hands on her hips, she took a step toward him. "Besides, who would they believe, you or me? The big corrupt banker or the hardworking small business owner."

"Hmm. Hardworking, maybe. Honest, never." His head thrust in her direction. "They'll believe me when I show them proof."

"What proof? You've got nothing. The banks are going to take the blame for this crisis, and the government will bail them out just like they did with Enron, and business will return to normal. If you'd sold your properties like I told you to, then you could be starting something new right now. I just launched a medical supply business, and I'm getting into writing. If you'd taken my advice you wouldn't be freaking out right now."

"Didn't you hear what I said? My bank is getting audited next week. If they find out what we did—"

"What you did." She walked away. After several steps, she turned and addressed him over her shoulder. "Compared to the bank fraud you committed, I didn't do anything."

He spoke to her back. "Don't you understand? You're destroying lives. Real peoples' lives."

"Like you care. Fool. You waited too long. Should've cashed out last year."

Before she could enter her car he ran up on her. Seized her by the left arm and spun her around. He stuck his nose mere inches from her face. His eyes squinted as he squeezed her arm tighter. Their eyes locked.

With her right hand, Candace thrust her purse in his direction. Despite the traffic noise, she heard the click. Her eyes narrowed and stayed fixed on his face. Her heart raced, but she swallowed her fear. She focused on her anger. Should she shoot to kill or just maim him?

He relinquished her arm.

From inside her purse, she strengthened her grip around the gun.

Hands raised, Charles stepped backward into a puddle and soiled his shoes.

She gritted her teeth, brought the gun outside her purse and leveled it at his chest. "Don't ever touch me."

Once she returned to her car, she transferred the gun to her left hand and entered her vehicle with the weapon trained on him. She tasted blood from where she bit the inside of her lip.

He spoke to her through the window. "You're messing with the wrong people this time, Candace. I'm warning you. Watch your step."

"Go back home. Worry about yourself." She smirked.

Opening with a rancorous anger, the sky unleashed a torrent of rain. She drove away. Skirted around the puddles, and observed him from her rearview mirror.

Drenched from the rain, Charles stood in the same spot where she left him. His piercing black eyes followed her car. From her rearview mirror, she watched him draw his index finger slowly across his neck.

Chapter 4

Traffic on Elm Street usually moved at a decent pace. The rapid heavy downpour stalled transit. Impaired visibility forced Myaisha to slow down. Fortunately, the rain slackened as quickly as it started. She checked the time, she should be on time for their meeting.

Her cell phone beeped, she received a text. At the stop light, she glanced at her phone. Deniece wrote she'd be late. She decided to wait for her inside the café.

She had heard about the Green Pastures café, but hadn't tried it yet. At the stop light, she rechecked the address. Three years ago, two of her church friends, Lottie and Mary, started the Greensboro Women of Color Writing Group. At its peak, their group numbered ten members. Now their group would have a permanent meeting space. She hoped this would lead to an increase in membership.

For the past three years, their group maintained a consistent fragility. Meetings often included simply her, Mary and Lottie. Tonight would move their group in a positive direction, provide a larger audience to share ideas, feedback and inspiration. Maybe they could hold conferences, invite speakers, published authors. Excited about this new chapter for their group, she sped up.

Cool air to refreshed her senses as she rolled down the car window. The smell of wet piney trees filled the car. A ray of sunlight burst from behind the gray clouds. She brought down the visor and considered the evening ahead. A real writing group for women of color in Greensboro—about time.

She secured her Honda in the Greene Street parking lot. As she waited at the crosswalk, sharp breezes caused her to zip up her jacket. Around the corner stood the Woolworth building where in 1960 four African American students from A&T State University held the first lunch counter sit-in of the Civil Rights Movement. Efforts were underway by community leaders to establish a memorial to commemorate the event. She knew some of the members on the committee, maybe she could interest them in joining her writing group.

Conversations spilled out of Green Pastures and onto the sidewalk. People dawdled outside the establishment. Encouraged by the crowd, she stepped inside.

The café bustled with a cacophony of sounds. Jazz music floated around the room from a hidden entertainment system. Red brick walls gave the space a warm welcoming ambiance, provided a neutral background for the decor. Black and white pictures of historic icons of the civil rights era adorned the walls along with various multicolored cultural artifacts. Despite the many items, the atmosphere didn't feel cluttered.

A diverse mixture of people circulated around the café. Some were professionally dressed; others wore business casual. With so many people, the space felt overly warm. She removed her jacket and readjusted her beret. Most of the women, like herself, were African American. Women wore Sunday hats, others kente cloth, hijabs, or saris. She felt her attire too informal, but at least she hadn't worn scrubs.

She wished Deniece would hurry, she wanted her to see the turnout. Deniece's interest in the group had been lax. She hoped her friend would be encouraged by the large attendance.

At the counter, she ordered tea. Aromas of fried chicken, barbeque and—curry? Alluring smells emanated from the kitchen. Her stomach growled. The last thing she'd eaten had been a peanut butter and jelly sandwich for lunch. Unsure about the arrangements for the meeting, she decided not to order food hoping snacks would be provided. Before she could step away from the counter with her beverage, someone tapped her shoulder. She turned around to find her friend standing behind her. She smiled.

Candace gave her a tiny peck on the cheek. "Myaisha," she said, "come with me. I want you to meet Harriet. She owns the café."

Without waiting for a reply, she took her by the arm and led her away. They snaked between the patrons, and she escorted Myaisha up to an older woman. Candace addressed the older woman. "Harriet, this is my good friend, Dr. Myaisha Douglas."

Dark skinned with a beaming smile, the older woman shook her hand. Missing a front tooth and a canine, the remaining teeth were all shiny white. Harriet's face glowed with the sweat of labor. Her jaw grinded. Graying dreadlocks draped down her shoulders, chest and back.

"Please, call me Myaisha," she said.

Harriet's eyes opened wide, her jaw froze. She leaned back on her orthotic shoes. "Well, God bless you sweetheart. Ain't that somethin'. A beautiful young lady like you a doctor."

She accepted the compliment with grace. Many of her older patients made similar remarks, amazed to meet an African American female physician. "Your restaurant is very nice. How long have you been here?" she asked.

"I just moved here in January. I had a place off Wendover. I'd been there forever. Then Candace here showed me how I could afford a better place." The woman beamed at Candace and patted her hand.

Before Harriet's praises continued, Candace pulled Myaisha close. "Oh, Harriet, excuse us. I have to introduce Myaisha to some people."

"I was hoping we could chat for a minute." The café owner looked toward her. "If the doctor doesn't mind."

"No problem." She stepped back to give Harriet and Candace space.

Harriet continued. "I wanted to ask about—"

Candace cut her off and pushed past her. "Later. Myaisha needs to meet some people."

As Candace whisked her away, she regarded Harriet, who gnashed her jaw as her smile dissolved, a limp wash cloth in her aged hands.

She frowned, stopped and asked, "Candace, can't you give her a moment?"

"Don't worry about her." She walked Myaisha up to a petite African American physician with long black hair and hazel eyes. "Myaisha, this is Cathy. She's a urologist. Correct?"

She shook hands with the urologist.

"Yes, that's right," Cathy said. "I moved here three months ago. I finished my residency in Alabama last year."

"Where are you working now?" she asked.

After she inquired about urologist's practice, they conversed about medicine and exchanged information. Before she could question Cathy about her writing, she heard glass clinking. Someone tried to gain their attention. At first, because of the crowd, she couldn't see who made the noise. Peering through the throng, she spied a short woman with an afro, who tried and failed to quiet everyone. She recognized Mary Thompkins, co-founder of GW-CWG.

On her tiptoes, Mary raised her voice. "Everyone. Please. We need to get started." Her eyes pleaded, but did nothing to stop the multitude of conversations.

Myaisha recognized Lottie Williams standing beside Mary.

Average sized with a pleasant face and dark complexion, she cast stern eyes upon Mary. Her head shook, she cleared her throat and addressed the throng. She yelled. "Ladies. We need to get started."

The restaurant fell silent. Lottie directed the women toward a conference room behind the café. A queue formed as people gathered their refreshments and personal items.

Myaisha's stomach growled its displeasure. She contemplated ordering something to eat. Instead, she entered the room as instructed. *Please let there be refreshments.* She followed behind Cathy.

As they entered the room, Cathy said, "I'm going to grab a seat up front."

"I'm going to grab something to eat," she said.

"Okay, I'll catch up with you later,"

Opposite the entrance, Lottie and Mary stood together along a wall decorated in an African motif. To her left she spied the refreshment table and headed in that direction. Unfortunately, many other women had a similar idea and she found herself in another queue. She contemplated whether to wait for food or obtain a seat. Her stomach ached another growl as the meeting started.

With a large smile, Mary welcomed everyone and began introductions.

Myaisha felt the enthusiasm from the women, it electrified the room. She looked around and saw beautiful beaming faces, people she didn't know were excited about writing. An evaluation of the line suggested little likelihood she would obtain any food. She searched for a seat as introductions continued. In a short time, she resigned herself to standing against the back wall, hungry. As Lottie detailed the origins of their group, she struggled to concentrate on the speech. She startled when someone tapped her arm.

Deniece joined her against the wall. "Did I miss anything?" she asked.

"No, not really."

A loud growl from her stomach made Deniece laugh. Her friend handed her a muffin. She mouthed the words, "Thank you". Shoulder to shoulder, they directed their attention toward the speaker.

As the meeting progressed, she noticed Lottie picking at the back of her hand and using a pencil to scratch her scalp. *Damn.* She just remembered Lottie had asked her to bring some medication samples from the office. She felt bad, and made a mental note to apologize.

As the meeting continued her concentration wandered. Standing near the doorway, her eyes drifted back into the café where a handful of people lingered. In a far corner, her attention focused on a couple, their heads bent together engaged in earnest conversation. For a moment she thought she recognized the man as Adán, Candace's husband. She could only view the back of the man's head and a tiny portion of his profile. This guy seemed to be flirting with his companion, who appeared to be a woman in her twenties.

She had no desire to become involved in someone's personal drama. All too familiar with life in a small southern city, she understood the danger of gossip. Candace was a grown woman capable of keeping track of her own husband. Disinterested, she immersed herself into the meeting.

Bright canned lights illuminated the space. Cabinets and shelves held small collections of books in individual pockets of the room with authors as diverse as Gwendolyn Brooks to Dr. Deidre Carter

Owens, from Lilia M. Schwarcz to Nalini Singh. Someone took time to compile a unique diversity of women authors. *Impressive.* Laughter and applause brought her attention back to the speakers.

Lottie said, "We'll meet here at Green Pastures the second Saturday of each month. Every Thursday, we'll meet at the downtown library for one hour of writing."

"We call it, '*Think it, Ink it*'," Mary said, interrupting her.

Myaisha noticed Candace waited off to one side. She figured Lottie and Mary prepared to thank her for the donating the space for their meetings. After acknowledging the contribution, Lottie stepped back and invited Candace to speak.

Searching the room, Candace came forward. She peered over the women seated before her. "Let's not forget to thank our hostess. Where's Harriet? Anyone see her?" she asked.

Everyone followed her eyes to the back of the room. Someone near the doorway went inside the café. In under a minute, wearing a head scarf and carrying a dish cloth, Harriet entered the room to a standing ovation.

Candace clapped along with the women. "Let's all thank Mrs. Harriet Tubman Carter, for welcoming us to her café," she said.

With a wave to the group and a smile, Harriet came forward, gave a half bow and said something Myaisha couldn't hear. The café owner departed as quickly as she arrived, her jaw still ruminating.

A glance at her watch caused her concern. It was late and tomorrow she had a full schedule of patients. She motioned to Deniece with a tilt of her head. "It's getting late."

Deniece's head tilted toward her in return. She whispered, "I know. I have work tomorrow. Wednesday bible study ends earlier than this."

She smiled and agreed. They made their way between the women toward the exit.

Lottie started to excuse the attendees when Candace interrupted.

"Before we end this evening, I have an important announcement to make," Candace said.

Many women had already vacated their seats, but turned back around as she spoke. Some continued toward the door and left.

With a smile worthy of a million-dollar toothpaste contract, Candace said, "I wanted to announce I have published my first novel."

The exodus from the room ceased. Women shouted their delight with boisterous applause.

Candace looked radiant, she bathed in their approval. "I am represented by one of the largest publishers in the country," she said. "My book has already received positive reviews, *and* I'm starting a new business to help other aspiring authors. My first ten clients get a discount on my services."

She couldn't hear everything Candace said because of the excited voices. People talked amongst each other and shouted their delight.

Deniece shrugged and angled her head toward the exit.

She joined her and the funnel of women collected at the doorway attempting to depart. As she waited her turn to exit, her gaze reverted toward the back of the room. She watched women congratulate and hug Candace.

In her element, her friend seemed to enjoy every minute of it. Her eyes moved beyond Candace off to the side where she spotted Lottie. The group leader's prior calm demeanor experienced a metamorphosis. Her average face drooped with a deep frown. *What was she angry about?* Unsure what upset Lottie, the wave of women swept her out the door before she could witness anything else.

Myaisha murmured an expletive and executed a sharp U-turn. She pointed her Honda back toward the café. As she left the café, her conversation with Deniece distracted her. On her way home—not two blocks from the restaurant—she reached over to increase the temperature in the car and realized she left her jacket in Green Pastures. A vague recollection of placing her jacket on a stool teased at the back of her memory.

She could have waited to pick the jacket up tomorrow, but she knew what would happen. She would become engrossed in work and forget. This jacket mattered, it had belonged to Sammy. The hospital returned it to her the evening he died, curled up in a clear plastic bag with the rest of his belongings. When she closed her eyes, she could still smell his cologne on the garment, feel him hug her tight when she zipped it up.

Traffic around the café had decreased by the time she arrived. She parked on the street directly in front of the establishment, rushed from her vehicle and ran inside.

A handful of people, not including staff, were still present.

Mary conversed with another woman at a side table.

She waved, but didn't stop. A quick survey of the room failed to uncover her jacket. There should be a lost and found somewhere. She looked around the café for someone to help her, chastised herself for being careless. She was tired and hungry, not necessarily in that order. *Get the jacket and you can go home.* As she stood at the counter waiting for assistance, her shoe tapped against the floor.

She noticed Candace and Lottie immersed in a conversation with two other people. Behind the kitchen counter, she noticed Harriet cleaning the kitchen. She made eye contact and waved the owner over.

Harriet smiled as she slowly walked over. "What can I do for yah, sugah?"

"I don't know if you remember me, I'm—"

"I remember yah. The doctor, right?"

"Yes. I lost my jacket. It's dark blue with a thick plush lining." She described the jacket in further detail.

Harriet dried her hands on the towel around on her waistband and led her to a large closet which held several grass braided baskets like the women make at the old slave market in Charleston. Items hung from a clothes rod and spilled out the baskets and onto the tiled floor.

This must be the lost and found, she thought. "Thank you, Harriet," she said before she dove in. She picked through the clothing, heard Harriet's clicking jaw fade away.

Maybe a minute later, she heard raised voices. They increased in intensity then became hushed whispers. The vacuum felt eerie, she was curious. She stopped her search and took a moment to see what caused the tumult. She peeked around the corner.

Near the cash register, Harriet held onto the edge of a towel while she spoke with Candace. "I'm worried about the café. You never tol' me about these expenses. I don't know how I'm gonna pay these bills."

Candace frowned and pointed a finger at Harriet's chest. "I brought in a large crowd for you tonight, didn't I? Well, stop worrying. My job is to bring in the customers, yours is to sell," she said, then stormed away from the older woman.

Removing a tootsie roll from the pocket of her apron, Harriet stared at Candace's retreating back. She placed the candy in her mouth and drifted back toward the kitchen.

Confused by the conversation, Myaisha set it aside and returned to her search. She located her jacket, embraced it and left the closet. She returned to the register, leaned across the countertop and addressed her comments to Harriet, who worked in the kitchen. "I found it. Thank you, Harriet."

"No problem, sugah. You drive safe now."

By that time, the café had been deserted. Chairs were turned upside down on the tables. The floor swept clean with a light scent of bleach. Outside, a sprinkling of people remained in the vicinity. Myaisha spotted a few people in the parking lot across the street.

Her adrenaline dissipated and left her chilled. She slipped into her jacket and zipped up. When she looked up she heard loud voices coming from her left.

Down the street, Lottie and Candace stood nose to nose engaged in an argument.

Though their conversation appeared animated, but they weren't physically assaulting each other. She didn't worry, she'd known both women for years. The two women were cousins. Family always fought about something or other. She presumed their disagreement concerned the meeting. After Candace mentioned publishing her book, she had noticed Lottie's displeasure.

Lottie neck veins distended as she vented and wagged her finger in Candace's face.

Candace stood stoic, her lips formed into a grim line. She placed her hands on her hips, and shook her head.

Myaisha strained to understand what they said, only able to pick up an occasional word in the conversation. *Should she intervene?* She had seen them argue before without consequence. She doubted anything more than hurt feelings would result this time either.

A police car cruised down the street.

No intervention would be needed on her part. The two women looked at the police vehicle and stepped away from each other.

Myaisha hadn't realized she blocked the doorway. Harriet exited the café and plowed right into her.

"Sorry," she said, and moved aside.

"No problem, sugah." Harriet locked the building and walked toward a sedan parked a few yards away.

She watched the car's brake lights come on. When she glanced down the street toward her left, Lottie and Candace were gone. She turned back around and saw Harriet signal a right turn and her vehicle disappear.

Alone in downtown Greensboro, at night—she sprinted for her car.

As she drove home, she wondered why Candace's announcement would upset Lottie. Maybe she should reach out to Candace, talk to her about her behavior. Candace had been rather curt with Harriet. Perhaps she was under some stress.

Their friendship had finally mended after years of being estranged. They weren't as close as they were in college, but they were friends again. She wanted to return to their previous relationship—rekindle the level of trust and affection they once shared. *How many years had passed since they shared confidences?* Not since—forget it. She didn't want to think about it. She was hungry and tired. Tomorrow she'd call Candace, ask her what was going on.

Cold slithered up her spine and she turned up the car's heater.

Chapter 5

Ten minutes between patients allowed Myaisha an opportunity to read a few pages of Candace's new book. LaDonna, Candace's office assistant, sent over an autographed copy. Flattered, she wasted no time examining its contents.

After a short perusal, she set the book aside and rubbed her tired eyes. Her gaze wandered out the window and onto the trees behind her office. Reflecting on the book, her admiration for Candace grew. In college, when other students wavered about their career choices, Candace unhesitatingly declared she would be a business woman—a successful business woman.

Myaisha had believed her, but she never knew the girl could also write. She could understand why someone would want to keep their writing a secret. Especially when you're successful in your field, it's hard to adjust to not being a success at something else. Maybe she would ask Candace to become her mentor. A noise brought her out of her reflections.

Dina rapped on the office door, her gloves muffled the sound. "Your next patient is ready," she said.

Myaisha hurried to the exam room. Once inside, she introduced herself to her patient and his wife.

Elbows perched on his knees, Mr. Abioye, a retired lawyer, leaned forward and looked up at her through bushy white eyebrows. His dark blue-black skin wizened by time and stress.

After she completed the history and exam, she washed her hands. She sat in front of the computer and pulled up the EHR, electronic health record. "Mr. Abioye, your blood pressure is still elevated, your weight and your blood sugar have increased—we need to do something different."

"I want to try another pill," he said, crossing his hands over his chest.

"We've tried five different blood pressure medications this year."

"I don't care. I want another pill."

She paused, felt her irritation increasing. "We need to try lifestyle changes—diet and exercise—"

"I told you, I'm not eating rabbit food—and I exercise enough."

She pivoted her stool away from the computer to directly face him. "What exercises have you done this week?"

"Are you calling me a liar? I told you I exercised. It's none of your business what I do."

"It actually is my business, Mr. Abioye, you're my patient. If you don't make the lifestyle changes we discussed, you're going to get worse."

Though she focused on Mr. Abioye, her gaze fell upon his wife as their discussion continued. She walked up to the exam table and handed him a piece of paper with information for the nutritionist and a wellness program. From the corner of her eye she glimpsed Mrs. Abioye, who winked at her. For the past year, they struggled to convince him to improve his lifestyle. With a barely perceptible nod toward Mrs. Abioye, she exited the exam room.

Mentally exhausted, she trudged into her office. She barely slipped out of her exam coat before her office manager popped inside the room.

Lips pursed and hands on her slim hips, Yvette said, "Mrs. Doctor, have you heard from Mrs. Knight?"

Yvette's daughter had been a patient of her husband, Sammy. Board certified in adult and child neurology, he cared for the infant, who eventually died from a neuro-metabolic disorder. A few months after the funeral, Yvette showed up at her office seeking employment. Her office manager had distinguished her and Sammy by the monikers Mrs. Doctor and Mr. Doctor respectively. The sentiment still touched her heart.

Looking in her purse for her sandwich, she said, "No. Why? What's wrong?" With the sandwich in hand, she looked up, noticed the glint in Yvette's eyes and braced herself for a long explanation. Under the desk, she shook off her Birkenstocks and stretched her feet.

Rolling up her sleeves, Yvette counted off from her fingers. "We still haven't received the spirometers we ordered *four months* ago. We never received the peak flow meters. The glucometers you picked up last week don't work. The tape measures for the head circumferences haven't arrived. The health fair is in two weeks. We—"

She held up her hands to block the verbal onslaught. "Okay. I get it. Did you call Mrs. Knight's office?"

Before she completed the sentence, Yvette sent her a pointed glare—the expression answered her question.

Her wavy long ponytail danced in the back of her head as she gesticulated. "What do you want me to do?" Yvette asked. "No one answers the office phone. I told you we should've stayed with our usual supplier. Knight Medical is unreliable. They don't know what they're doing. They've never delivered a single order on time. No one has anything good to say about them. Whenever I—"

Her hands gripped the table and lifted her weary body up out of the chair. "Enough. I get it. I'll talk to Mrs. Knight. The supplies are probably in her office." She slipped her shoes back on, opened her desk drawer and retrieved her purse while she gave Yvette instructions. "Call the pediatric pulmonologist, ask if we can borrow some peak flow meters and spirometers. Then call our usual supplier. See how long it'll take them to deliver the items we need. I'll be right back."

After she closed and locked her office door, she slung her purse over her shoulders and exited the office from the rear.

A mile away down the road, Myaisha struck the steering wheel. *Damn.* She forgot to bring her sandwich—no lunch again. Perhaps she should take Deniece's advice and loosen the purse strings and have lunch delivered to her office. She had always been frugal. *It wouldn't kill you to occasionally eat out.* Maybe she should consider it a treat to herself.

Smiling, she turned on the radio. *California Dreaming* by the Mamas and Papas played as she pulled into the office complex located off Friendly Road. Mostly deserted, the parking lot stood as a testament to it being lunch time. She spied Candace's sports car in a secluded corner of the lot.

Inside the building, she climbed the narrow staircase two steps at a time up to the third floor. In the hallway Knight Enterprises was positioned on her right. She entered.

The waiting area was empty. Three rectangular rooms composed Knight Enterprises' place of business, a waiting area, a middle room containing LaDonna's desk, and the final room constituted Candace's office. A door separated each room. She crossed the waiting area to the reception window. *Where was LaDonna?*

Inundated by silence, she became uncomfortable. A hollowness pervaded the space. Nothing looked out of place. The ugly flower prints hung on the walls. Furniture didn't appear disturbed. But the absence of Candace's office assistant signaled something amiss.

She never knew LaDonna to be absent from the front desk during office hours. If she went to lunch, she would've locked the door. Perhaps Candace expected someone.

She tapped on the countertop and waited. No one came. The longer she stood there the more her unease increased. On her tiptoes, she leaned across the countertop and peered through the cubicle opening. To her surprise and dismay, Candace's office door was ajar.

Her heart raced, she gripped the counter and shouted. "Hello? Candace?" Her voice echoed through the space.

Something felt wrong. She abandoned the window and tried the door leading to the back office. Her assumption the door would be locked proved incorrect.

Goosebumps erupted along her arms. She proceeded through the doorway. Shaking, she covered the distance between the door and Candace's room in seconds. With her foot, she pushed the partially open door against the wall to display the entire office. On the floor in front of the desk, she found Candace.

In an instant, she ran to her friend's side, knelt down and started CPR. In her head, she recited ABC— airway, breathing, circulation. Her purse dropped onto the ground as her hand went to the face of her friend. The back of her hand didn't detect any breaths. Slipping her fingers underneath the scarf around Candace's neck, she felt warm skin. She bumped up against a thick gold chain and searched for the carotid pulse. Absent.

She straightened her friend's bent body and prepared to deliver chest compressions. Surprised, her hands hovered over the chest cavity. A sticky maroon colored patch soaked an otherwise pristine unwrinkled blue silk blouse.

Her knuckles pushed down hard on Candace's upper inner eye lid but failed to garner any movement—no positioning or response to pain. Her stomach lurched. She gazed over at her friend's vacant face. Tears pooled in her eyes.

She retrieved her cell phone and dialed.

A flat southern drawl asked, "911. What's your emergency?"

"I need an ambulance. My friend's been shot. She's dead."

Chapter 6

Myaisha felt her heart pound against her chest. She glanced around the room to be sure the murder had left. Once satisfied she remained the only living person in the room, she called her office manager, who answered after one ring. "Yvette?"

"Mrs. Doctor, did you get the supplies?" Yvette asked.

She scanned the office while she spoke on the phone. "Mrs. Knight's dead."

Yvette shouted. "What happened? Are you okay?"

She didn't answer the question. Her mind focused on the scene. "Call the afternoon patients. Reschedule them for tomorrow. I'm not sure when I'll get back. The police are on the way."

"What happened? Was it a robbery?"

"I don't know. I have to go." She hung up, unable to give Yvette answers she didn't have.

Years spent reading Walter Mosley, Ellery Queen, and Agatha Christie taught her the importance of studying the crime scene. She listened—no sirens yet, she had time. *What did she see, hear, smell?*

Spartan in décor, the office held the absolute minimal amount of furniture required to conduct business. Steel file cabinets hugged walls on both sides of the room, with shorter cabinets on the right side. A large desk loomed behind Candace, who was sprawled on the floor at the front corner of the desk.

No personal or family photos hung on the off-white walls, only diplomas. Nothing added warmth to the office. She had never appreciated how cold and bereft of personality the room felt. That was because her friend had brought so much vitality to every space she occupied. Now, the room resembled simple business efficiency.

She gazed down at Candace's contorted body which had one arm bent underneath her torso and the other arm lay outstretched reaching for nothing. She examined the coagulated blood on Candace's shirt, careful not to touch it. *Too late.* She noticed a tiny amount of blood on her shirt sleeve, probably from when she prepared to deliver chest percussions. She tried to remove the substance with a wet wipe from her purse as she continued to examine the room.

A diamond from the ring on Candace's finger sparkled up at her. She counted three other pieces of jewelry—diamond earrings, a gold necklace and a jeweled bracelet. Their presence made robbery less likely. Besides, she couldn't fathom what anyone would want to steal from a realty office.

Wary of her surroundings she retreated away from the desk and noticed the lopsided chair. *Did Candace fall against it after the murderer shot her? Did the killer move it?* Her gaze took in the large desk. Folders, stapler, pens—everything looked to be in order except the papers strewn across the floor in front of and beside the desk.

Wait. The computer. She remembered Candace kept an Apple computer on the desk. *Where was it? And if the murderer took it—why?*

She heard siren noises. She had to hurry. Once the police arrived, she would be removed from the scene.

Smell. She sniffed the air, her nose wrinkled. A velvety scent of Candace's perfume lingered in the space. She never did get the name of the fragrance—now she'd never know. *Forget the perfume.* She closed her eyes and tried to focus. She detected another odor in the air. Her head tilted to the right as she strained to identify the scent—faint, acrid. *Cigarettes?* Candace didn't smoke. Maybe the murderer did, or perhaps it came from the gun. She heard the sirens pitch increase.

She rushed around to the other side of the desk. Her hand reached forward to slide open the desk drawer when the police arrived.

Relegated to the lobby, Myaisha watched the police process the crime scene. Through a slight crack in the doorway leading to the back rooms, she could still see Candace. Police scurried through the office like ants at a picnic. Positioned around the large desk, paramedics packed away their equipment. She presumed they needed permission to transfer her friend to the gurney then to the morgue.

Knowing what awaited Candace at the autopsy—her beautiful friend cut open and dissected—it made her ill. Nauseated, she closed her eyes until the feeling passed.

Police officers and emergency personnel conversed as they worked. She listened for details, any information to explain what occurred. By an act of violence, her friend had been relegated to being referred to as 'the deceased'. With everyone distracted, she attempted to call her office.

To her left, she heard a police officer clear his throat. A large imposing male officer approached and gave her a stern glare. "No calls," he said.

In her left hand, she held her phone. "I want to let my office know I'll be here a little longer."

"I'm sorry, ma'am. You're a witness and the homicide detectives are gonna want to question you."

"I have a schedule full of patients. I need to check with my staff to make sure they rescheduled them for tomorrow."

"No calls. Those are my orders."

She studied the officer. His stoic face, sunburnt and clean shaven. *Did he suspect her of complicity in the death of her friend?* He could, and perhaps he should. Anyone who discovered a dead body would be suspect. She'd read enough police procedural crime stories to understand how they developed a suspect list.

If she couldn't call her office, perhaps she could leave, speak with the detectives later at her office. She asked and the officer refused. She tried one last time. "Officer. I'm a doctor. My patients need me."

His face motionless, he said, "Murder trumps medicine." Conversation ended.

She would never admit it, but the real reason she requested to leave wasn't because of patient obligations. She had to get out of there—go anywhere—to remove the image of Candace lying broken on the ground from her mind.

Another officer, a woman who stood perhaps a foot shorter than the male officer, advanced from her right. Her gentle face remained as impassive as her counterpart.

Before she could make a request, the officer asked, "You're Dr. Douglas, correct?"

"Yes."

The officer removed a notepad and clicked her pen. "I'm in charge until the homicide detectives arrive. You said the receptionist wasn't here when you found the body. Correct?"

"Yes."

"Do you know where we can find her? Do you have her phone number?"

"No, I'm sorry. I don't."

Another police officer came over and interrupted their conversation. While the two of them conferred, Myaisha relaxed.

Now the initial shock wore off—and she no longer played amateur detective—her emotions took over. Tears trailed down her face, a sticky salt residue of sadness. She was understandably upset, but the murder also left her confused. The semblance of order that existed in her world had been disturbed. People like Candace didn't get murdered. Her friend created a successful life for herself—knew the right people and did the right things. Other than a failed marriage, her friend succeeded in every venture she undertook.

Homicides could be random, yet she felt something incongruous about this crime being arbitrary—the scene inconsistent. Candace's computer had been stolen, but not her jewelry. Before the police ordered her out of the office, she spied Candace's purse in the desk drawer. All items a killer would take if robbery were the motive.

Her mind became a tangled web of disjointed thoughts which refused to coalesce into a concrete idea. She chided herself for being foolish. She fought to understand what bothered her. Candace's death, the circumstances, the mechanism. No, something else. An explanation eluded her for the moment.

She straightened her back, and suppressed her emotions. Allowed her analytical brain to take command. With her tears suspended, she concentrated on the events of the morning. Yvette mentioned the equipment for the medical fair around 11:10. She calculated the amount of time required to drive to the building and figured she had entered the office about thirty minutes later. Two minutes were spent in the waiting area while she stood at the reception desk. Next, she discovered Candace and started CPR. Possibly half a minute elapsed before she noticed the gunshot wound.

She brought what she witnessed at the murder scene to the forefront of her mind. Candace's body still felt warm, in addition, the blood on the blouse had coagulated, which suggested death occurred within two hours of her arrival. A lax estimate, but her limited exposure to forensics had been her anatomy and pathology courses in medical school and residency respectively. The police coroner would establish the actual time of death, but this gave her an approximate time frame for now.

She glanced at her phone, considered doing a quick internet search for calculating time of death. Her eyes pivoted left and she noticed the large male officer watching her. After a moment, she returned to considering how the crime occurred. Bullet wound to the left anterior chest, type of gun unknown. There was no visible residue on the blouse, but forensics would test the fabric for microscopic particles. The entrance wound suggested a small caliber bullet, but forensics wasn't her strong point. She had no training in bullet wounds or how to calculate the time of death.

What else could she deduce? She evaluated the front office. Nothing struck her as unusual. She peered again through the small opening into Candace's office. She commanded her brain to disregard the officers and medical personnel.

The female officer finished her discussion with the other officer and resumed her questions. Her writing pad and a pen poised to take notes. "Tell me what happened when you arrived at the office," she said.

Myaisha readjusted her position to face the officer. "I knew something was wrong right away. LaDonna always greeted me when I entered," she said. "I walked up to the reception desk and called out, but no one answered. I poked my head through the opening and noticed Candace's office door ajar."

Even as she spoke with the officer, her mind struggled with the question of why both doors were unlocked. LaDonna could have forgotten, but she never struck her as absentminded. Perhaps Candace requested the doors remain unlocked, which would imply she expected to meet someone. Another possibility, LaDonna did lock the door but Candace unlocked it herself later. Again, the assumption being Candace expected to meet with someone. Did the person she met with kill her? If so, why?

"Yeah? Continue. What happened when you got to the back office?"

She frowned as she recalled her steps. "I—I noticed Candace on the floor. I ran over to her. I started CPR. Checked her airway, breathing—" Her jaw tensed as she stopped to get her emotions under control.

The officer watched her.

She said, "I was about to start chest percussions when I noticed the blood on her chest. I called 911."

The blue eyed officer studied her.

Myaisha maintained her composure.

"Did you touch anything?"

"No. Wait—I touched her desk when I bent down."

"Anything else?"

She shook her head. The officer repeated the same message as the earlier officer, no phone calls until the homicide detectives arrived. She watched the officer leave and join her colleagues.

Alone, her thoughts returned to Candace. She focused on the murder. *Who? How? Where?* Colonel Mustard with a candle stick flashed into her mind. Josiah, her son, loved to play *Clue* as a child. Instead of a library, her murder involved 'Mrs. Scarlett with a revolver in a business office'. Even in tragedy, the brain made surprising connections. Pushing the game *Clue* from her consciousness, she thought about what else she knew. These exercises helped pass the time, but she got no further into the who or why.

A police photographer arrived and chronicled the homicide in pictures. Even in death, Candace caused a stir. Intentional or not, she had always commanded attention—whether as a college student or real estate broker. Her friend thrived on publicity, possessed a magnetism—a strength of personality—she enthralled people.

Not everyone admired of her though, especially women. *Could jealousy have been the motive? A disgruntled admirer?* Myaisha's head tilted up and to the right as she considered the word disgruntled. It reminded her of something.

A memory rose in her consciousness. She recalled the last conversation she had with Candace in the office. Again, she had rushed over to retrieve some glucometers Yvette had ordered. That day, she had interrupted Candace on a phone call.

"Sorry," Myaisha had said. "LaDonna told me to come right back."

"Don't worry. It wasn't important, just a disgruntled customer. Let me get your order." She located the boxes resting on the floor next to the shorter cabinets.

Myaisha had accepted the boxes, and said, "Sorry about your client. Hope the rest of your day is better."

Propped up against the corner of her desk, Candace had twirled a pen between her fingers. "No problem. He's not my first unhappy client. Won't be the last for a while—not with this market."

"What do you mean?"

Candace's chuckle had made her feel moronic. "Where have you been? I'm talking about the housing market. People are freaking out. Blaming everyone but themselves. Girl, the market is crashing. A lot of people are going to lose a lot of money."

With a frown, she regarded her friend. "I'm sorry Candace. Are you going to be okay?"

Green eyes sparkled at her under long lashes. Candace dropped into her chair, a grin crossed her face. "I'm going to be fine—actually more than fine. I saw this coming a year ago."

"But you're a realtor. Aren't you invested in a lot of real estate?"

"Was. I sold most of it. Made out very nicely." Preening, she leaned back in the chair and crossed her legs. "It's all about timing. I bought at the bottom of the market and sold at the height. Perfect."

"What about your clients?"

With a shrug, she considered her nails. "It's business. Real estate is the biggest investment most people will ever make. They should pay more attention to the market. If they don't, that's their problem."

"Candace, most of your clients are church members—friends."

"They're adults. If they made poor business decisions too bad."

"Is this how you conduct business—how you treat people?"

Brows furrowed, Candace had jumped out of her chair. "Why are you always judging me, Mya?"

She had leaned across the desk and touched Candace's hand. "I'm not judging you, I just want you to think about how you treat people. Don't you care about your clients?"

"Don't lecture me about business. After what you did to me."

Myaisha had withdrawn her hand, recoiling as if slapped.

The desk telephone had rung and interrupted the increasing tension between them. Candace had answered the phone and after a few seconds, she covered the receiver. "I'd love to talk more, but I've got work to do."

She hadn't appreciated the sarcasm in Candace's tone but gathered up the boxes and departed. Relieved she hadn't employed Candace as her realtor.

She shook her head free of the past and returned her attention to the crime scene. Now, her college friend lay murdered on the office floor. She zeroed in on the large desk without the computer. *Where did it go, and why would anyone take it?* It must contain something important. *Did it suggest premeditation?* Unsure, she made a mental note to mention it to the detectives when they arrived.

Noise from the gurney being rolled next to Candace brought her out of her recollections. Her gaze skimmed the lobby, absorbed every detail. Her stomach grumbled. She thought about her abandoned sandwich waiting on her desk. Before she continued along that line of thought, she noticed a woman technician, who wore a jacket with the word 'forensics' in large block letters, kneel down beside

Candace. Myaisha observed her employ tweezers to remove an item from Candace's hand. Too far away to be sure, from the manner in which the technician handled the object, she surmised it must be either a hair or a fiber.

She reflected back upon her arrival. *Did she recall any strands on Candace's fingers?* Her brain failed to produce a memory of anything on friend's hand. A whiff of something reached her nostrils. Trying to identify the scent, she turned to see a man glance in her direction.

He stopped to speak with the police officer beside the door. After a short conversation he strode in her direction. Once he stood about a foot away from her he displayed a shiny badge and introduced himself. "Dr. Douglas, I'm Detective de Jesus. I'd like to ask you some questions," he said.

His presence disturbed her concentration. She didn't answer right away. Some thought teased at the back of her mind. She smelled his cologne, spicy.

He raised his voice. "Dr. Douglas? We're ready for your statement."

His tone bothered her. She had remembered something, but now lost her train of thought. She regarded him. He stood about an inch shorter than her with thick jet black hair pulled into a ponytail. A notepad in hand, his suit jacket hung open revealing a gun in his shoulder holster. The suit, though inexpensive, fit him well—bulging biceps tugged at the fabric. *He must work out a lot.*

A gentle touch to her arm brought her back to the present.

She pulled her attention away from his gun. "I'm sorry, detective."

"I understand," he said. "Finding your friend murdered—you're upset. But I need to ask some questions to clarify your statement, then you'll be free to go."

As he spoke, she watched the police process the scene. Her attention bounced from him to Candace. She felt like she was keeping vigil over her friend, ensuring the police did right by her—treated her with dignity. She wanted the killer to be held responsible, to atone for their crime. A murder had been committed, and no matter Candace's failings she deserved justice.

Paramedics placed Candace on a litter. A large sheet shrouded her friend's body. Tears dripped from her eyes as they wheeled her into the lobby and outside. Candace, in body and spirit, had departed.

She watched police file out the office. Not until then had she noticed a distinct difference in tint between Candace's office door and the door between the waiting room and LaDonna's room. The waiting room door looked—newer? She hadn't noticed a difference when she came by to pick up the glucometers the week before the murder.

The detective continued to question her so she couldn't give the door further consideration at the moment. He must have perceived her distraction because he guided her by the elbow outside Candace's office and into the third floor hallway.

People from other offices stood in the hallway gawking at them. Death as a spectator sport. *Ghouls*

She pulled herself from his grasp and asked, "What did you ask me?" She hugged her shoulders, steeled herself for a barrage of questions, impatient to leave.

Mouth open to ask a question; the detective's gaze fell over her body. His vision zeroed in on her legs.

She grew self-conscious. Before she could comment on his inappropriate behavior, he bent down and pointed at her leg.

"Is there a hair on your pants?" he asked.

Down her long legs, her gaze fell on the area he referenced. On reflex her hand reached to brush the substance away.

He caught her hand in mid-air and called over a member of the forensics team.

Her body stood woodenly. She feared any movement might dislodge the evidence. DNA could identify the killer. Once the woman from forensics secured the hair in a small clear container, Myaisha relaxed.

"It must have got on my pants when I checked on Candace," she said, unsure why she felt it necessary to provide an explanation.

He made notations in his writing pad, turned back several pages and read something else. After half a minute, he asked, "What brought *you* to the office?"

His subtle emphasis on 'you' caught her attention. Her body stiffened. "What do you mean?"

"Why you? You're a doctor. Why didn't you send one of your staff? And why did you come by the office today, during lunch?" He crossed his arms over his chest. His pen tapped against his bicep as he waited.

Her forehead creased in frustration. She had answered these questions. *Didn't he have them written down in his notebook?* She sighed. "We ordered some equipment for an upcoming medical fair. Since it was lunch time, I decided to run over and pick them up."

He stared at her. She knew he wanted more. At first she returned his gaze, then she broke eye contact and glanced around the area. Neither spoke. Her hand bumped up against the keys in her purse. Realizing the quickest way to leave would be to give him more, she explained. "I needed to get some equipment for my office and I wanted to speak with Candace about the delay in our order."

The detective opened his mouth, but she cut him off. "I came because I didn't want to inconvenience my staff—because it was my fault."

As his eyebrows knitted into a question, she hastened to clarify.

"We usually ordered our medical equipment from a different retailer. Candace recently started a medical supply business and she needed customers. Since we're—were—friends, I switched my business to her company."

She cleared the lump in her throat and waited for more questions. Her weight shifted to her left leg. Keys dangled in her hand. His silence aggravated her, but also stimulated her to provide more details. Briefly, she informed him about how Yvette ordered the equipment four months prior. Instead of cancelling the order and returning to their previous supplier, she wanted to give Candace a chance to make things right but they needed the supplies for the health fair. She decided to come over and speak with her in person.

Clicking his pen, the instrument hung in the air ready to write. "Why didn't you call?"

Her eyes squinted. "I did—we did. Yvette called. No one answered the office phone." Until he asked his question, she hadn't considered the significance of the call.

"Didn't you try her cell?"

"No. I wanted to speak with her in person. Besides, we needed the supplies. Someone had to make the trip. It made more sense for me to do it."

With a nod he scribbled more notes on his pad. "Do you know what time your officer manager first tried calling?"

"No. The office phone should have a record of all outgoing calls." He scribbled some more.

Peering over the small gap between them, she tried to read what he wrote.

He snapped the booklet shut and motioned for another officer to join them. A female officer eyed her, arms at her side one hand near her weapon. This officer matched her height, but looked younger and more fit.

Myaisha stepped back and sized up the woman. She wondered what they had in mind.

"Dr. Douglas, if you don't mind, Officer Tan will now conduct a body search," he said.

If she minded? Her eyes narrowed as she considered him. Nothing in his demeanor suggested he spoke in jest. "You can't be serious," she said.

The female officer remained detached, unspeaking.

"We're looking for the murder weapon, doctor. This is a homicide investigation. With your permission, we would also like to check your car."

Without responding, she considered his comment, weighed her options. She understood his logic, and wanted to assist in the investigation. She handed him her car keys then allowed the female officer to guide her to the restroom.

Minutes later, relieved the search didn't involve her getting undressed, she exited the ladies room. No longer needed at the crime scene, she exited the building to find Detective de Jesus and several technicians surrounding her Honda. She watched them place her spare tire and miscellaneous items into the trunk. Without a word, she held out her hand into which the detective inserted her keys.

"Thank you, doctor. We have your information. We'll verify your statement. Are you returning to your office?" he asked.

"Yes."

"We know how to contact you if we have any further questions. You're free to go." He stepped away from the car, but remained nearby.

She walked past him and settled into her vehicle. Before she started the engine, she hesitated. Conflicted about wanting to ask her own questions and leave at the same time, she tapped her fingers on the steering wheel. She looked out her side window at the detective. He stood with his arms crossed over his chest observing her. His rigid countenance didn't invite questions. She put the car in gear and drove away.

Chapter 7

A clipboard fell and smacked onto the tiled floor. Clacking reverberated around the exam room. The sound brought Myaisha back to the present. She made no attempt to pick it up. Instead she sat up straighter on the stool, mortified that she hadn't heard a word Mrs. Martin said for several minutes

Her staff managed to reschedule most of the afternoon patients, but some insisted on keeping their appointments—unsympathetic to her tragic loss. She forced Candace's death into the far recesses of her mind and concentrated on her patient.

"I think she needs lab work," Mrs. Martin said. The mother's eyes rested upon the teenager seated on the exam table. The teen tapped away at her cell phone, oblivious to the conversation concerning her health.

Myaisha regarded the gangly teen, who held a cell phone with head phones over her pierced ears. A quick glance at the computer refreshed her memory on the child's medical status. Healthy. Vaccines up to date with normal height and weight. The young woman passed her vision and hearing tests. From her perspective, a regular adolescent.

She slid her stool closer to the mother. "What exactly are you worried about?" she asked.

Large arms gesticulated as Mrs. Martin's eye's enlarged. "Just look at her. She's too thin. I'm worried she's anemic. Can't you check her iron?"

Angling the computer toward the mother, she positioned the screen where the mother could view her daughter's chart. "We checked a complete blood count last month, remember? You were worried about her menstrual cycles. Tests showed no anemia."

She gave her time to read the display, and tried to mask her distraction as images of Candace flashed in her mind. Her jaw clenched. She hid her displeasure at not being able to mourn her friend.

Mrs. Martin shook her head. "I don't understand it. Why is she so thin? I feed her all the time. Nothing sticks. She's fading away. You have to do something."

"Your daughter's weight is fine. She's not having any symptoms or complaints. Her exam today was normal. There is no reason to do further testing."

"Something's wrong. She looks pale, and she's always tired."

Myaisha tapped the teen on the foot. The boots reminded her of Candace, who wore them almost daily.

The teen jerked her head away from the cell phone screen. "What?"

"Cammie, your mom says your tired all the time. Is that true?"

Cammi rolled her eyes so high astronauts saw. "No. I'm fine. There's nothing wrong."

"What about last night?" her mother asked. "You were too tired to eat."

Cammi pulled the headphones from her ears. "I told you, I ate before practice."

"A couple slices of pizza?"

"That's all I wanted."

"That's not a meal."

Cammie jump off the exam table and faced off with her mother. The two argued.

An image sprang into Myaisha's mind of Candace yelling at her over their business deal. She remembered the anger in Candace's face, felt the sting of the unkind words they hurled at each other like it happened yesterday.

It took several minutes, but she managed to intercede and squelch the argument between the Martin women. She reassured the mother Cammie was fine and directed them to follow up with any concerns.

Fatigued and hungry, she retired to her office. She quickly unwrapped her neglected meal and devoured the sandwich. In the middle of a bite someone tapped on her door.

With her head inserted through the doorway, Yvette said, "Mrs. Doctor, there's a cop here to speak with you."

Jelly dripped down her chin. She grabbed a tissue. "Let him in." *Where's a napkin when you needed one?*

Yvette misspoke. Two officers crammed into her small office while she wiped sticky jelly from her face. A long angular African American gentleman accompanied Detective de Jesus.

She stood and extended her hand in greeting. Peanut butter glued her teeth together. She struggled not to mumble. "Please come in. Take a seat," she said.

Accepting her hand, this new officer introduced himself. "I'm Detective Gamble," he said. "Sorry to bother you doctor, but we have a few more questions. We'll be quick."

She set her sandwich aside and resumed her seat. The detectives sat. She waited for questions while subtly trying to remove the peanut butter from the roof of her mouth with her tongue.

Detective Gamble delved straight into questions. "Did you speak with anyone about the death of Mrs. Knight?"

She took a sip from her water bottle. The lukewarm liquid did nothing to dislodge the peanut butter from her palate. She used the few seconds to consider the purpose of his question. It had to mean something if they traveled all the way to her office to ask. "I called my staff from Candace's office," she said.

Stern dark brown eyes looked back at her. He said, "Yes, you already told us that. I meant have you notified anyone since then."

"No, I haven't had time. I started seeing patients as soon as I got back."

"Would you please call Mrs. Knight's husband? We'd appreciate your cooperation."

"Sure. I'll call him when I finish."

"No, ma'am. I meant would you call him *now*."

The emphasis he placed on the last word concerned her. She wanted to ask why, but it seemed easier to simply comply. From her exam coat pocket, she removed her cell phone and pulled up Adán in her contacts.

As the line rang, she kept her eyes positioned on Detective Gamble—noting from her periphery Detective de Jesus, though quiet, also kept his eyes fixed on her. Their close observation unnerved her. An image of Candace's outstretched hand holding a phone darted in her mind. She dismissed the idea, recalling Candace held nothing.

Seconds ticked by. The call went to voice mail. She showed him the phone screen and hung up.

He slid forward to the edge of the seat. "Why didn't you leave a message?"

She grimaced. "That would be inappropriate. That's not the type of message you leave on a phone."

Silence hung between them. Neither relented as they engaged in the staring game. Detective Gamble, his gaze hard, didn't waver.

She studied him. His military haircut added to the intensity of his glare, with a face too young to be a homicide detective. She didn't mind obliging the police but refused to be bullied into breaking with common decency. Leaving Adán a phone message about Candace's death would be unkind. *How would she have felt if someone left a message about Sammy having suffered a stroke on her phone? Obscene.*

An image of Candace spread across the floor flashed in her mind. The events of the day became too much. A wave of grief washed over her, compounding her fatigue. Overwhelmed, tears flooded her eyes and her vision blurred. She dropped her gaze, fought to not allow tears to escape. She remembered Candace always said never let them see you cry.

Detective Gamble remained impassive.

Detective de Jesus broke the détente. "We wanted to know if you could reach Mr. Knight because we've been unable to notify him about his wife's death," he said.

She considered the significance of Adán not responding to calls. *Could he be hurt, another victim of this killer?* No, too farfetched. Someone killing both him and Candace in two different locations on the same day seemed improbable. The more likely scenario would be Adán murdered Candace and fled to escape the authorities—or to establish an alibi.

She didn't believe either scenario, but suspicion naturally fell upon the surviving spouse in a murder investigation. Possibilities cycled through her mind. Her fingers tingled at the memory of the cool gold necklace around Candace's neck. She noticed the detectives exchanged glances with each other. It meant something.

She said, "If I reach him, I'll tell him to contact you right away."

Detective Gamble ignored her statement. "How did you get blood on your clothing?" he asked.

His sudden change of topic made her head ache. She sipped some water. "I was about to perform chest compressions when I saw the blood on Candace's shirt. My sleeve must have brushed against the wound. I noticed the blood had coagulated."

Detective de Jesus consulted his notebook. Detective Gamble observed her.

Accustomed to difficult situations, she reciprocated his steadfast expression. His attitude started to grate on her nerves. Hunger and fatigue drained her patience. She massaged her temples.

"Did you have a business relationship with Mrs. Knight?" Detective Gamble asked.

"Other than ordering medical supplies from her, no."

"Did you engage in any other financial transactions with Mrs. Knight?

"No."

"Had you argued recently with Mrs. Knight about anything?"

"No."

"Do you know of anyone who wished her harm? Might have threatened her?"

"No."

"Who do you think killed her?"

"I don't know."

"Would you tell us if you did?"

Her left brow rose. "What are you insinuating, detective?"

"Not insinuating, doctor, just asking."

Doubtful. She wondered what information the detectives could have gathered on Candace in such a short time. Her curiosity piqued. *Why were they really here?* She would have to figure that out on her own. The detectives rose.

Detective Gamble handed her his card. "Thank you, Dr. Douglas. Call us as soon as you hear from Mr. Knight."

When they departed, they left her office door open. She rose to close the door and noticed her staff watching. She realized they had been listening. They couldn't have heard much since little had been said.

She powered down her computer, stared at it without seeing. It took a moment for her to process what occurred. Out of deference to the police, she hadn't told anyone about the murder, hadn't called mutual friends or their pastor—not even Deniece. But since the authorities had processed the scene, she could make those phone calls. She deferred calling Adán.

She held her cell phone as she recalled five years ago a crying Yvette had barged into the patient room where she examined a toddler. One look at the face of her office manager signaled something terrible had occurred. Her husband had been rushed to the hospital after suffering a stroke. If someone had left a message about Sammy on her phone—she would have gone ballistic.

Her hands trembled. Emotions racked her body. Visions of Candace's blood soaked shirts sprang before her eyes, Sammy's pained anguished expression as he lay in the hospital bed. She closed her eyes and recited a prayer. Minutes passed as her heart rate moderated. Her grief calmed and her nerves relaxed. She made her calls.

After she informed their pastor and Lottie about Candace's death, she grabbed her jacket and purse, locked up the office and departed. Myaisha headed for Jamestown. On the drive, she phoned Deniece. After being chastised for using her phone while driving, she informed her about the murder and hung up. As she merged into traffic, she contemplated the difficult conversation ahead. *How would Adán react?* He had been married to Candace for three years. They had no children. *Would he grieve as deeply as she had?*

Wendover Avenue west led her into Jamestown. The setting sun mirrored the decline in her energy level. She understood speaking to Adán in person would be the proper thing to do, but secretly she hoped he wouldn't be home, or the authorities would have arrived first—let them notify him about Candace's death.

Her cell phone pinged consistently on the drive to Jamestown—probably messages about Candace. Before she left her office she tried to call Mary and some other mutual acquaintances. Now, in the car she ignored the phone, she didn't want to speak with anyone right then. She rehearsed what she would say to Adán. Throughout her medical career she had delivered death notifications to family members, but she never told anyone their loved one had been murdered.

Thirty minutes later, she turned onto a narrow street of an exclusive enclave in a picturesque neighborhood. Spacious homes were situated on large lots with verdant manicured lawns. Dusk settled peacefully over the majestic trees. The mid-century home at the end of the street on the right belonged to Candace.

As her Honda traveled down the street, she spied a non-descript vehicle parked at the curb two houses away from her destination. The murder had her senses on high alert. The older model generic vehicle didn't fit into this neighborhood. As she passed the car, she glanced at the driver—a uniformed police officer. They were staking out the house. The officer didn't blink as she viewed his profile. He maintained a watchful forward gaze, focused on the Knight home.

She noted he wasn't either of the detectives that had interviewed her earlier. Her Honda inched up the driveway. As she set the parking break, headlights flashed in her rearview mirror. She remained in her car.

Adán pull up beside her and acknowledged her with a smile complimented by his deep dimples. By the time she exited her vehicle and circled around his SUV, he was waiting at the front door. On the walk up to the entrance, she studied him. At 6 feet tall, with honey colored skin and short fine wavy hair, Adán had often been mistaken as being Mediterranean. He was bi-racial, his mom a Filipina chef and his dad an African American Army sergeant.

His smile suggested he was unaware of Candace's murder. *Was he a victim or a perpetrator?* No time to tell. She had a duty to perform and she would do it. At the doorway, her face softened.

"Adán," she said, "I need to speak with you. Something bad has happened to Candace."

The smile slipped from his face. His dimples receded. "What? Where is she? What happened?" he asked.

Without answering his questions, she led him by the arm inside the house. He permitted her to guide him. In the foyer, she faced him. His tan puppy dog eyes seemed to appeal for understanding. *Did he love Candace?* Nothing in his countenance suggested he was anything other than what he purported to be. She held his hand. "I'm sorry, Adán. Candace is dead."

He fainted. Beginning with his face down to his limbs he folded.

Whatever she expected him losing consciousness out wasn't it. Securing her hands under his axillae, she leveraged his weight against the wall and lowered his body down onto the floor. Of course as she struggled with Adán the doorbell rang.

She positioned him with his head on the floor, his feet slightly elevated—*return blood to his brain.* Once she felt confident with his position, she answered the door.

The officer from the unmarked car stood on the doorstep, disappointment evident on his face. She figured he hadn't expected her to answer the door.

He looked past her into the house. "I need to speak with Mr. Knight," he said.

"He fainted." She stepped aside so the officer could view Adán lying across the floor behind the door.

The officer stormed past her and knelt down beside Adán. He spoke into a walkie-talkie attached to his arm.

She closed the door and joined the officer beside Adán. "We don't need an ambulance. He'll come around in a moment. He passed out when I told him about Candace."

The officer's frowned his displeasure. He made another call to his dispatcher.

It took a little less than a minute for Adán to regain consciousness.

She and the officer assisted him as he gathered his feet beneath himself and stumbled over to the couch in the sunken living room.

This provided her an opportunity to look around. The mid-century aesthetic had always been a favorite of hers—simple décor, but expensive. Candace had exquisite taste. Real estate had been profitable for her. She marveled at how her friend could afford it. Hard work from her many businesses, she presumed. She never inquired, figured it was none of her business. At least it hadn't been. Because of the murder, soon, everything Candace did would be public knowledge.

Her attention returned to Adán. She set him down on the couch then left him with the police officer and retreated to the kitchen to find some water. An alcove located off the living room, positioned near sliding glass doors, contained a large wine rack and wet bar. Before returning to the living room, she grabbed a bottle of brandy. Adán might find it more helpful than the glass of water.

She listened as the officer conducted his interrogation. Unconcerned by her presence, he kept his attention on Adán, who accepted the glass and continued to answer questions.

Instead of taking a seat, she decided to explore the home. Something about the questioning from the detectives in her office stimulated her curiosity. Also, she didn't believe Candace had been the victim of a random crime. More importantly, she didn't believe the police thought the crime had been random. If the crime was personal, Adán became suspect number one.

Floral hints of Candace's perfume permeated the air. As she proceeded down the hallway, she overheard the interrogation. She passed the bathroom, and stopped in front of the guest bedroom. *Should she check it out? Would they notice?* She felt like an intruder, interfering with an official police investigation. *What did she hope to find?* Unsure of her motives, she returned to the beginning of the hallway and listened to the interrogation.

Leaning across the table toward Adán, the police officer said, "We tried to locate you at your office, Mr. Knight. Your assistant said you left early this morning."

"I often work outside my office," Adán said, pausing to take a sip of water. "I'm a life coach. My office is wherever my patients want me to be."

"We tried to reach you by phone—left several messages. Why didn't you answer?"

Adán reached into his pocket and flipped his phone on. "I turn off my phone when I'm with clients. They pay for my time and I give them my complete attention."

She listened to Adán's tone. He sounded insincere. She detected a note of arrogance—defiance. A smirk hung at the corner of his mouth—or maybe not. Whatever she thought she saw on his face evaporated in seconds.

Adán again appeared his usual relaxed self. He didn't seem to require her assistance any longer, however, she wasn't ready to leave. She felt compelled to listen to the exchange.

"Where were you, sir?" the officer asked.

A knock brought everyone's attention to the front door.

On impulse, she answered it.

Detectives Gamble and de Jesus frowned at her. Without an invitation, they circumvented her and proceeded into the living room.

Close on their heels, she sat on the couch beside Adán.

The patrol officer stood upon their arrival and explained where his interrogation ended. He excused himself and left the living room but not the residence, maintaining his vigilance from the front door.

Detective de Jesus sat in a chair to the right of Adán. Detective Gamble sat opposite Adán, on the opposite couch. Both detectives gave him their full attention. Mean mugging, they settled into their positions and waited a full minute before they began their questions.

Since no one paid her any attention, she strolled around the living room. She viewed photos of Candace and Adán on the mantel, spied a picture of Santa Cruz on the wall near the large window looking out over the front yard. Memories of her and Candace on the beach studying for their college classes floated through her mind. She felt sadness welling up inside her chest and walked away before she cried. As she passed the hallway, something in the corner of her eye caught her attention.

The door to the master bedroom was wide open. She saw an object near the foot of the bed. *Was it a box, or a suitcase?* Several steps closer to the bedroom revealed the object to be a suitcase, actually several suitcases. Someone prepared for a trip. *Candace or Adán?* The suitcases looked dour, a bland tan color. She traveled with Candace before and remembered her friend had teal colored luggage. The bags must belong to Adán. *Where did Adán intend to go? Could he be fleeing? Had the police noticed the luggage?* While she studied the bags, she remained attuned to the interrogation. She returned to the front of the hallway, and positioned herself where she could simultaneously view the master bedroom and living room.

While Detective Gamble asked questions, Detective de Jesus took notes.

"Where were you this morning, Mr. Knight?" asked Detective Gamble.

Adán reclined against a pillow. More relaxed than perhaps he should be, she thought.

"With a client," Adán said.

"Who?"

With a deep sigh, Adán sat up straight. "No more questions until you tell me what happened to my wife. Myaisha said Candace is dead. What happened?"

Detective Gamble cocked his head to the side. He turned around looking, she knew, for her. He gave her a pointed glare until she returned to the living room. When she sat down on the couch his gaze flowed back to Adán.

"Your wife was murdered, Mr. Knight," he said.

Adán's eyes flew open, his jaw dropped. "Where? How? Who—who would do that?"

Detective Gamble didn't flinch, he observed with steady eyes.

Did he suspect Adán already knew about Candace's murder? She believed Adán's response appropriate—not overly done but concerned. Detective Gamble's eyes bore into him though, she got the impression that the detective didn't believe Adán. She decided Adán needed support and scooted closer to him on the couch.

Detective de Jesus unbuttoned his suit coat and slid forward on the chair. "She was shot, Mr. Knight," he said. "In her office. Now answer the question. Who was this client you were with?"

Seated on the left side of Adán, she couldn't obtain a clear view of Detective de Jesus. The tenor of his voice remained professional, but neither detective expressed sympathy toward the widower. *Did they know something she didn't?* Maybe they needed to remain aloof to be effective.

Adán mimicked the detectives' actions and leaned forward, his legs spread apart, feet firmly on the ground. "I don't like your tone detective," he said.

Detective Gamble leaned further across the table. "We don't care what you like. Where were you today, and who were you with?"

His head back tilted back, Adán gazed up at the ceiling. After a few seconds, he brought a different more determined face down toward the detectives. "You know what? How 'bout you get the hell outta my house. Right now. How 'bout that?"

With a slight nod to each other the detectives stood but didn't move from their positions.

She studied them and realized they had reached some mutual agreement in their silent communication.

"We'd like permission to check your residence. With your consent of course," Detective Gamble said.

Adán's lips curled to the side. "Not on your life."

"We can get a warrant," Detective de Jesus said.

Adán stood and headed for the foyer. "Get it."

"Why wouldn't you want to assist in the investigation of your wife's murder, Mr. Knight?" Detective Gamble asked.

Good question. Like the detectives, she awaited Adán's reply. None came. He continued toward the front door. The detectives followed after him.

"Why don't you accompany us downtown, Mr. Knight?" Detective de Jesus asked.

"Am I under arrest?"

"No, sir. We just need your cooperation to investigate the murder. Don't you want us to find your wife's killer? Just a few questions and we'll get you back home. We'll even give you a ride." Detective de Jesus placed his note pad in his jacket pocket.

She noticed Adán twirl his watch around his wrist. Having played cards with him and Candace before, she knew his tell. More nervous than he let on to the detectives, he seemed to ponder his options. She watched the players but remained seated during the exchange.

"I can answer questions here just as easily as I can downtown."

"Would you consent to a partial search of your home?" Detective Gamble asked.

Adán hesitated. For a minute, she thought he would consent.

"I believe I should consult my attorney first."

Detective Gamble crossed his arms over his chest. "Would you mind calling your attorney now, sir?"

This time he didn't hesitate, but pulled out his phone as he walked into the kitchen. In his absence, the detectives exchanged meaningful glances. Neither spoke a word to each other or to her.

In those few minutes, she examined the room. Draperies on each side of the sliding glass doors framed the darkness outside. A phone charger sat on a side table near the doors. Even from a distance, she could tell the charger belonged to a Samsung—she owned a droid too. However, just now Adán pulled out an iPhone to call his attorney. Candace loved everything Apple. She remembered how ecstatic Candace was when Apple introduced their first cell phone in June. He had two phones, which could be significant—or not.

Adán carried a glass of whiskey when he returned to the living room. "I left a message for my attorney. Until I hear back from her, this discussion is over," he said.

The detectives walked toward the front door.

Before they departed, Detective Gamble leaned into Adán's face. "We'll be waiting outside."

He followed behind them and secured the lock after they left.

She noticed him remove a second phone from a different pocket.

He started to make a call. The phone snapped shut when he glanced up and saw her seated on the couch. His dimpled face evolved into a frown, then flat. Guarded, the curtain came down over his expression again.

He placed it in his pocket and lowered the corners of his lips. "Myaisha, I really appreciate you coming in person to tell me about Candace but I need to be alone right now. I'm sure you understand."

She understood a dismissal when she heard one. Before she left, she gave him a big hug. "Adán. I'm sorry. Please let me know if there is anything I can do for you. Anything."

"Thank you."

After he shut the door behind her, she heard the locks click into place.

On the way to her car, she mulled over what transpired. Adán had two phones. He brought out the droid after the detectives left. *Who did he need to contact right after Candace's death?* She yawned. It was late and she felt spent. Her friend had been murdered and her husband kept secrets. Myaisha rolled down the windows allowing the air to slap her face.

Two more unmarked police cars parked along the street. A forensics van pulled up behind them and joined the forming queue. Porch lights dotted the street. Neighbors huddled together on their porches, whispered amongst themselves in the night. Lured from the safety of their homes by the death of one of their own. Curiosity overrode their need for security and comfort.

On the drive home, she wondered if by the end of the night Adán would lose his liberty and end up in a jail cell.

Chapter 8

Detective Todd Gamble stood outside the station, closed his eyes and turned up toward the sky. He tuned out the road noise. Sun rays warmed his face. Thursday had been overcast and rainy. Today, sunshine promised summer truly arrived.

Fresh air calmed his frayed nerves. He took several deep breaths. The explosive temper of his boss, the chief of police, raged all morning. Irate calls from business leaders, reporters, and city council members flooded their office. Greensboro's prominent citizens vented their frustration at the chief, who in turn unleashed his impatience at the perceived lack of progress by the homicide department.

Candace Knight had been murdered yesterday. It was Friday morning and he hadn't had an opportunity to question key witnesses yet. Adán Knight lawyered up. The receptionist, LaDonna Jefferson, had a mental breakdown and had to be taken to the emergency room and sedated. His two most important witnesses rendered unavailable—not helpful.

He knew the longer it took to develop a case and identify a suspect the less likely they were to obtain a conviction. He also understood the need for patience. Time brought out more facts. People remembered things they neglected to mention during their initial interview. Important details sometimes required opportunity to come to fruition. Phone records, forensics—data required time. A good detective understood when to wait and when to push.

They hadn't arrested anyone, but they had a promising suspect in the husband. Without probable cause the judge refused to sign a warrant to search the couple's home since the homicide occurred in the victim's office. Mr. Knight consented to a limited search—with his lawyer present of course. He and Ian were permitted inside, but not the forensics team. When they gained entry to the premises, the home appeared in order.

In the study, Mr. Knight produced a hand gun from inside the otherwise empty safe. He confiscated the weapon, but failed to locate anything germane to their homicide investigation. Given the circumstances of Mrs. Knight's death, he doubted they would uncover evidence of probative value in the couple's home. He hoped to discover evidence for a motive. Without reasonable cause sufficient for a judge, a search warrant would not be issued.

As the ringing in his ears diminished his pressure calmed. For a moment he basked in the peace. He scratched his head and stretched his arms.

In a flurry, Ian rushed out the station and careened into him. "Why are you standing in front of the door?" he asked before he walked off.

Rubbing his back where the door hit him, Todd caught up with Ian and together they headed for their vehicle. Both understood their next step without discussion. They worked together for two years. At 5'9", his partner looked like a Mr. Universe contestant. Ian de Jesus wasn't what most people expected in a police officer and he knew it—and didn't care. Their colleagues believed they had known each other for much longer. They seemed to be in synch most of the time, which made working together easier.

He slid underneath the steering wheel, removed his gun from its shoulder holster and secured it before he turned on the ignition. With a side glance, he asked, "What's your hurry?"

Ian grimaced and stared out the window. "Let's just get going okay,"

He recognized Ian committed the same dedication to his detective work as he did to his fitness workouts. His partner came to work every day ready to give 100%. Patience wasn't a job requirement, so Ian didn't exhibit it often.

Todd drove away from the station. Perhaps discussing the case would get Ian's mind off whatever had him in a bad mood. "Let's go over the case again. From the beginning," he said. "Right now, my money's on the husband. Not cooperating with us looks suspicious. What do you think?"

Ian clenched a muscle ball in his left hand. "Maybe. It's too early to say. We need to speak with witnesses. Find out more about our vic. What about the gun we got from the husband?"

"Clean. Not the murder weapon, and it's licensed."

"It's too early to narrow our focus on the husband. We need to interview her assistant. Any family besides the parents?" Ian tossed the ball into the cup holder.

"Siblings—in and out of state. None of them had contact with Mrs. Knight for years. There's a cousin in Greensboro. One of the patrol officers interviewed her yesterday. She was at work during the homicide. She's been cleared."

Ian stared out the front window. "Personal life?"

Headed north, Todd then turned off Elm Street. "Looks pretty straight forward. The wife is a successful business woman and controls the money. The husband is younger and self-employed." The conversation paused while he executed a left turn. "No kids. Married three years. What if he got tired of her? Had someone on the side. It would give him a motive."

Ian flipped through the pages of his notebook. "No forced entry at the scene. No signs of a struggle."

"Exactly."

"What about the hairs?"

"The coroner doesn't believe they belong to the victim. They're in forensics for processing. We'll check when we return to the station."

While stopped at the signal light, he took a moment to think over the facts of the case. Speaking out loud to himself, he said, "But if she fought with someone... There weren't any signs of a struggle. No furniture disturbed. No bruises on her body."

Retrieving the ball, Ian repeated his wrist exercises. "The chair was moved," he said.

Todd recalled the scene. One of the chairs had been disturbed. "Yes, but not like there had been a skirmish."

He took advantage of the silence to make a mental note to call forensics, verify they examined the chair for hairs, prints, and blood. Perhaps fibers were deposited on the seat. He eased the sedan into an apartment complex. "We'll know more after we question the receptionist."

A right turn brought him into a large apartment complex. He idled the car next to a map to confirm the unit's location. Tall thin pine trees surrounded three large buildings. He parked the vehicle in the visitor section.

Ian dropped the ball into the cup holder. "Assistant."

Muttering a curse word under his breath, he shook his head. "Whatever. Let's go." He set the emergency break and holstered his weapon.

Dropping his notebook into his coat pocket, Ian exited the vehicle first. "She was a mess at the office."

"Yes, but she's had time to calm down. She should feel better today. We need to find out more about Mrs. Knight and what happened in the office."

A cool breeze accompanied them as they proceeded up to the apartment. He straightened his tie before he knocked on the door. Reflexively, they stood on opposite sides of the doorway.

The day of the murder, LaDonna Jefferson returned to an office complex crawling with police. Informed about the death of her boss, the receptionist fainted. Later in the evening, when they tried to interrogate her in the ER, they found her weepy answers vague and useless.

He hoped she had sufficient time to recuperate. They needed answers. His chief wanted the murderer apprehended yesterday. Mrs. Jefferson would be their first witness interrogation of what promised to be a busy day. With a nod from his partner, he rapped on the door again. After several minutes, he heard shuffling inside.

The door cracked open. A metal chain stretched taut guarding the premises. A bleary eyed woman, a silk scarf over her head, squinted at them in confusion.

Both detectives removed their badges.

"Good morning Mrs. Jefferson," he said. "I don't know if you remember us. I'm Detective Gamble. This is Detective de Jesus. We need to continue our interview regarding your employer, Mrs. Knight."

In the background, he heard someone ask, "Who is it?"

Without a response, the woman shut the door.

He heard her converse with someone. He strained to understand the conversation, then looked over at Ian, whose shoulders briefly rose and fell. With a long large sigh, he knocked again—harder. "Mrs. Jefferson, open up. We can talk here or at the station."

Through the door, she said, "I'm comin'."

Locks turned and the door hurriedly opened.

She had removed her scarf, displaying a head half full of rollers. A deep frown crossed her forehead. "Why you screamin' down my door?" she asked. She pulled on the belt securing the terry cloth robe she wore. Stepping aside, she pointed them toward a large room.

From between the drapes he viewed glass sliding doors leading onto a balcony. Lights in the room were off but enough sunlight streamed through the windows for him to get a perfunctory look at the apartment. *Typical.* A couch, loveseat and various chairs scattered around the room—a heterogeneous blend of furnishings. Replicas of modern art work hung on the walls. They didn't align with his sensibilities, but he felt it worked with the decor.

Mrs. Jefferson flipped on the lights and opened the curtains, which further illuminated the room. The apartment appeared well kept, unlike Mrs. Jefferson. Her eyes were swollen, face puffy. Hard lines etched into her weathered skin. Without makeup she looked older than her reported age of fifty three. She either had a difficult night or she sorely mourned the death of her employer, or both.

She invited them to be seated and asked if they would like coffee.

He declined her offer, however, Ian accepted. Neither spoke while Mrs. Jefferson left to get dressed. He heard another voice coming from the bedroom.

She re-entered the living room, sans hair rollers, with a man.

Sporting a shiny black balding head, the man introduced himself and shook their hands. "Morning. I'm Glen."

Shaking the man's hand, he said, "I'm Detective Gamble. This is Detective de Jesus." Glen's handshake was firm and short. Todd regarded his jeans and tan work boots—he looked fit. He faced her. "We have some follow up questions for you Mrs. Jefferson. It won't take long, then we'll let you go about your day."

She stood straighter. "It's Ms. Jefferson."

"I apologize. Ms. Jefferson."

Ian gave her a slight smile. "It shouldn't take much of your time, ma'am. Are you feeling better?"

Her posture slumped. "Not really. I'm sorry I couldn't be more helpful before. When I got to the office—It was so upsetting." Tears tottered at the edges of her artificial lashes.

"Why don't I help you with the coffee," Ian said.

Thanking him, she headed into the kitchen.

After his partner left, Todd fixed his attention on Glen. He obtained his complete name and address, and inquired about his occupation.

Glen stated he worked in construction.

With the preliminaries completed, he dove into the interrogation. He liked to keep witnesses on edge. "So Glen, I take it you and Ms. Jefferson are an item?"

All five feet five inches of Glen's body tensed. Seated on the sofa opposite him, he rested his hands on his thighs. "Yeah. Me and LaDonna been together for years," he said.

"How many?"

"Too many. Twenty, maybe twenty-two."

"Do you know anything about the murder?

"Naw, just what I hear on the news, and what LaDonna told me."

Stock still, his ears perked up. "What did LaDonna tell you?"

Glen explained how LaDonna called him to pick her up from the hospital. He spent the evening at her place taking care of her. She told him the police were at the office when she got back from lunch on Wednesday.

With a slight nod of his head, Todd made mental notes. His ability to remember conversations served him well in police work. Instead of scribbling information during interviews, he could focus on the person—their movements, body language, unvoiced reactions. He believed how a witness reacted to questions helped the investigation as much, if not more, than what they said. Later, back at his desk, he could regurgitate entire conversations almost verbatim. Ian suggested they take his memory to Vegas and strike it big at the casinos. Unfortunately, it didn't work that way. His brain packaged the information differently.

Glen remained cool and collected—not nervous, but unenthusiastic.

He leaned forward, positioned his legs father apart. "Where did Ms. Jefferson go for lunch? Did she tell you?"

"She didn't have to tell me. We ate together. Something we do on Wednesdays at our usual spot."

According to Glen, LaDonna got there about 11:30 and she left around 1:30 to return to the office. He didn't hear from her again until she called him from the hospital.

"How often do you stay the night?"

Sliding to the edge of the sofa, Glen rubbed his hands along his jeans. Gritted his teeth. "What you saying?"

"Just asking questions, sir."

"Look. LaDonna and me, we serious. But we have our reasons for not getting married, understand? I love her like she my real wife."

"Do you live here too?"

With measured breaths Glen seemed to consider the question before he responded. "I have my own place. LaDonna prefers to live here, alone. I don't push her. She want her own place, that's fine by me."

Not sure how this related to his murder case, he backed off. Approached another line of questions. "What can you tell me about Candace Knight? Did you know her?"

"Yeah, I know her—knew her. Didn't care for her, but I'd met her."

"What was the problem?"

"No problem. She was a'right."

"Come on, Glen. The sooner you tell us, the sooner we leave."

With the topic off him and LaDonna, he loosened up, in body and tongue. He rubbed his bald spot and fidgeted with his hands. "Look, I didn't like Mrs. Knight, a'right. Thought she was too stuck up. Always acting all high and mighty," he said. "But she took good care of LaDonna. Paid her real well. Benefits and everything—even one of those 401Ks."

"So you don't know anyone who would want to kill her?"

He snickered. "Oh, hell. I know plenty of people liked ta kill her. Anyone that did business with her."

Sectioned off from the great room, the long narrow kitchen ended at a bay window which housed a small café style table for two. Ian glanced out the window at the swaying trees. The kitchen smelled of stale food, but appeared tidy.

LaDonna directed him to where the cups and cutlery were housed. While she prepared the coffee, he set cups on a serving tray. While he collected utensils from a drawer, he gave LaDonna a side glance and noticed her shoulders slouch. She wept softly. He walked up to her and guided her to the table.

"Here. Sit down," he said. "I can make the coffee." He tore open a packet and poured it into the machine.

She stared out the bay window at the sunlit yard, unfocused on anything in particular it seemed.

As the aroma of coffee filled the galley kitchen, he noticed her wipe her nose on the kitchen towel. *Remember not to touch that towel.* With two brimming coffee mugs, he joined her at the table. Tasting the lackluster coffee, he allowed her a moment to compose herself.

She held her mug, but didn't drink. Her reddened eyes looked vacant.

"Are you ready to answer some questions?" he asked.

"Yeah. Go ahead." Sniffling, she wiped her nose again with the towel.

In one swift movement he removed his note pad and pen from his pocket, never taking his eyes off her. "Tell me when you started working for Mrs. Knight."

Her eyes drifted out the window. "I started working for Mrs. Knight when she was still Ms. Jones—her maiden name. Then she married her first husband, and became Mrs. Scott."

"Did you know her first husband?" Although he already had information on the deceased from their background check, he allowed her to continue, let her tell her story in her own way. He jotted an occasional note. Made the necessary supportive sounds of condolence.

Her brows wrinkled as if she tried to remember. "No, not really. He came by the office a few times, but he never spoke to me. He'd just look my way and I'd buzz him through to the back office. He wasn't a nice man. I could tell he didn't make her happy. He didn't treat her good."

He nodded for her to continue.

"Then one day, she told me she cut him loose. Just like that." She snapped her fingers, dabbed her nose with the towel.

"Are those the words she used?"

"No, but something like that. Basically, she let me know she ended it."

"When did Mr. Knight enter the picture?" He watched her calculate the time in her head.

"Not sure. Maybe four years ago."

He knew the length of the marriage from the background report. Given how long LaDonna had worked for the victim, it seemed strange she didn't know. "You're not sure?"

Adding sugar to her coffee, LaDonna stirred while she thought. "Well, you see they lived together for a while, at least a year I think. Then one day she comes into the office and says they got married. Showed me the largest ring I ever saw. She was so happy."

Tears flowed down her sunken cheeks.

Ian took the opportunity to refill his cup. When he returned to the table he invited her to continue. "So, no ceremony?"

"Nope, nothing. Just ran off to the Bahamas and got married on the beach. Mrs. Knight showed me pictures and everything. She was beautiful. No fancy wedding dress." Her face looked pained.

"You didn't approve."

"It wasn't my place to approve or not. I just didn't understand why she had to rush? They'd been together a while. What did it matter? These days, people don't care. She already had one bad marriage. She didn't need another."

Apparently, LaDonna wasn't a romantic. "Did Mrs. Knight seem happy with the marriage?" he asked.

Taking a sip of coffee, she pinched up her face and pushed the cup away. "Yeah. She was happy. Real happy, at first."

He gave her a moment, let her emotions marinate. He took her cup and refilled it. Placed it before her and resumed his seat. "Then what happened?"

"She found out he was a cheat." LaDonna took a large gulp of coffee. A few moments passed as she consumed more coffee. She walked over to the pantry and removed a container of Danish and placed it on the table.

As a courtesy he accepted one but let it languish untouched on the saucer.

After several bites of pastry, she continued. "I could have told her he cheated."

"How did you know?"

She licked sugar from her fingers. Wiped them on the towel she used to blow her nose.

Ian winced.

"It was obvious. Lately, he didn't even try to hide it. Coming home late. Having *meetings* at all hours. Smelling of perfume. What hard working man wears perfume?"

He ignored her question and asked one of his own. "Mrs. Knight told you all this?"

"She told me some things. Other stuff I saw on my own."

He tried to sum her up. *Could she be vengeful toward Mr. Knight?* Upset about the brutal murder of the employer she obviously adored. *How reliable were her recollections?* He needed her to elaborate. "How did you know Mr. Knight cheated?"

LaDonna explained how they at a seminar he gave on personal empowerment. Her boss signed up for his life coaching sessions.

Her brows raised. "Most of his clients are women, you know. Next thing I know, they started dating. I didn't think nothing about it at first. Mrs. Knight was older than him but she was beautiful and smart. She could take care of herself but she felt lonely. Working hard. It's tough being a successful black woman—not too many pickings when it comes to men. She was excited about a younger man giving her attention. And he looked good, acted charming. But then I started to see what he was all about. It didn't take long after they married. Men always show they true colors after you marry them."

She finished her Danish. Ian held fast, letting her story evolve.

"He came around the office less often," she said. "Didn't call her like before. Mrs. Knight came into work wearing more makeup."

His radar when up. He sat up straighter. "Did you ever see bruises on her?"

She stammered, but finally admitted she never saw any bruises. "I didn't have too. I knew he hurt her. Inside or out, it's still abuse."

Careful not to agree or disagree, he pursued more. "So you never actually saw him cheat. You just assumed it from his behavior?"

Her eyes flashed on him. "I didn't say that. I know what I saw."

Careful. He needed to maintain her trust. "Tell me what you saw, LaDonna."

Seeming to accept his unvoiced apology, she explained. She and Glen always lunched together on Wednesdays—the same spot, same time. One day while they were at lunch, Mr. Knight came into the deli with a woman.

"Could it have been a client?"

She snorted. "No way. They weren't acting like it was business. Their heads were all close together, whispering and stuff. It wasn't decent. Acting like that in public."

Would it be proper if he conducted his affair in private? He kept his thoughts to himself. "Did you tell Mrs. Knight?

She jumped up in her chair. "Of course not.

"What do you mean 'of course not'?"

She dressed him down with her eyes, a grimace on her lips. "You ever hear about killin' the messenger? I wasn't gonna be the one to destroy her marriage. Let someone else tell her Adán screwed around. I loved my job, and I loved her."

Tears followed. Ian retrieved a glass of water for her. After a minute, he asked, "Do you believe her husband could've killed her?"

She choked back sobs. "No—and not because he loved her. Because he didn't. It's just—he doesn't have the balls to do it. Big jerk. Nothing but a lady's man. Never done a hard day's work in his life."

"Who do you think killed her, LaDonna? You knew her as well as anyone else, probably better." He wasn't sure he believed that, but flattery wouldn't hurt.

"I don't know."

He glanced down at his notebook. "Did she have any enemies?"

Because she paused, his gaze darted up from his paper and fastened upon her. Something descended between them—a roadblock. He smelled secrets, and he loved secrets. "LaDonna?"

She avoided his eyes. "No, none I knew about."

Liar. He let it go. He'd return to it soon enough.

Todd looked up to find Ian and Mrs. Jefferson rejoining them in the living room. She carried a carafe of coffee on a tray with Danish. His partner took a seat in a straight backed chair. The scent of caffeine sent a jolt of energy into him. He accepted a cup, but declined Danish.

He sipped the coffee. "Thank you, Mrs. Jefferson."

Setting the items down on the coffee table, she said, "Ms. Jefferson, but call me LaDonna."

"I apologize. Thank you, LaDonna." He set his cup on the side table.

She curled up on the sofa beside Glen, who placed his arm around her shoulders. Giving her a hug, he brought her into his chest. At least four inches taller than him, she assumed an almost fetal position to nestle under him. Blond streaked relaxed hair fell down both sides of her chest. Her red-rimmed eyes closed as she melted into him.

Todd exchanged a knowing glance with Ian, and signaled he would lead the interview. Their routine had been perfected over the past two years. Divide the interrogation of their suspects, then one of them would close the interview. Their rendition of 'good cop, bad cop'. Since Ian established a rapport with her, he would conclude the interview.

Once he determined the couple were comfortable, he started his questions. "So, LaDonna, Glen says your employer made a lot of enemies."

She sat up abruptly, pushed herself off Glen's chest. "How could you?"

Glen held her hand. "Baby, I told them the truth. Just tell them what you know, then we'll be done with this. It doesn't concern us. She's dead. No one can hurt her now. You kept her secrets long enough. There's no one to protect anymore."

She glared at him, removed his arm from around her shoulders and slunk to the opposite side of the sofa. He slid toward her but stopped when she waved him off. Like a guilty child, he hung his head and maintained his position.

He and Ian watched and waited. But she remained steadfast, gave them what he presumed to be her most evil scowl. Undeterred, he detected back pedaling and he wasn't going to allow it. He reminded her of their official status.

Her large lips remained closed, defiant.

His lips set in a firm tight line. Chin raised, eyes level, he said, "This is a homicide investigation. Sooner or later we're going to find out you held back information. I promise you, if you make us work to get information you already had, we will not be pleased."

She glared at him. Unlike Ian, however, he didn't offer comfort or understanding. He returned her glare and bore through her façade.

Her gaze averted, readjusted herself on the sofa. "I have nothing to say."

He signaled Ian, and in unison they rose.

"Fine," he said "We'll continue this conversation downtown."

Crossing her arms around her body, she curled up into herself. "Why do I have to go downtown? Am I being arrested? For what?"

"Ma'am, this is a homicide investigation. You're a material witness. We need information and we mean to get it. Since you refuse to cooperate, you're going downtown. Grab your purse. Let's go."

He stood, arms crossed over his chest.

Ian jingled the handcuffs in his jacket pocket.

Great touch.

LaDonna searched his partner's face. If she desired sanctuary, she found none. She turned to Glen. He slid over and hugged her again. This time she didn't push him away, but rested her head on his shoulder. She cried.

Glen kissed her forehead. "Go ahead, baby. Tell 'em what they want to know."

They maintained their position. He watched her for a response.

One look at Glen and she acquiesced. "Okay. I'll tell you."

Without checking with each other, in unison they sat back down.

Ian removed his note book as he questioned her. He said, "Tell us who wanted to kill your boss?"

Adán removed a bundle of clothes from the bedroom closet. Jazz beats reverberated around the room. He dropped items onto the bed and took a swig from his beer bottle. Cool and mellow, the barley warmed his belly. On the way to retrieve another load, his cell phone buzzed. Removing it from his back pocket he sat at the foot of the bed.

"Why are you calling me?" he asked.

A shrill voice emanated from the phone. A woman asked. "Why am I calling you? Are you kidding me? I haven't heard from you in a week. Yesterday your wife was murdered. I'm freaking out."

He returned to the closet and grabbed some shoes off the floor with his free hand. "Calm down. Getting upset won't help."

"Adán, someone murdered her. The police are going to suspect you, especially if they find out about us."

"Exactly why you shouldn't be calling me, Kelley."

"This is your other phone, right? The police don't know about it, do they?"

"No, but they can find out. Don't call me. It's too risky."

"Okay, but when can I see you?"

"When I call you." He hung up. Powered off the phone.

Chapter 9

Zion Baptist Church sanctuary buzzed with isolated conversations. Myaisha looked around, it was packed with people. The ushers brought in additional seating, some people stood along the back wall. Yesterday, Candace died. This evening, church members, colleagues, clients, people from all over the Triad came out to pay their respects. She sat in the back row, two pews behind Mary and her husband Greg.

Seated in the front church pew were Adán, his parents, and Candace's parents. She didn't recognize any other family members. She had met Candace's parents before, but none of the extended family. Estranged from her siblings, Candace rarely spoke about her brother and sisters. Business associates and friends filled the sanctuary—her sorority sisters occupied the second and third rows.

Pastor Matthew opened the event and led the congregation in singing hymnals. Yolanda Adams, *Still I Rise*, a favorite of Candace's, played before testimonies began. People shared their stories of how her friend touched their lives.

LaDonna waved to her from a seat in the front row across the aisle from Adán. Myaisha's heart went out to her. She seemed to mourn Candace's death more than anyone present. She didn't mention Adán in her eulogy. In fact, she sent him a cold stare on her way down from the podium. Bypassing him when she paid her respects to Candace's parents.

During the homecoming, no one mentioned the circumstances surrounding her death. Sympathy poured out for the grieving widower, especially from the deaconesses and other women of the church.

Myaisha glanced around the sanctuary viewing the mourners. Sorrow mixed with anger. An image of Candace sprawled along the floor flittered through her mind. She heard her heart beat in her ears. Her skin flushed. The coarse paper from the evening's program crinkled between her fingers. A whispered vow to assist the authorities identify the killer escaped her lips.

A horrible thought crossed her mind—*the murderer could be someone in the church masquerading as a friend or family member.* From her bookcase experience with mysteries, the spouse became the primary suspect followed by family and friends. Robbery didn't appear to be the motive behind the murder, which suggested Candace had a relationship with her killer. After family and friends would be associates, which would explain the unlocked office doors.

Her eyes narrowed, she surveyed the attendees with suspicion. *Did one of these people kill her friend?* The person with the most to gain sat front and center. Scooting to the edge of the pew, she tried to get a better view of Adán. *Did he truly grieve Candace's death, or had he played a role in her murder?*

The choir sang a hymnal. She set aside the murder to focus on the memorial. Many people, like her, would miss her friend. For the past few years their relationship steadily improved. They weren't back to sharing confidences like they had in college, but Candace appeared to have forgiven her. She blamed herself for not trying harder—sooner—to mend their friendship. Tears drenched her cheeks as one by one people came forward to share their memories. Testimonies lasted for over two hours.

Her mind reverted back to the same place five years prior. She and Josiah had sat together on the front pew, clutched onto each other afraid to let go. Sammy lay in a casket below the pastor's podium. She had cried to exhaustion, hollowed by grief. Like a black hole, her emptiness would have consumed her if not for Josiah. Caring for him anchored her. She couldn't fall apart as long as he needed her.

Would Adán have anyone? His parents flew up from Florida for the service, but planned to fly home tomorrow according to local gossip. Their church would have to step up, become his surrogate family. *Would Adán want to stay here?* He wasn't originally from Greensboro. As a life coach, he could work from anywhere. She couldn't image him selling that beautiful home. When she got a chance, she would ask him what his plans were. Perhaps she should drop by the house to check up on him. It would also give her an opportunity to ask him why he had packed to leave before the murder.

She wondered if the police still surveilled the home. As much as she hated the thought, if she intended to investigate Candace's murder she would have to question Adán—obtain answers to tough questions. As a physician, she asked uncomfortable questions every day—it came easily for her. This would be different. These people were her friends, like family to her. They took her in and made her feel like she belonged. With her biological family on the opposite coast she depended upon her church. Her attention returned to the service as Pastor Matthew stepped up to the microphone.

He closed down the remembrance with his personal memories of Candace. He invited anyone in need of prayer or support to contact him or the church elders. With the choir swaying in the background, Pastor Matthew held his hands out toward the congregation. Eyes closed, he said, "Lord, I ask you to put your arms around Brother Adán. Help us support him during this difficult time. Welcome Sister Candace into your bosom dear God. Keep her safe until we are all joined together again, at home with you in heaven. We ask in the name of our Lord. Let the church say, Amen."

The congregation repeated amen. A beat later, the sanctuary stirred. People looked for acknowledgement they could depart. The elders opened the back doors. A tide of people began to exit. As some people departed others approached Adán.

On the platform, a dark skinned woman took Pastor Matthew aside. He nodded his head repeatedly like as Pez container as she spoke. He exchanged words with one of the elders before escorting the woman up to the podium.

Curious, Myaisha watched.

Pastor Matthew stood beside the woman. Again he raised his hands. Unable to get peoples' attention, he tapped the microphone. "Brothers and sisters. If we could trouble you for a moment." He paused as people either sat or remained standing in place.

From her seat, she strained to see Adán's response. He twirled his watch. *Was he nervous from worry or surprise?*

When some semblance of order returned, Pastor Matthew said, "I want you to give Sister Joi a moment of your time." He stepped back and slightly to the side, made room for the woman to address the sanctuary.

Short and round, Joi had a voice which belied her size. She didn't require the microphone to project her voice. "Good evening, friends," she said. "A horrible tragedy brings us together to mourn our sister, Candace Knight. We, the members of the Greensboro Black Professionals Alliance, are offering a reward to anyone with information leading to the apprehension of the person who murdered our dear friend. I'll leave the details with the pastor. Anyone with information should contact the police."

Sister Joi paused and cast her eyes upon Adán. Her countenance relaxed. "Brother Knight, we promise to do all we can to bring justice to you and our sister."

Little areas of applause erupted. Pastor Matthew came up from behind Sister Joi. He guided her down from the platform and thanked the congregation.

With the statement Candace had been murdered people expounded their theories about what occurred.

Myaisha kept her seat and watched and listened as people drifted down the aisles and out the sanctuary. She caught tidbits of gossip as people speculated upon Candace's death while rendering judgment upon her life.

Her gaze returned to Adán. Her heart tore for him anew. Public opinion would designate him guilty until proven otherwise. She had heard rumors about his dalliances. *Had infidelity led to murder?*

People streamed out the sanctuary. Like a fish swimming against the tide, a woman entered the sanctuary.

Myaisha stared, but didn't recognize her.

Attired in an impeccable business suit, the woman scurried along the pew in her direction. Confused, she scanned her immediate vicinity, even looked behind herself, as she wondered who the woman sought. In seconds, she had her answer.

Extending a soft hand, lightly scented of lavender, the woman addressed her. "Are you Dr. Douglas? Dr. Myaisha Douglas?" she asked.

She accepted the limp handshake and regarded the woman with caution. Her left eyebrow arched. "May I help you?"

The woman provided her name and said, "I'm the estate lawyer for Mrs. Candace Knight." Lifting a briefcase onto the bench, the woman clicked it open and extracted a large manila envelope. She handed over to her. "Mrs. Knight appointed you executor of her estate."

Generally, quite good at hiding her emotions her eyes widened and her lips parted. Aware she gawked at the woman, she shut her mouth. Intrigued, she hung on the attorney's every word.

The woman suggested they talk in a less conspicuous area in the sanctuary. When they were alone, the attorney stated next week she would contact Myaisha to arrange a more formal meeting.

"There are a lot of responsibilities involved in being an executor," the lawyer said. "I wanted you to have time to think it over before we met. Understand what the position entailed. If you accept, we'll discuss the legalities involved. It will require a time commitment on your part."

Tapping the envelope, the attorney detailed the documents inside. Explained what and where Myaisha needed to sign if she agreed to act as executor.

"Think it over. I would appreciate a decision by Monday. My assistant will contact you at your office. If you decline, I'll need to designate a replacement. If you accept, I'll send a courier to your office to retrieve the signed documents."

Questions flooded her already saturated mind. Her head felt thick. Overwhelmed, she simply stood there, watched as the attorney drifted away along with the other attendees. Up to this point, she considered herself a bystander in Candace's murder. A witness to the murder after the fact. A dear friend who wanted justice upheld. Now...

If Candace requested she serve as executor, of course she would accept. Candace had assigned her a role as an active participant. As executor, she would have to become more involved. Execute means to carry out fully, do what is required. *Could she fulfill her designation as executor without assisting in the apprehension of Candace's murderer?*

She felt dizzy with exhaustion. She followed the mourners out of the sanctuary. Except for the ushers, she was the last person to depart. A tad unsteady, she gripped the package as if her life depended upon its contents. The crisp envelope contrasted with her fluid emotions.

Once in the vestibule, she considered telling Adán about the lawyer. Since a horde of people surrounded him, she decided later would be best. Perhaps she should let the lawyer notify him about her assignment as executor. *Should she read the documents tonight?* Distracted, she startled when someone slipped up from behind her.

Mary gave her a hug and kiss. "Myaisha, is it true you found her body?" she asked.

Returning the hug, she then turned to Greg and hugged him too. "Yes," she said. "How are you guys holding up?" As she spoke with them, she wedged the large envelope into her purse—it barely fit.

Mary alerted onto the package, a question behind her eyes. Myaisha didn't satisfy her curiosity. They linked arms and walked toward the church exit.

"I still can't believe it—Candace dead," Mary said. "The last time I saw her, she looked... I don't know how to explain it."

She understood. Candace had been dynamic—alive, a whirlwind of constant motion.

Greg rubbed his wife's back. "It's such a shock—to everyone. We couldn't believe it when we heard it. Could we, babe?"

Mary hugged Greg around the waist and agreed.

"What do you think happened, doc? Robbery?" he asked.

She shook her head. "I don't know, Greg."

Cool night air greeted them outside.

Mary secured her crocheted shawl about her shoulders. "Goodness. Such a large turnout tonight. I hadn't realized Candace had so many friends."

Her eyes darted onto Mary. She viewed her profile, heard something odd in her voice. *Did her friend intend to be sardonic?* The stay-at-home mother appeared her kind gentle self.

"The service was nice. Pastor gave a good sermon," Greg said.

Mary rolled her eyes. "It wasn't a sermon Greg."

"You know what I mean. Pastor Matthew speaks well. We're lucky to have him."

Myaisha smiled. She recognized Greg's usual refrain. He enjoyed church. Always on time, he sat in the front pew. Usually alone because Mary and the children preferred to sit in the back. Greg had been a church elder for years. Until last month, when he stepped down from his position. Myaisha never understood why. She never asked.

Interesting. Although curious about medicine and her patients, her inquisitiveness hadn't extended into her personal life. With Candace murdered, things had changed. Greg was born to be an elder. He took his responsibilities to heart, proud of his commitment to the church and service to others. *Why would he relinquish his position as elder?*

Mary and Greg walked beside each other.

With her thoughts on recent events, she had fallen a step behind. They said their goodbyes.

"It was a nice memorial," Mary said.

"Yes it was. The entire church turned out, except Lottie. Drive safely, Myaisha," Greg said. "See you on Sunday."

She crossed the graveled lot, which held a few cars. A small Toyota Corolla idled at the edge of the church property. The first vehicle she ever purchased had been a Toyota Corolla hatchback. Many pleasant evenings were spent in her Corolla. She and Candace would drive down the coast to Monterey. Seated in the hatchback, they ate popcorn and watched movies at the drive-end. *Did drive-end theaters still exist?*

Her thoughts were all over the place. She needed rest. With a wave to the pastor, she drove away.

Half a block from the church, something Greg mentioned scratched at her consciousness. Down the darkened streets, she struggled to remember. Slamming on the breaks, she watched the signal light turn red. She blew out air, relieved she managed to stop in time.

Greg's comment about Lottie returned to her consciousness. *Where was Lottie?* As Candace's cousin, she should have been in the front pew with the other family members. Myaisha knew the women weren't close, but they were still family.

What would keep Lottie from attending a memorial service for her murdered cousin? Opposites in many ways, Candace and Lottie were both strong independent women. Gregarious ambitious Candace countered the content reserved Lottie. Those differences never kept them from supporting one another. In fact, Candace had helped Lottie secure Green Pastures for their writing group.

Steering her Honda through the winding streets, she hoped Lottie was fine. A glance in the rearview mirror brought her attention to more pressing issues. Two cars back, she noticed a Toyota Corolla that looked eerily similar to the one in the church parking lot. Of course, Toyotas were common. It could simply be her imagination. She'd had a long day. To be sure, she made a turn at the next left and waited to see if the vehicle followed. It did.

Her fatigue evaporated. She clenched the steering wheel. Unable to get a view of the driver, her eyes darted between her mirrors as she considered her options. She considered driving to a police station. At the next intersection, she executed an illegal U-turn. Now, she headed toward the Toyota. She peered through the windshield at the driver. Glare prevented a good appraisal of the individual, but she breathed a sigh of relief when it continued straight ahead.

Why would someone follow her? Could there be a connection with Candace's murder? With one eye trained on the rearview mirror for Toyota Corollas, she drove home.

Chapter 10

Cumulus clouds marched along the sky threatening rain. Miniscule pollens and danders floated through the air. Dressed in sneakers and a slicker, Myaisha parked in the garage at Moses Cone Hospital. Saturday mornings should be for rest. Instead, she prepared to take an ACLS, advanced cardiovascular life support, class. With Candace's murder on her mind, she preferred not to attend. She felt distracted. However, her certification would lapse by the end of the month. Unless she attended a class in Raleigh or Charlotte, it would be months before Greensboro offered another course.

If she didn't moonlight at the urgent care center in Kernersville, she would let her ACLS certification lapse. Since Josiah started college last fall, she appreciated the extra money. She didn't struggle to provide for his education—Sammy left them financially comfortable. A prudent saver, truth be told, she didn't need to work at all. With modest living, she could survive on his life insurance and her savings. She needed work for more than money though, caring for people gave her purpose. She enjoyed practicing medicine. When it became a chore, she would quit.

The three-story parking structure stood bare except for about a dozen vehicles. She grabbed her fedora and headed into the hospital. From the stairway she accessed the physician entrance on the first floor. She had an hour before class began, so she went to the medical records department to complete her patient charts. Afterward, she checked in at the nursery.

Lecture rooms were on the opposite side of the medical center. After class, she intended to stop by her favorite bakery and pick up some delicacies for her and Boomer. A relaxing evening at home would be a perfect ending to the day. Maybe she would tackle her work in progress—a cozy mystery. *Damn.* She almost forgot. She agreed to stop by the police station to sign her statement. At least it would also give her an opportunity to check their progress in the homicide investigation.

Once she entered the lecture room, she signed in and took a seat. A stale odor permeated the room. Plastic mannequins contributed to a musty smell of regret and boredom. She had taken the ACLS class many times and could probably pass it from rote memory. All the videos, didactics, and testing sessions with the mannequins drove her crazy. A vision of Candace's dead face flashed into her mind. She turned away from the mannequins and surveyed the room.

A reserved-looking gray haired older man took the other seat at her table. He introduced himself and stated he worked as an anesthesiologist. She liked the way his pale light blue eyes shined when he smiled. They exchanged pleasantries and returned to their own preoccupations. She skimmed through her manual—it never hurt to study. Failing the course would be embarrassing, not to mention a waste of her time and money.

Overhead fluorescent lights added to the drab atmosphere. A slow parade of dour faced individuals entered the classroom. An audible collective whisper grew as people conversed, afraid to speak too loudly their desire to leave and enjoy North Carolina's fickle summer weather before it changed—again.

She checked her watch, fantasized about sumptuous pastries with her favorite teas. Her mouth salivated at the idea.

Once all seats were occupied, the instructor called everyone to attention.

Half her brain listened, the other part contemplated surprising Josiah tomorrow with a visit to his college. She tried to give him space, but she missed him terribly. Especially with Candace murdered, she really wanted to be with him—touch him and give him a giant hug.

The instructor's stentorian voice interrupted her thoughts. The woman said, "Okay, partner up. Work in groups of two. Each group will rotate through the stations at least once. Feel free to return to a station if you need extra help. After the didactics, we'll watch videos. Remember ...."

Tuning out the instructor, she and the anesthesiologist arrived at their first station. He looked even more disinterested than she felt. In two minutes, they completed their first clinical.

She walked beside him to the next didactic, slouched from one leg to the other while they awaited their turn. After they finished, she stepped away from the open chest mannequin. Before she got far something heavy crashed upon her foot.

"Ouch!" She cried out, bent down to check her foot.

A very tall man turned around at the same time she bent down. He stumbled against her, overcorrected, and bumped into the table causing the mannequin to fall onto the ground. People gathered around to retrieve the CPR model and reassemble it upon the table.

The mannequin head rolled on the ground and bumped up against her leg. The hollow empty eyes stared up at her. Myaisha fought the rising nausea in the back of her mouth as the broken mannequin conjured up another memory of Candace's dead body on the office floor. The acid burned her throat.

The towering stranger looked from her to the table. He said, "I'm sorry. I didn't see you. Let me help you up." He gaped down at her, and offered her his hand.

After checking her toes, she gingerly rose on her injured foot. Hobbling, she accepted his hand to regain her balance. "How could you not see me?" she asked.

Standing at five feet eleven inches, she found herself facing the man's neck. With a frown, she stepped back and viewed the man attached to the hand. Her eyes widened in surprise.

His mouth dropped open and he released her hand. "I'm sorry. I'm such a klutz."

Limping—*her foot really hurt*—she gaped at probably the tallest man she'd ever seen in person.

Short curly hair, soft brown eyes, he stared back. People moved around them, disregarded their mishap. She searched for her partner, regained her composure.

She mumbled. "Don't worry about it." She left and caught up with the anesthesiologist at the shock table.

As they completed the didactics, she occasionally side-glanced at the stranger. He had a muscular frame with rich brown skin. He was kinda hot—not like she cared, because she didn't. But she found it hard not to admire his physique.

The instructor asked her a question about hydration. *Focus on the didactic.*

After she finished the exam, she collected her certificate. On her way out of the classroom, she sent Deniece a quick text.

Going to bakery. Want something?

Misty air and a few clouds met her outside. She reached forward to open the door leading to the garage.

A large hand reached in front of her and grasped the knob before she could.

Her heart raced, and her hand dove in her purse for her mace.

"Sorry, did I scare you?" he asked. The tall stranger from the ACLS class smiled at her. "Let me get that for you," he said.

The good-looking man had manners. His bass voice sounded nice. She entered the stairwell, conscious of him behind her.

He followed her into the staircase.

Neither spoke, at first. She resisted the urge to look at him.

"I'm sorry again about your foot. Are you sure you're okay?" he asked.

Her foot still hurt, but she tried not to limp. *It didn't look—why was she worried about her appearance?* "Don't worry. I'm fine," she said.

He held the door to the parking deck open for her again.

She felt flush, and wanted to check her hair. In a rush that morning, she fashioned her hair into a ponytail. By now, she probably had a nice big pouf ball on her head.

"You're still limping."

"I'm fine, really." She pulled out her keys and the fob beeped.

Hand outstretched, he strode in front of her. "My name's AJ. AJ Thomas."

She accepted his handshake. "Myaisha Douglas." His grip was firm, but not rough. She glanced up into his face. Such a charming smile. His hand felt warm and strong.

The day was cool but she felt hot. Electricity traveled from his firm calloused hand into her palm and up her arm. Realizing they still held hands, she dropped his palm as if it burned.

"Next time, try another way to get my attention." She smiled.

"Sorry about that. Want to grab something to eat?" He flashed her a smile which could have come off the cover of GQ. Full lips curved into an enormous grin.

She liked his grin. But she didn't date. It *had* been five years. *But was she ready?*

"Are you alright?" he asked.

"No—I mean yes. I mean; I should go. Thank you for the invitation, but I have to pass." She headed toward her car, but could feel him right beside her.

"I didn't mean to be so forward. I just wanted to apologize. Make it up to you with lunch—my treat."

She opened the car door and paused. Her cell phone beeped, a text from Deniece. She sent a quick text back, and noticed him standing there waiting for a reply. "AJ, I don't go out with guys I don't know," she said.

He smiled again. "How does a guy get to know you?"

She suppressed a giggle. *Was she flirting?* Oh, no. This had become dangerous. "Usually through a friend, or church."

"Will this do?" He brought out his phone and waved it in her direction.

She regarded the phone and considered his proposition.

"We can talk. Get to know each other wirelessly."

With a grin, she said, "Calling would be fine." She accepted his number and gave hers in exchange. Before she entered the car, she received a text addressed from AJ. Confused, she frowned. From the corner of her eye she noticed him grinning.

"Just wanted to make sure I got the right number," he said.

Okay, he was flirting. She touched the brim of her fedora and placed the car in reverse. She heard him say 'thank you', and started to reply when she saw something familiar. Her hands tightened on the steering wheeling. She froze.

A Toyota Corolla idled in a corner of the garage.

She squinted, strained to view the occupant. A head was visible, but no distinguishing features.

When she glanced to her left, she noticed AJ had departed. In the garage alone with the mystery Corolla, she quickly pulled forward and exited the garage.

Careful to check her rearview mirror for the Toyota, she turned left out the lot and observed the Toyota duplicate her actions. She maintained the speed limit and headed for the downtown police station. Since she had a follow up interview with the homicide detectives this morning anyway, she would mention to them she had a stalker.

Chapter 11

Sunny skies did nothing to ameliorate Myaisha's discomfort. Her eyes darted between her mirrors as she tracked the Toyota. It slipped behind a moving truck, but continued to follow her. Sweat beaded on her forehead. She tried to control her breathing, focus on her upcoming meeting with the detectives.

The day of the murder, she neglected to mention Lottie's argument with Candace the night their writing group met at Green Pastures. Nor did she mention an argument Candace had with Adán after church four days prior to the murder. She omitted those incidents from her statement because she doubted Adán or Lottie murdered Candace. Their arguments seemed insignificant. *Why worry the police about a domestic disagreement?* But domestic violence ranked as the number one cause for homicides against women. *How many victims of domestic abuse had she treated in her career?*

She was determined to tell the police everything she knew, and to mention the Toyota Corolla.

The air inside the police station felt stale, a stink of sweat and cigarettes added to the unpleasantness. Dull lighting heightened the gloom. In the background she heard phones ringing and people conversing. She placed her sunglasses in her purse, but left her fedora on.

In the lobby, she wondered if she should she ask for assistance or wait for the detectives to come looking for her. She regarded the police officer behind the plexiglass. He appeared to be reading something.

She glanced down at the angled tiled floor extending away from her in a winding zigzag formation like a maze. As she considered what to do, Detective de Jesus came through a door along the same wall as the reception window.

After greeting her, he escorted her into the station.

She had never been in a police station. It didn't look anything like she expected. On the left side of the hallway, she noticed several smaller rooms. She presumed they were used for interrogations. On the right, she viewed a larger office space containing groups of desks. In this larger room, police officers were working, on computers or phones. *Where was he leading her, surely not to an interrogation room?*

As if in answer to her question, the detective opened a door on the left side of the hall. He held out his hand and directed her to enter.

Her left eyebrow rose as she craned her neck to peeked inside. Small and boxy, the room held a desk and four chairs. Her eyes darted down the hallway from where she entered and back at the detective.

"Why are we going in there?" she asked. "I thought you only needed me to sign my statement."

A grin sat flat on his face. He moved in her direction, edging her toward the door as she backed away from him. "We like to conduct our interviews in here," he said.

She studied his face, but it gave no hint of his intentions. "Am I a suspect?"

"Everyone's a suspect right now," Detective de Jesus said. "Please come in."

Detective Gamble's sudden arrival from behind caused her to gasp.

"Sorry," he said. "I didn't mean to startle you." He entered the room, swung around and waited for her to follow.

Looking from one detective to the other, she considered the situation then acquiesced. She figured it was routine.

Detective de Jesus brought up the rear and closed the door.

She heard a click. *Did the door lock?*

Ecru walls held no adornment. Peeling laminate flooring and a table missing a coaster, the drab décor made her sad. *How many people entered this room and never left? Don't be morbid, they didn't die, they were arrested.* That failed to lift her spirits. She would give her statement and leave.

Across from her sat Detective de Jesus. He placed a manila folder on the table. It remained unopened half way between them. To her left, Detective Gamble took a seat away from the table with his back against the wall.

Removing a note pad from his suit jacket, Detective de Jesus asked, "Would you explain what brought you to the office on Wednesday, Dr. Douglas?"

Her forehead wrinkled, she regarded Detective de Jesus then Detective Gamble. Neither made an attempt to speak. They watched her, waited for a reply. A standoff.

She cleared her throat. "What progress have you made in your investigation?"

"We're still conducting interviews," Detective de Jesus said. "We need to clarify witness statements. Answer my question, please." He tapped his pen against the table and stared at her.

Arching her left brow, she gave him a dead glare. "Am I a suspect?"

Detective de Jesus sighed. "Doctor, this will go faster if you just answer the questions."

"I'm not answering any questions until you answer mine." She slid her chair beyond the table, putting distance between them. She chanced to look up into the corner of the wall. A red dot blinked back at her. Her gaze fell back over Detective de Jesus. "Are you recording this?" Her heart pounded. *Would they Mirandize her?*

Without waiting for a reply she stood and advanced toward the door. He intercepted her, but not before she grabbed the door knob. Locked. She pivoted on her left foot, and glared at him.

The hand he extended toward her retreated under her glare.

She squared her shoulders. "Why am I locked in here? Am I under arrest?"

"No, doctor. The door automatically locks. It opens from the outside."

Her arms crossed her chest. "Then tell someone to open it."

"Dr. Douglas—"

"Now. I came here voluntarily to provide a statement, not to be interrogated." She clutched her purse and maintained her position. Her heart raced, she felt sweat trickle down her back. She was upset, but didn't want to lose her temper—not in a police station.

Detective Gamble approached her from the right. "Dr. Douglas, take a seat," he said. "We'll finish up our questions, then you'll be free to leave."

Her head snapped to the right, she eyed him. Her head swiveled back to Detective de Jesus. "Open the door right now."

No one moved for half a minute. She opened her purse and removed her phone. Before she could dial, Detective de Jesus tapped on the door.

A uniformed officer responded and released the lock.

As soon as the gap proved wide enough to accommodate her frame, she maneuvered around the officer and fled.

Detectives de Jesus and Gamble pursued her.

"Wait, Dr. Douglas," Detective de Jesus said. "Dr. Douglas."

Detective Gamble also called after her.

Quickening her pace, she rushed out the station.

Detective Gamble ran out in front and overtook her.

She slackened her pace, not wanting to plow into him.

He held up his palms. "Dr. Douglas, please. We need your statement. Let's start over. Come back inside."

Attempting to walk around him failed as he stepped in front of her again—cautious not to touch her. Her chest rose and fell rapidly, she felt sweat pool in her lower back. When she swung to the other side, he again obstructed her progress. From her peripheral vision, she saw Detective de Jesus waiting in the rear.

She gritted her teeth. *Breathe. Don't lose it.* "You already have my statement. I have nothing to add. Next time you want my cooperation, don't treat me like a criminal."

Detective Gamble waved his hands out in front of himself as if in surrender. "We apologize. I apologize. Our mistake. We really could use your help. Please, come back into the station."

She placed her left hand on her hip, as the right hand held her bag. "Have you made any progress in the investigation?"

The detective dropped his hands at his side. "I'm not at liberty to discuss facts in the case. Our investigation is ongoing."

"Why not? If you want my help, I want to know where you are in your inquiry."

"That's not how this works. We ask questions, you answer. Come back inside."

She slipped on her glasses. "That's not how I work. You have my statement. If you want to speak with me again, make an appointment. You can call my office or my attorney."

Her keys jostled in her hand. She walked straight toward him. This time he stepped aside. She strode away. Her body shook with rage. She knew they watched her, she dared not glance back. Instead, she decided to walk over to the Green Pastures café. Calm down before she drove home.

She waited at the corner for the light traffic then crossed over two streets. A block further she entered Green Pastures.

Flavorful aromas greeted her at the door. She breathed in fried chicken and Arabica beans. She hungered for the former, could do without the latter.

For a Saturday morning, the attendance seemed light. While she waited in line she perused the menu on the wall behind the counter. With her elevated heart rate, she considered whether to order caffeinated or decaffeinated tea. As she paid for her beverage, someone tapped her left shoulder. She startled and hiccupped, dropping her credit card on the ground. After he picked up the card, she stood up to find Harriet smiling at her.

"I'm sorry, sugah. I didn't mean to scare yah," she said.

Myaisha returned the smile and took a deep breath. "No, it's my fault. I'm a little upset." She paid for her chai tea latte and stepped away from the countertop. To her surprise, Harriet followed.

Harriet frowned. "I'm sorry sugah, you not feeling well, but could I speak to yah?"

"Of course." Not in a hurry presently, she settled into a small table in a secluded corner of the eatery and scrutinized Harriet.

The woman seemed worried, her face somber, her jaw clicked. She hoped Harriet wasn't about to ask her for medical advice. She always felt awkward when people waylaid her at inappropriate times to ask about their medical ailments. She didn't mind giving free medical services, but in the office please. She sipped her tea while Harriet wrung her hands. *Perhaps she should give the woman some assistance.*

"Did you want some medical advice?" she asked.

Harriet chuckled. "Oh, no, sugah. I got a nice doctor over in High Point. No, it's about Mrs. Knight."

Her eyes widened. She set aside her tea. "Candace? What about her?"

"I heard about the murder."

"Do you know anything about it?"

"Nah. I don't think so." Harriet's forehead wrinkled. She pulled a towel from the belt around her waist and absently wiped the table clean of debris it didn't have.

Myaisha slid her chair closer to the table and whispered. "What do you mean, you don't think so?"

"I don't know who shot her, but I might know why."

Weary eyed, the older woman's jaw clicked and clacked as she relayed her story. Over the next thirty minutes, Harriet detailed how she came to purchase the café. Candace had been trying to get her to sell her building off of Wendover for years. The restauranteur had refused until Candace presented her with a plan to provide both of them with a guaranteed income.

"Mrs. Knight told me she'd published this book, and she was gonna start this club—a book club," Harriet said. "She'd make money telling people how they could get published like her. I'd buy the café and Mrs. Knight would bring in customers from her group. Writers and professional people who could pay good money. She promised me she'd rent out the conference room and I could charge fees."

"Did you ask Candace to explain the details on how the business would operate? Did you sign a contract?"

Head lowered, the woman's jaw snapped hard. "Nah. She didn't give me no details, just said it'd be easy. People would spend money trying to publish they books. They'd come to the meetings and eat and drink. That's how I'd make my money."

She nodded, encouraged Harriet to continue.

"But she also tol' me, I'd get a discount on the rent—and some of her money from the book. I know it's wrong to think about my problems—her being killed and all—but I got this bill yesterday. It said I owed all this money. And I ain't got it. I don't know what to do. Mrs. Knight's gone—her office closed. I don't know if I should call her husband, but I can't afford all this." She returned to wringing the towel.

Even as she listened she looked outside past Harriet. She wondered if the police would contact her again—if they suspected her of being complicit in the murder. Her attention oscillated from Harriett to the homicide detectives. She spoke absently. "I understand."

Harriet's tone increased. "No, you don't."

Her attention returned to their conversation. She saw Harriet glaring at her. "I want my old place back," Harriet said. "I can't stay here. I ain't got all this money. Mrs. Knight got me into this d—into this d—"

"Dilemma."

"Yeah—and I heard she done it to other people too."

Harriet related rumors she'd heard around town about how Candace swindled people. She heard Candace cheated her real estate clients and broke business deals.

With each allegation, Myaisha felt her temper rise. Her heart started to race again. She tried to remove any defensiveness from her tone. "You don't have a signed contract where Candace agreed to this arrangement, do you?" she asked.

"Nah. Mrs. Knight said we couldn't write up no agreement. Not until after I bought the property. It weren't legal, she said. We could get in trouble. But she promised to get me the papers after the closing, but she never did." Again, she wiped away at the imaginary debris. She hung her head, her jaw click-clacked.

Myaisha weighed Harriet's story. There was only her word about Candace's involvement in any improper business arrangements. The woman had no proof. With nothing in writing, she couldn't prove her statements. *Wasn't it her responsibility to look after herself?* Candace couldn't be faulted if a business transaction failed. Business was fickle by nature. *Right?*

With the kitchen smells and side conversations, Myaisha felt over stimulated—dizzy. Her eyes closed. A picture of Candace's dead face flickered in her mind. First, the detectives treated her like a suspect. Now, Harriet accused her friend of being dishonest. She couldn't accept it. Candace had been her friend for years. Harriet, she knew nothing about her. She needed to get out of there, she needed air.

Grabbing her tea, she rose and started to leave. Before she could escape, Harriet lightly touched her arm.

"Please, doctor, help me. I don't want to lose everything. I don't know what I'd do," she said.

Without responding, she exited the café. Outside, she leaned up against the side of the building. She closed her eyes and took several deep breaths. *Get it together girl.* The light breeze cooled the perspiration on her skin. Each moment brought her reason under control. Sunlight warmed her eyelids.

When she opened her eyes, she saw a woman approach. A frown grew under her fedora. She scrutinized the woman. Short, with a scarf on her head, the woman appeared headed for the café.

Her gaze wandered toward the street. She saw a Toyota Corolla parked at the curb. Her eyes widened, senses on high alert. She reached for the canister of mace in her purse.

The woman must have noticed because she raised empty palms as she passed by the entrance to the café and walked up to her.

"Don't shoot me, spray me, or hit me with whatever you have in your purse," she said.

Though the woman was much shorter than her, she appeared muscular and guarded.

Myaisha disregarded the woman's statement and kept her hand on the mace. "Who are you?" she asked.

The woman removed a card from her pocket and handed it over to her. "I'm a private detective. Mrs. Knight hired me."

She ignored the card and asked the woman, "Is that your Toyota Corolla?"

"Yes."

She straightened her back. Her nostrils flared. "Have you been following me?"

"Yes."

"Why?"

"Can we go somewhere else to discuss this?"

Her eyes darted from the woman, to the Toyota, and back to the café. She noticed Harriet watched them from the window. *What a day.* She met an attractive guy at the ACLS class. A twinge from her foot reminded her it hurt. The police insulted her. *Did they or could she be over sensitive?* And Harriet accused Candace of malfeasance, which bothered her the most because she knew it could be true.

She released her grip on the mace canister. "Okay. Let's go inside the café."

The private detective returned the card to her pocket. "Good. I'm thirsty," she said.

"If you tell me why Candace hired you, I'll buy you a tea."

"Tea? Aren't you fancy. I'll take a coffee, thank you."

Maybe they should meet in a bar. Myaisha had a feeling after she spoke with the detective, she would need a drink.

Chapter 12

For Myaisha, the mocha latte whatever the private detective ordered looked more like a milky hot chocolate than coffee. Whatever the concoction was it cost more than her tea. They sat together in a corner of the café near the window. From her periphery, she noticed Harriet watched her. She knew she had been rude, but—

"So, who goes first?" the private detective asked.

Focused on the woman in front of her, she said, "You. Explain yourself."

The woman laughed. "Who are you, Easy Rawlings?"

Myaisha touched the hat on her head. She started wearing hats shortly after Sammy died. Saturdays, she always wore the fedora—his favorite hat. Emboldened, she said, "How about you start with your name, and why you want to speak with me?"

"Grace Jones," she said with a wide grin.

Myaisha laughed. "Really? Are you making up names?"

The woman handed over a card which read Grace Jones, private investigator.

Her brows knitted into a question. "Your mom named you Grace Jones?"

The investigator shook her head. "No. I use it professionally. In my business, it wouldn't be prudent to divulge my real name."

She removed her cell phone and took a picture of Grace's business card. "Fine. Why did Candace hired you—and why you're following me?"

"I'll answer the second question first. I followed you because I need to get paid."

Her lips formed into a question, but Grace answered before she could speak.

"I know; you're going to ask why would you should pay me. It's the answer to your first question. You want to pay me to find out why Candace hired me."

Frustrated, she stretched her back as she sat in her chair. Her head felt thick. "Do you know who killed Candace?"

"No."

"Is it in the information you have?"

"Could be." A smirk teased at the corner of Grace's mouth.

She leaned her elbows on the table. "What does that even mean?"

"It means I don't know—from my own knowledge—who killed Mrs. Knight. But clues to her killer may be in the information I accumulated."

Suspicious, she studied the woman. Grace wore jeans and a blazer, and carried herself like a no non-sense kind of person. However, the woman wanted to get paid. Evidently, she provided some service for Candace. Since dead people couldn't pay, she shopped the intel around to what she considered interested parties. *Could she trust her? No.*

"Why don't you give it to the police?" she asked. "Turn it in for the reward."

Grace drank her coffee concoction then licked her lips. "Because, if the police don't connect the information with solving the crime, I don't get paid."

"What about Adán? Have you tried him?"

"You mean dimples? He doesn't have any money. Mrs. Knight kept him on a tight leash."

A flinch escaped her body.

"My comment surprised you? Then you must not have known Mrs. Knight as well as I thought." Grace finished off her latte.

She studied the PI. Her gaze wandered across the café at no one in particular. Myaisha didn't trust her, but she wanted the information. "How much?"

"Ten thousand."

"Liar. No way Candace ever agreed to ten thousand dollars. Her expensive tastes didn't extend to the people she employed."

With her head thrown back, Grace let out a loud cackle.

People turned around and looked at them. After a few minutes, they returned to their coffees.

Unashamed, the PI continued laughing, tears streamed from her eyes. "Sorry. I had to try it on. I guess you knew Knight better than I thought. That's actually how I got the job. In case you couldn't tell, I'm new at this. First lesson of business, get paid up front."

"How long have you been a private investigator?" she asked.

"Don't worry about it. How about five?" Grace scooted her chair closer to the table.

She peered into Grace's eyes. "Two."

The woman held her gaze, didn't flinch. "Three. And if you find it useful, another thousand—and you give me a recommendation."

"A recommendation? How? Facebook?"

She chuckled, her cherubic face lit up with a large smile. "Tell your friends. Send work my way. A girl's gotta eat."

"Agreed."

They shook hands, and made payment arrangements.

While Grace went to her vehicle, Myaisha considered what Candace was up to and whether it involved her murder.

The PI returned from her vehicle carrying a large folder and handed it to Myaisha.

Accepting the package, she asked, "Grace, you have *no* idea who could have killed Candace?"

Grace gathered up her food, prepared to depart. "Sure, anyone burned in her business schemes."

For a quarter of an hour, Myaisha sat in the café reading the dossier Grace compiled for Candace. Traffic in the café increased and she decided it would be better to continue reading the documents at home.

Before she left, she approached the counter. She asked the cashier if she could speak with the owner. Her wait wasn't long.

Wearing a scarf and holding a dish towel, Harriet left the kitchen and joined her at a nearby table. Her jaw grinded.

She sighed. "Harriet, I want to apologize. You asked for my help, and I neglected to give you an answer." She folded her hands on the table. "I will help you."

Harriet placed her hands over hers and smiled. "I knew you would, sugah. You good people."

A smiled crossed her lips. She squeezed Harriet's hands. "So are you."

Chapter 13

Ding dong!

Adán stacked boxes near the door in the master bedroom. He would miss living in this house. He loved Candace's taste, the mid-century esthetic appealed to him. It was one of the few things they shared.

Between the police and visitors from church, he hadn't managed to finish packing. It took longer than he expected. He'd been at it for two days. It amazed him how much clothing Candace owned. His parents offered to stay and help, but he preferred to be alone. He needed time to process everything.

Ding Dong!

Damn. Whoever it was they weren't giving up. His lawyer wasn't due until three. He feared it might be the police. Tossing a hand full of clothes onto the bed, he made his way to the front door. Through the peep hole, he saw Kelley. He exhaled.

She stood there with her arms wrapped around her torso, shivering.

His eyes narrowed. He cracked open the door. "Kelley, what are you doing here? I told you not to come by."

She pushed him aside and bolted through the entrance. Ran past him and rushed into the living room.

Speaking to the air, he said, "Come in."

Before he closed the door he peered around outside—no police cars. For the past two days at least one unmarked vehicle stationed at the end of his driveway. Relieved the authorities seemed to have abandoned their vigil, he joined Kelley in the living room.

She paced back and forth in front of the large sliding glass doors.

He glanced outside at the large trees at the edge of the yard swaying in the breeze.

Kelley's leg bounced up and down. She spun around to face him. "Adán, I know I shouldn't have come, but I had to speak with you."

He stepped away from her. "Kelley, the cops are watching me. It's too risky for us to be seen together."

"I know, but I'm getting nervous. The school will be audited next month. If I don't get the money back..." Crying, she abandoned the windows and took a seat on the couch closest to the fireplace.

He twisted the watch on his wrist, sat on the couch across from her. "I can't help you. I don't have any money. You made a deal with Candace, not me."

"I could go to jail."

"I understand, and I don't want that for you. But I—there's nothing I can do. I can't help you."

Her eyes filled with tears. "Did you at least get the video back? It was your idea to break into the office. If the police get the video, I could be charged with robbery. Embezzling from the school is bad enough. But if the police find the video—I could be charged with burglary too."

"Come on." He stood and led her into the kitchen.

Head down, she followed, picking at her finger nails. She waited for him beside the island and chewed on her battered fingernails.

He exited the pantry with one fist covered in flour. His hand opened to displayed a thumb drive.

With a gasp she snatched it from his palm. She closed her eyes and trembled. Her left leg shuddered. Her silent lips moved in prayer.

Water dripped over his hands in the sink. After he washed up, he gave her a few minutes to collect herself.

"Candace never cooked a day in her life," he said. "The kitchen became the ideal hiding place. I got the thumb drive from the safe before she cleaned it out. Kelley, you'll figure something out about the money. Maybe I could speak to my lawyer for you."

Her head shook. She said, "Not unless he promises to represent me too. I'm not telling anyone what I did unless I'm protected."

"She, not he. By the way, did you bring the items you stole—took, from the office?"

"Yes, here." A thick stack of papers tumbled out of her leather backpack.

He gathered up the documents, scanning through them as he stacked them together. A notarized document with an official seal landed on the ground. Picking it up, he scrutinized the heading. Puzzled, he frowned, deciding to read it later. He added it to the pile. First, he had to get rid of Kelley. "Is this everything?" he asked.

She picked at her nails, and watched him arrange the papers. "Yes. You said my money and documents were in the office safe. It was the reason I broke in."

"I know."

"How come you didn't know about the security cameras?" She squinted, studied him closely as he answered.

"You think I set you up? Why would I do that? I needed your help as much as you needed mine."

"Yes, but I was the one your wife caught on video breaking into her office. And the safe didn't hold anything I needed, just a bunch of legal papers, contracts—you have to help me."

He exited the kitchen and headed toward the front door. "I will. I promise."

"When? I don't have much time. I need money. If I lose my job, my husband will find out what I did. I'm scared." She followed him into the foyer.

Leading her by the elbow, he assisted her across the threshold and outside. He had no intentions of taking on her problems. He had his vices, but stealing wasn't one of them. He felt sorry for the teacher, she seemed like a nice girl. Young, attractive—if she had money he'd think about helping her. Right now, he had no desire to take care of anyone, let alone a woman stupid enough to embezzle money from her employer.

She approached him several months ago, explaining the arrangement she'd made with Candace. She'd invested money she stole from her school's athletic account, believing the transaction would earn her quick money she could replenish before the school discovered. She understood her mistake too late. Kelley stole money from the school and Candace stole it from her. The cycle of crime.

He had explained to the teacher he couldn't help her, but offered a solution. She could burgle Candace's office and retrieve her money and financial documents from the safe. It astounded him when the teacher took him up on his suggestion. For his part, he provided her with the combination to the safe. Kelley had located her contract, but unfortunately for her the safe held only a few hundred dollars.

Adán had hoped she would locate financial documents to help him locate where Candace deposited money in overseas bank accounts. Unknown to him at the time, his wife had installed a surveillance camera, but she hadn't called the police. After Candace identified Kelley as the culprit, she threatened to send the video to the police if the stolen documents weren't returned. Kelley had tried to negotiate return of the documents for the money she invested, but his wife refused.

He couldn't help Kelley. In fact, Candace accused him of infidelity with the young teacher. He considered the teacher attractive, very much so, but adultery also wasn't one of his vices either. A comfortable life funded by an undemanding financially successful woman had been his goal, which he thought he had secured in Candace. Shortly after their marriage though, he discovered his mistake. His bride had goals of her own.

Now single again, he intended to enjoy his life. Once he inherited her estate, he would be leaving Greensboro and all its problems behind. First, he had to satisfy the cops of his innocence, which he would accomplish later today after he and his lawyer met with the detectives. Admiring her doll-like eyes, he felt a twinge of guilt—only a twinge.

"My wife just died. I need time to think. To be alone," he said.

She slipped from his grasp, poked her finger in his chest and shoved him back. "You didn't even love her. You told me she treated you like dirt. Like you were something to show off to her friends." She shoved him in the chest again. "I broke into her office because you told me I would find my agreement *and* my money. You're the only person who benefited"

He backed up, blocked the threshold so she couldn't get inside. Held the door knob with one hand behind his back. "No one made you break into the office, Kelley. Just like no one told you to steal the money from the school."

Smack.

She slapped him hard across the face. "You, jerk. I risked my job, my marriage. For what?"

Prepared to hit him again, but this time he anticipated the assault and grabbed her hand. They wrestled for a few seconds until she escaped his grasp.

Her finger flew into his face. "You'll regret this, Adán. I swear." She took several steps away from him, then swung around. "You'll get yours, just like your wife."

Before he returned inside, he noticed the neighbors. From their porches, the neighborhood watched. He shook his head. This had to end soon. He bent down to pick up the newspaper. When he stood up he appreciated someone off to his left.

Before she returned home, Myaisha decided to stop by and check on Adán. Her head hurt, but she worried about him. The church had organized a schedule where someone would bring him food each day. She hadn't placed her name on the list, but decided to drop something by anyway. Not a great cook, she was an excellent baker. But even with her sweet tooth, she couldn't eat all the bake goods she prepared—although Boomer made up for her deficiencies. Today, however, she picked up something from her favorite bakery.

The visit to the police station hadn't gone as planned. The incident still bothered her. *Why had they treated her like a suspect?* They were probably just doing their duty, but she still resented it. She really wanted to know how the case progressed. There hadn't been any updates in the press. No one in church knew anything more than she did. Then Harriet—and the private detective. It was almost too much. She was tired. After she checked on Adán she intended to take a long hot bath.

She also had a few questions for the widower, especially about the argument at Pastor Matthew's home the week before the murder. She needed to sort out the information she learned and establish a plan on how to investigate the murder. Right now, she felt the case directed her.

As she drove down Candace's street, she noticed a police car conspicuously parked at the corner. Making eye contact with the officer, she continued toward the house. Parked in the driveway, she removed the cake from the back seat. In a flash, the front door of the house flew open. Surprised, she stood there, gripping the dessert container to her chest.

On the door step, she saw Adán speaking with a woman. In her early twenties, attractive, the woman wore long box braids which extended down her back. The woman gestured wildly, made no attempt to lower her voice. Not exactly shouting, the quiet early morning heightened her tone.

In contrast, Adán stood there detached. At least until the woman slapped him across the face. The sound echoed down the street.

Stunned, Myaisha increased her grip on the container—it almost dropped. Out of the corner of her eye, she spied the police vehicle stealthily approach the home.

The woman hurried from the porch, jumped in her car and sped away.

Focused on retrieving the newspaper from the ground, Adán failed to notice her approach. When he stood upright, she greeted him. Face to face with her, his eyes enlarged. His mouth hung open.

"Hello, Adán," she said. "I thought I'd come by and check on you."

"Dr. Doug—Myaisha. Hi. Come in."

With the box tucked under her right arm, she stood in the foyer. She gave him a moment to recover. A red hand print on his left cheek.

Once inside, he dropped the newspaper on the table. "Thanks for coming by. Let me take that. Can I get you anything?"

"No, thank you. I'm good."

He accepted the cake container and withdrew to the kitchen.

While he stepped away, she seized the opportunity to look around. She scrutinized the living room, noticed things had been removed—pictures of Candace, pictures of him with Candace. Cautious, she tiptoed into the hallway. The bedroom door stood ajar.

With her limited view, she saw clothes strewn across the bed. Boxes assembled around the room. *Already packing?* It took her years to part with anything belonging to Sammy—in truth, she simply relocated his items to a guest room. In contrast, Adán required only two days. It could be some kind of record.

Hearing him return, she hastened into the living room and stood beside the fireplace.

He held a cup in his hand. "Can I get you a cup of coffee?" he asked.

Her nose twitched. "No, thank you."

"Thanks for stopping by. It's been a difficult time."

"I'm sure. Have the police told you anything about their investigation?"

"No. Actually, I have an appointment to meet with them in a few hours. They want me to give an official statement." Sitting on the edge of a chair, he sipped his coffee.

She sat on a chair near the fireplace. "Are you going alone?"

"Oh, no. My lawyer will be stopping by later. We're gonna drive down to the station together."

"That's good. Smart." As she viewed the room, an uncomfortable silence descended between them. She'd always liked Adán. He appeared amiable enough, but they had never been friends—independent of Candace. She accepted him because of her friendship with her. Now that she took the opportunity to observe him up close he seemed superficial. But out of respect for her friend, she wanted to be supportive. She believed Candace would want her to. At the very least it would be the Christian thing to do.

"Do you need anything? Is there anything I can do to help?" she asked.

"No, thank you. Everyone's been great." He placed his cup down on the table and stood. "I'll be fine. I just need some time to sort my life out."

Taking his cue, she also rose. On her way toward the front door, she felt him fall in behind her. On a whim, she spun around. She caught him off guard and they plowed into each other, knocking heads.

He sputtered. "Oh. Sorry."

She rubbed her forehead. "I'm sorry. My fault. By the way, what's the name of that woman?"

For a second his mouth hung open, then his face went blank.

She waited. The machinations of his gray matter were evident from his wandering eyes. She decided to be more transparent. "You know, the woman who slapped you at the front door."

His smile fell, no more dimples. The cockiness dissipated. He raised his voice. "I'm sure you can understand this isn't a good time for me."

"What about the argument you had with Candace at Pastor Matthew's house last Sunday? What was it about?"

He strode to the front door, stood beside it as he held it open. "I don't have to explain my relationship with Candace to you."

"No, you don't. But it would help clarify why—"

"Myaisha, I need to be alone. My wife was murdered, and this has been stressful for me."

"Of course. I understand. But it would take a second for you to tell me the name of the young lady, and why she assaulted you." She stepped outside.

His jaw clenched. "I can't believe I have to say this to you, of all people, but mind your own business." He shut the door in her face.

She shrugged it off and returned to her car. Intrigued, she thought about the woman with the braids. Apparently, one of his paramours. *But who was she? And what did he do to deserve a slap?*

She touched the brim of her hat with her fingertips, thought about how she could find out. *Just because you're wearing a fedora, doesn't make you Easy Rawlings.*

Chapter 14

The early evening sky cleared to a nice robin blue hue. A light wind fluttered the leaves. Myaisha walked Boomer along the sidewalk around the neighborhood. A few children rode their bikes. Scents of grilled meats wafted on the breezes.

From behind, an excited dog on a long leash gained on them.

She stepped into the street.

Boomer barked and whined, his tail beat rapidly.

She tightened the leash and directed him to heel at her side.

The dog passed within inches of them as its owner conversed on his cell phone.

With a deep frown, she shot him a wicked glare. *Rude.*

He avoided eye contact and continued his chat while taking up the entire sidewalk.

Boomer, an older black lab—with manners—didn't tug on the leash. He accepted his discipline and gazed up at her. His wide doggy eyes seemed to ask, 'Can I sniff, Mommy? Can I, please?'

"Sit, Boomer," she said.

With a low whine in his belly, he remained at attention as the large classic poodle strolled by. He turned his head up toward her and barked. His look said, 'Killjoy'.

She loosened the leash and they continued their walk.

Boomer sniffed along the sidewalk and tried to catch up with the quickly departing poodle. He accepted the fruitlessness of his endeavor and picked up the scent of some squirrels. He growled half-heartedly at the trees.

Fresh air hadn't cleared her head, she remained conflicted. At least the walk provided her with some exercise. She could lose a few pounds.

A lawn mower threw up whiffs of fresh cut grass. Sunlight beamed across the lawns its final rays before it set.

She smiled at a neighbor pruning roses in the front yard. With her free hand she waved to another neighbor on her porch in a rocking chair.

How to proceed with investigating Candace's murder? Reading murder mysteries wasn't enough preparation to solve a true homicide.

As they made their way home, her phone rang. She transferred the leash to her right hand and dug her phone out her pants pocket. "Hey, D. What's up?" she asked. She could barely make out her voice from the background noise.

"Where are you?" Deniece asked.

"I took Boomer for a walk. Where are you?" She strolled up to her front door.

"We're just leaving church. You should come next week. A visiting pastor will be preaching."

"No, thanks." With her cell phone balanced between her shoulder and ear, she felt in her pocket for the house keys.

Boomer bounded inside the house.

"How did it go at the police station?"

"Not well. I'll tell you about it later. You and Barry got plans?"

"No, why?"

"I need to talk about Candace." She swallowed. "I didn't tell you everything."

<hr>

As crickets chirped in the woods at the end of her yard, Myaisha grew more frustrated. Her knees hurt from kneeling on the stone patio. Twilight and hedges provided privacy and blocked prying eyes. Her neighbors couldn't see her wrestling with Boomer. Holding a shampoo bottle in one hand and a hose in the other, she attempted to give him a bath.

"Sit still," she said. Setting the shampoo bottle down, she held him by the collar and sprayed him. "We're almost done."

Despite her pleas, Boomer edged further away from her and shook his body free of what little water and soap she'd managed to get on him. Determined to complete his bath, she lathered him up again, showered him from the nozzle, and scrubbed him from his head to his tail. Minutes passed and she became drenched. She ignored his whining and completed the bath. Before she could start to dry him off, she heard jingling keys. *Strange.* She turned off the hose and listened.

Her lab used the opportunity to shake again and scamper into the house.

"Boomer, come here." She gave chase, cornered him inside the laundry room and threw a towel over the labrador.

The front door bells chimed.

Dropping the towel, she headed for the front door. She slipped on the tiled floor slick from soap and water and grabbed onto the wall to break her fall.

She made it into the kitchen, with Boomer at her side, when she heard the door open. He barked and trotted to the door.

"Hello? Who's there?" she asked,

Not able to see anyone, she heard Deniece's voice answer.

"Myaisha? Mya. Where are you?"

"Over here." She exhaled and returned to the laundry room to retrieve the towel and wipe up the water she trailed into the kitchen.

Paws scratched along the floor boards as Boomer dashed around the house, rubbing his wet body against the furniture.

She sprinted after him. "Boomer, come back here."

He delivered several short barks before he jumped onto Deniece.

Kneeling down, she ruffled his hair. "Boomer. You been a good dog. Huh?"

His large tail smacked rapidly against the floor and nearby wall. It confirmed, yes indeed, he had been a good dog.

Myaisha ordered him down off Deniece. He barked. She herded him back into the laundry room.

Minutes later, she returned to the living room wearing clean clothing and collapsed into a chair. She wiped her hands on her t-shirt, and scratched her head between two thick French braids.

A drier, but still damp Boomer trotted behind her with a treat between his teeth and took up a position beside the couch near Deniece. He snorted at her and pawed affectionately at Deniece, who responded by scratching behind his ears. He jumped up on her lap.

Myaisha stretched her legs forward. "Boomer, get off the couch."

He gave a short bark, obeyed her command but remained near Deniece.

She bent over to sniff his coat. "Looks like someone's not happy about their bath," she said. "Umm. You smell clean Boomer."

"He's not alone. I'm not happy either. Thanks for coming."

Deniece laughed. "Girl, you look exhausted. What's wrong?"

With a large yawn, she stretched her back and tightened her braids "There's too much going on. Today, has been crazy. I thought the ACLS would be the most stressful thing I had to do."

"What happened?"

"I don't even know where to begin, but I need help. I'm investigating Candace's murder—"

"Why? Leave it to the police. They'll catch her killer—it's their job." Dressed in a calf length dress, Deniece slipped out of her heels and curled her legs under her torso on the couch. "You realize you arrived minutes after murderer left. Imagine what would've happened if you got there a few minutes earlier."

She looked beyond Deniece into the backyard, watched birds alighting on branches of the trees. "I didn't think about that."

"Well, think about it. You understand you could have been hurt—or killed. Leave it alone."

"I know I should, but I can't. She was my friend. How can I ignore her murder?"

Deniece tossed her purse on the table. "Easy. You have other priorities."

Her gaze fell on Boomer as he chewed on his treat. "I can't understand why anyone would murder Candace," she said. "I can understand people being angry with her, but murder? It seems drastic."

Leaning forward with her elbows on the coffee table, Denise asked, "What's going on? What's really bothering you?"

Warm brown eyes invited her to confess her perturbation. She sighed. "Candace was my friend. I've known her—" Tears brimmed at the edge of her lashes. It took a moment for her to reign in her emotions.

Denise rose and sat on the couch next to her, gave her a side hug.

She cleared her throat. "Someone murdered her in her office. This wasn't some random crime, someone targeted her. It was personal. Someone wanted her dead for a specific reason. And I have a feeling searching for her killer means discovering stuff about her I don't want to know."

Their conversation stalled.

Pivoting on the couch, she faced Deniece. Having resolved to sharing everything she knew, she detailed what occurred. She began with the police station, purposefully leaving out the tall stranger at the ACLS class.

Her eyes widened, she asked, "You think they suspect you?"

The tone of her friend's voice made her frown. "Well, yes."

"Why?"

"I don't know." She shrugged. "Maybe they don't suspect me. It might be their normal protocol. The point is, they aren't looking at strangers. Whoever murdered Candace knew her and she knew them. That's why she left the office door unlocked. She expected her killer. She wasn't afraid of him."

"Him?"

"Or her." She slid to the edge of the sofa, spoke conspiratorially. "There's more." She explained what Harriet told her at the café about Candace's intention to make money off their writing group. By the time she described the incident with the young lady at Adán's place, her friend gaped at her.

At the end of the monologue, Deniece sank back into the sofa pillows. "I'm not surprised," she said. "I always thought Adán was a mooch."

"Really? I think he's a nice guy. A little lacking in brains, but sweet."

"Um hmm." Deniece rolled her eyes, flattened her lips. "Like everyone else, you fell for his cheap charm. Girl, he's just eye candy with dimples."

"I did not. I saw how he treated Candace—like a queen."

Stretching her feet under the table, Deniece smirked. "Easy to do using her money."

"That's not fair. It's not his fault he didn't make as much money as she did."

"Okay, fine. What's so great about him? He's a life coach. He makes his living telling women how to *effectuate* their potential. What a bunch of crap."

"There's nothing wrong with being a life coach. They can be helpful." She picked up a stray glass from the table, stepped over Boomer and headed for the kitchen.

Deniece followed behind her. "Yeah, right. Whatever. The point is, he lived off Candace. She supported him."

"I thought we were liberated. Is it supposed to matter if the wife makes more than the husband?"

"I'm just saying it's easy to be generous with someone else's money."

Boomer lumbered off the floor, licked up the remaining crumbs of his treat from the floor and brought up the rear as everyone entered the kitchen.

After dropping the glass in the sink, she went to the refrigerator and started removing items. "You hungry?"

Shaking her head in the negative, Deniece joined her at refrigerator. She grabbed the juice container and then sought a glass from the cabinet.

Myaisha prepared dinner.

Like a tennis ball, Boomer's head volleyed between both women.

While she assembled a frittata, her friend filled Boomer's bowl with dog food. He gave the bowl a sniff, then returned to the side of his mistress to await droppings.

Sipping her juice, Deniece asked, "So, what's the problem? Like I said, leave it alone. Let the police handle it."

Garlic and shallots sizzled in the pan releasing their pungent aromas. Delicious scents floated around the kitchen. She added eggs and seasonings, and last the cheese. Focused on the dish, she gave her a side-glance.

"I haven't finished." The skillet went into the oven. She relayed the separate arguments she witnessed involving Candace with Adán and Lottie, keeping the fact she hadn't shared the information with the police until the end.

Placing her glass in the sink, Deniece asked, "What's wrong with you? What're you doing? No wonder you believe the police suspect you. It's your guilty conscience."

Snatching up a dish towel from the countertop, she wiped her hands. "I don't even know what the arguments were about. What if they had nothing to do with the murder? I don't want to get anyone in trouble."

Her eyes enlarged, her arms flew wide. She leaned across the island and peered into her face. "That's the point, you don't know. Mya, you're a great doctor, but you're not a detective—and it's none of your business. Tell the cops what you know and leave it alone."

"I want to help. Candace had to be murdered by someone she knew. That's where I have an advantage over the police. I knew her—know her friends. The killer could be a mutual acquaintance."

"Not necessarily. It could be someone Candace met through her work—club, sorority, or some other organization she belonged to."

Casting her eyes over the kitchen, she thought it over. "That's possible."

They discussed different scenarios as she prepared water for tea. Sliding the frittata onto a plate, she took a seat beside Deniece at the kitchen island. As she ate, two pairs of eyes watched her.

Boomer's mouth hung open. He panted, a trickle of drool hit the floor.

After retrieving a fork and plate, Deniece joined her in attacking the frittata. She asked, "So again, what's the problem?"

Her fork hung in the air as she chewed her eggs. "The problem is; I might know the murderer. It could be—"

"Adán. It must be Adán."

She dropped her fork. "What is it with you and Adán? Why would he kill her?"

With a sly grin, Deniece counted the reasons off on her fingers. "Murder 101, the spouse is always the first suspect. Murder 102, the most likely suspect is usually the murderer. Murder 103, he was having an affair—probably not his first. Murder 104, she had all the money. Did you know Candace had been listed as one of the thirty under thirty to watch in *Charlotte Magazine*?"

She laughed, sipped her tea. "Candace passed thirty a long time ago."

Deniece speared some eggs and peppers with her fork. "I related an example of her success. I read in the paper she had been listed as a top performing realtor in Guilford County five years in a row. *And* I heard from some friends she owned properties in the Carolinas, Georgia and Florida."

"Aside from rumors, we don't know he committed adultery. Hercule Poirot always said to confirm everything you hear from another source. And, Adán had to know he would be the first person the police suspected. He might not be a genius, but I don't believe he's a fool."

Grinning, Deniece asked, "Your conducting your investigation based on your experience with Agatha Christie?"

She sneered. "Bite me."

"Maybe she planned to divorce him. I heard they had a prenup. She would've annihilated him in a divorce. But now, as the surviving spouse, he gets everything."

Climbing down from the stool, Myaisha deposited her remaining food into Boomer's bowl and placed the plate in the sink.

Duplicating her actions, Deniece scraped her meal into the bowl too. "I bet there's life insurance. He'd make out simply selling that house. The place must be worth a fortune."

Turning on the faucet, she started cleaning the dishes. "It's possible. I have to contact the lawyer on Monday. I'll find out the details of her will."

Elbows rested on the quartz countertop, Deniece watched her. "What lawyer?"

Soap suds covered her forearms covered in suds. "Candace named me executor of her estate," she said.

Jumping up off the stool, Deniece startled Boomer. However, in seconds his attention returned to his food bowel.

"How did you not tell me you'd been appointed executor of Candace's estate? All this time we're discussing her death and you never thought to mention being her executor."

Her soapy hands shrugged. "I forgot, okay."

They exchanged a look.

Grimacing, Deniece shook her head, picked up her mug and went into the living room.

Minutes later, Myaisha joined her on the couch. Her fingers curled around the mug, the warmth gave her comfort as she stared out into the darkening sky. The window glass reflected her face, which dissolved into a picture of Candace—eyes closed, her face a death mask. She gasped.

"What? Deniece asked.

She blinked the vision away. "Nothing. Sorry."

With a start, Deniece tapped her on the shoulder. "What's the name of the detective who interviewed you again?"

"Detectives Gamble and de Jesus."

"First names."

"I don't know. Let me get their cards." Setting her mug on the table, she went to find her purse.

When she returned, Boomer lay at Deniece's feet. Handing the cards over to her friend, she asked, "Why don't you get a dog?"

"I hate dogs." Deniece read the cards.

Boomer looked up at her, shook his coat and laid back down across her bare feet.

"No you don't," Myaisha said, smiling. "You love dogs. You had a dog for years."

She tossed the cards on the table. "Exactly, and she went and died on me."

Her eyes softened. "She didn't die on purpose."

"Maybe not, but she broke my heart. One broke heart in a lifetime is enough." Avoiding eye contact, Deniece scrolled through her phone.

Sipping her tea, she regarded her friend. All her family lived out west, therefore Deniece became like a sister to her. They'd been through much together—Sammy's death, Deniece's infertility. Despite being a physician, she'd been useless to help her friend conceive a child. Neither prayers, diligence, or research helped. Through it all, she remained true, listened and supported her friend. After Sammy died, she suffered her own personal breakdown. Her friend rose to the challenge, took care of Josiah when she couldn't. She wondered if friendships had life expectancies. *Had her friendship with Candace exceeded its life expectancy?*

A shout brought her out of her reflections.

"Got it," Deniece said.

Her eyebrow arched in question.

Handing her back the business cards, Deniece said, "Your Detective de Jesus, I know his mother. We worked together at Cone Hospital years ago. She's a nurse, *and* a member of our writing group."

"Are you sure?"

"Of course. How many de Jesus's can there be in Greensboro?"

Probably more than her friend realized. Greensboro's Asian diaspora increased significantly in the '70s and '80s, some from refugee resettlement. She said, "You think she can get information from him?"

"Absolutely, she's fierce, like us." Deniece sent a text to Mrs. de Jesus.

She winced. "Don't get him in trouble—or me."

"I won't. I'm just gonna ask her to speak with him about the case. Everyone likes a little gossip."

Gathering up their cups, she retired to the kitchen, speaking over her shoulder. "Still in church clothes and already gossiping."

"Hey, you want help or not? No judging. By the way, when are you coming to church with me again?"

Not raised in the church, Myaisha's dad stated he met God on the battlefields of 'Nam and since he made it back home in one piece he figured they were already on good terms. Her mother, agnostic on a good day, never cared either way. Sammy invited her to his church when they were in college. She joined the faith right before her marriage.

Back in the living room, she set a glass of water down on the table. "I have my own church, thank you very much."

"Fine, but it's not a sin to visit another church." A large grin grew along Deniece's face. "Speaking about sin, I know a guy who'd be perfect for you."

Her body tensed. She avoided her friend's gaze and looked outside. "Since when were we talking about dating." She moved across the room to a recliner in front of the bookcase.

With a wink, she said, "We are now. Mya, it's time. Aren't you interested in meeting someone?"

"No."

"How about just getting something on the side? You know, for those lonely nights." Her eyebrows rose suggestively.

She laughed. "Stop it. No, I'm good."

"What am I going to do with you? If I don't find you someone, you're going to die alone."

"I can find my own man."

"Yeah, right. Where? In a book store. At the writing group."

Or at an ACLS class. "I can find a man on my own."

Denice chuckled, came over to the recliner, and knelt beside the chair. "Girlfriend, its time."

"I don't need a man."

"No one needs a man." Deniece sat on the arm of the chair. "They're accessories, like those rat dogs women carry in their purses. Nice to have along for the ride."

She smiled as she studied her friend's face, searched for confirmation. She feared acknowledging what she knew to be true, she was attracted to AJ. He awakened something deep inside her, buried for years—neglected. Her rational mind fought against her tender heart. Embarrassed, her arms encircled her knees and curled into her chest. She wasn't ready to share her feelings toward AJ with Deniece. She wasn't even sure what she felt.

"D—I don't know. Sammy was the only man I'd ever been with."

She smirked. "Let's start with a date first. You can worry about the other stuff after we find someone you like."

They laughed. Deniece slid down the arm of the chair and fell against her side. She rested her head against her shoulder as her friend gave her a hug. They held each other.

Was she ready for a relationship? Candace had been murdered and she was thinking about a man.

She hugged Deniece and kissed her temple, determined not to let down another friend.

Chapter 15

The downtown police station buzzed with activity. Adán had to lean close to his attorney to hear what she said as they waited in line. Once he arrived at the Plexiglass window, he provided his name and then waited in a corner of the lobby with his attorney. He used the time to rehearse his statement—his attorney made him practice in the car. *Remember, wait for her signal before you answer, and be brief.*

After a short wait, they were escorted to a dull square interrogation room. Glad to leave the lobby, with all its noises and odors, he didn't mind the wobbly table and uncomfortable chair. Two detectives sat across from them. They looked as unfriendly as they did the other night at his home.

As advised, he provided the police with a statement about his activities the day of the murder.

His attorney rested her arms on the table. "I want to mention the intrusiveness of the police surveillance around Mr. Knight's home. It's a violation of his rights, and disruptive to his neighbors."

Sitting directly across from him, Detective Gamble rested his hands on the table. "I apologize for any inconvenience. I'll see what I can do."

Considering the smirk across the detective's face, Adán doubted anything would change.

Detective de Jesus brought out a note pad, and clicked a pen. "We don't want to keep you any longer than necessary, Mr. Knight," he said. "Where were you specifically between ten and twelve the morning your wife was killed?"

The lawyer touched his forearm, signaled him to be quiet. "Mr. Knight already stated he had an appointment with a client," she said.

He noticed the detectives exchanged side glances. They were tag teaming him. He wondered which would be the good cop.

Detective de Jesus asked, "We need the name of your client, to verify your alibi."

"Mr. Knight explained he needs to obtain his client's consent before revealing her name," his lawyer said.

Detective Gamble pounced. "Her?"

His lawyer sat up straighter. "Just a figure of speech."

"Umm hmm." Detective de Jesus's pen hovered above his writing pad. "Would *she* be the same woman the patrol officer witnessed strike you this morning at your home?"

Leaning over to whisper into his ear, the lawyer asked him about the veracity of the detective's statement.

He inclined his head slightly in her direction and waited for instructions.

Facing the detectives, the lawyer said, "We'll answer that question at the proper time."

Tapping the table with his fingers, which caused the rickety table to shake, Detective Gamble said, "The time is now, counselor. This is a homicide investigation. A prominent citizen had been murdered in her office, in broad daylight. The person with the strongest motive is your client. If he's innocent, why not help us clear his name, then we can focus on the real culprit."

With a snort, the lawyer lifted her briefcase off the floor. Her other hand rested on his shoulder. "Unless you have more evidence, or a warrant, this interview is over. Let's go."

The interview terminated after half an hour.

Back home, Adán sauntered over to the wet bar. He removed a short glass added ice and poured in a healthy dose of brandy. He listened as the ice crackled then drank long and deep, savored the warm burnt orange fluid. Licking his lips, he carried his glass into the living room. Removing his shoes, he stretched his legs along the couch.

Speaking to no one, he gazed longingly into the glass. "Candace, my dear, you had exceptional taste."

If she were alive, he would not be drinking her twenty-year-old brandy—because it belonged to her. Everything belonged to her, and she'd been particular about telling him that. He came into the relationship with little—in fact, less than zero. He carried a lot of debt into their marriage, debt she never let him forget she paid off.

Entranced by the brandy, he thought back over their short marriage. From the moment he met her he sensed something different about Candace—a strength, dynamism. They lived together for close to two years before they wed. Back then they were good together, got along great. Traveled. Dined. Shared their dreams and ambitions.

Antsy to legalize their relationship, she proposed to him while they vacationed in the Caribbean. That day on the beach, she looked beautiful. A crystal blue sky mirrored the calm azure seas. For a brief moment, he actually believed in love. The honeymoon—and marriage—ended when she discovered the extent of his debts. As husband and wife, she gained fifty percent ownership in his liabilities. The night he detailed the extent of his financial obligations, they fought. It was the first time she had called him stupid. From that moment forward, stupid became almost a pet name.

He remembered when she had paid off his last loan. It was evening and they were in their bedroom. Clothed in a bath robe, she complained about paying his bills.

"You're so stupid," she had said. "Don't you know what debt does to your earning potential?"

He sat up in bed and tossed back the sheet. "Candy, I told you. I'm working on paying you back."

"Don't call me Candy." She glowered at him. Her hands rose to her hips.

"Sweetheart, I'm sorry." He scooted to the side of the bed. Arms outstretched, he hugged her about the waist. Pulled her body toward him and caressed her supple perfumed skin. "Let's go back to bed. Come on, babe. I'll make it up to you. I promise. Let's not argue—not tonight."

She leaned away from him. "You know what I want? I want you to take care of your business. This is supposed to be a partnership and I expect you to pull your weight."

His ego wasn't the only thing deflated. He took another sip of brandy.

Candace had intended for them to become Greensboro's black power couple—expected his success to rival her own. Whatever love he once had for her evaporated after he repeatedly failed to meet her expectations. She had managed his life coaching business for a short time. Changed his client profile to include professional people able to pay the salary she felt he deserved. With the increase in his fees, her expectations for him also grew. Gone were the lectures to youth groups and the mentoring programs he had sponsored. She chided him for believing charitable causes mattered. Her motto, 'you only give to charity as much as you get back', in recognition, awards, favors. There had to be some return on investment.

At first he had conceded to her demands. Eager to satisfy her and interested in growing his business. But soon he discovered the secret to her success—she cheated. Going forward, he resisted her input. Pushed back and regained control of his business. He liked success, but he enjoyed his freedom more.

As a teenager, he had a brief encounter with the legal system and had no intention of reliving the experience. Candace negotiated deals with some serious investors. If they couldn't get satisfaction—

Bam, bam, bam.

Startled, he spilled his drink on his trousers. Sitting up, he scanned the vicinity for the source of the noise. His gaze landed on a figure standing on the back patio deck. He set down his glass and hurried to the sliding doors. He recognized Charles Marshall.

He slid back the glass door a crack and stood on the threshold. "What are you doing here?"

Charles started forward, but Adán's frame blocked entry.

Lips tight, eyes bloodshot, he asked, "Aren't you going to invite me in?"

For a moment, Adán considered his unexpected guest.

Wearing cargo pants and a windbreaker, Charles looked nothing of the respected banker he knew only a month prior. He had read in the paper that the state's attorney had begun an investigation into Charles' bank. *The police harassed him, Kelley nagged him, now this.* He didn't want to be bothered with more drama.

He said, "Look man—"

Charles bum-rushed his way inside. He stalked around the living room, his eyes in constant motion. "I don't have time for this. The cops are watching your place. I need to get out of town and I need money."

A frown creased his face as he remained beside the door. "What did you come here for? I don't have any money."

"You don't, but Candace did. She owed me, and I need to collect it—now."

"Man, what do you think? Candace left money lying around the house."

"Idiot, I know that. When can you get access to her accounts?"

"I don't know."

"Dammit." Charles paced around the living room, uttering more expletives. "Have you met with the attorney yet?"

Hands in his pocket, he said, "No, I don't speak with her 'til Monday."

Charles rushed toward him. He braced for an assault.

Laughing, Charles said, "Don't worry. I'm not going to hit you." He removed a card from his pocket and handed it to him. "You can reach me at this number. *Call me*. I need to get out of North Carolina. I'll tell you where to send my money. Oh, and I might not hurt you but I know people who would." A snarl crossed his face.

He opened his mouth to speak, but Charles fled before he could say a word. He locked the doors, closed the drapes. His heart raced.

After he refreshed his drink, he again reclined on the couch.

His fear had materialized. Worried her clients might seek retribution, he had warned her. Candace had laughed—called him weak. Her solution had been to hire a bodyguard—*guess she never got around to it*. She believed she could overcome any complication. Confidence could be a liability.

What could he do about Charles Marshall? Did he have any recourse? He could call the police, but not without revealing he knew about Candace's illegal activities.

Concentration became difficult as the intoxicating liquid dulled his mind. Grinning up at the ceiling, he placed a pillow under his head and laughed. Candace planned to dump him, leave him with nothing—less than nothing if she held him to their prenuptial agreement. Her death came right on time. Now everything would be his. The empire she created would all go to him, her next of kin.

He made a toast, held his glass up toward the ceiling. "To you, Candace, my dear. Guess I got the last laugh after all." With one large swoop, he swallowed the remaining brandy and clumsily placed the glass on the coffee table.

He needed to speak with Myaisha about the money. Before they drove down to the police station, his lawyer informed him Candace had designated her executor of the will. He wished he'd known that before he slammed the door in her face. He needed to find a way to get the money and flee Greensboro before Charles came around looking for a cut.

Worry about it tomorrow. His head extended against the pillow and he slept.

Chapter 16

There was never a good time for a funeral. Overcast skies fit the mood of the attendees, somber without tears. Since most of Candace's extended family lived in North Carolina, Myaisha expected more of them would attend the services. The distance to travel for the funeral shouldn't have been prohibitive. She surveyed the people in attendance. Her brow wrinkled as she wondered why less people attended the funeral than attended the memorial.

Adán sat front and center in the first row of the church sanctuary. With a polite smile, he greeted those who walked by for the viewing.

From her seat two pews behind him, she viewed his profile. Jaw set, he stared straight ahead. In her opinion, an open casket seemed a violation of the deceased's privacy. She passed by the coffin without looking inside. Images of Candace strewn across the office floor remained imprinted upon her brain. She didn't need more visions haunting her sleep.

Lottie and Herman sat on the far right side of the church. He positioned his wheelchair up against the wall across the aisle from the pew. Unable to walk or stand for any length of time since his accident, he looked content—the new wheelchair improved his mobility. The accident that caused his disability occurred two years ago. Lottie doted on him. At almost fifteen years his wife's senior, he seemed a perfect match for her.

He might have been more successful in his rehabilitation, if she had allowed him to physically exert himself more. Perhaps being his doctor biased her opinion. After a month of rehab, he withdrew from the program, consigned himself to his wheelchair. Lottie's devotion to him only increased. Overall, he maintained a positive outlook. He possessed a sharp wit and a keen mind, which she appreciated.

Myaisha smiled when she noticed the couple holding hands—*so adorable*.

When services ended, he waved to her as they exited the sanctuary.

She hurried to her vehicle, anxious to leave the church before images of Candace or memories of Sammy brought her to tears. In addition, she didn't want to be at the end of the procession of cars traveling to the graveside. Fortunately, the event occurred on an early Sunday morning in a small southern city. All awake God-fearing citizens were ensconced in church, which decreased road traffic.

On the way to her car, she made an unsuccessful attempt to catch Adán's attention. A gaggle of women surrounded him. His face remained solemn. Whatever he felt, he kept hidden.

At the graveside, Myaisha stood in the grass next to Mary and Greg. Pregnant with their second child when she met her, Mary wanted to be a teacher. For now, church Sunday school would have to suffice. Instead of pursuing a career in education, she married during her senior year in college and never completed her degree.

From what she saw, Mary had no regrets. Her husband, Greg, worked in hospital administration while she pursued her interests in writing and raised their children. She wished to publish her poems, which she occasionally sent out to contests and magazines. One of her poems featured in Sammy's obituary.

At the graveside service, her thoughts reverted to Sammy. Her eyes wandered toward the mausoleum where he was interred. She trembled, remembered it rained the day of his funeral. The cold, windy weather gave her a visible excuse for shivering. Her tremulousness stemmed from fear. Sammy had been part of her life for over twenty years. When he died, she forsook part of herself at his graveside.

Her hands clenched, she directed her attention to the service for Candace, sent thoughts of Sammy to the recesses of her mind. *Focus on the pastor's words.*

Her gaze centered on the casket hovering over a large hole. This time, her friend would be constrained to a small plot of earth. Into her mind came an image of Candace, her hand reached forward trying to touch her—asking for help. Her friend's dead body lay on the office floor. As Myaisha zeroed in on the image in her mind suddenly Candace's eyes flew open. Startled, she hiccupped, her stomach contracted. Nauseated, she forced away the image, struggled to keep her tears in check.

Taking some deep breaths, she smelled rain in the air. She cast her eyes skyward and viewed gun metal gray clouds above. The pastor's words broke through the fog in her mind. Thoughts of Sammy—visions of Candace—her nerves were raw.

What did the outstretched hand mean? Had Candace reached for something? Did her friend attempt to halt the bullet about to pierce her heart?

Pastor Matthew concluded the service and people dispersed.

Recalled to herself, she realized someone spoke to her; but they left before she could respond.

Looking around, she tried to identify the person. "Who was that?" she asked Mary.

Adjusting the shawl around her shoulders, she said, "I believe a cousin or somebody. There aren't many family members present, are there?"

She frowned. "No, there aren't." Maybe she should have helped Adán and Lottie contact the family. It's possible, with the investigation into Candace's death, Adán had been too preoccupied with other concerns and neglected notifying family members.

Head bowed, Adán approached the casket and tossed a hand full of flowers onto the coffin. Long stemmed roses slipped off his fingers, fell on the casket and tumbled into the hallowed out earthen pit. He turned aside, his shoulders heaving.

As the pastor placed a hand on his back and led him away, Candace's parents dropped their flowers on the casket. The congregation followed behind Adán. People drifted away.

Funeral attendants lowered her friend into the grave. It all seemed precipitous.

Perhaps they were concerned about rain.

She watched Adán's head bob. He appeared to be crying. A deaconess hugged him around the shoulders. His parents stood by his side. Pastor Matthew led the family away toward the parking lot.

Could she be mistaken—she didn't notice any tears.

A breeze sent a smell of raw soil into her nostrils. Water impregnated the air, but no rain fell. The temperature cooled.

Mary and Greg hugged her and said their goodbyes.

Watching them walking away, she remained graveside and said a silent prayer over her friend. Part of her vow, a commitment to bring the murderer to justice.

Over the past two days, she communicated with Candace's parents and members of the Greensboro Black Professionals Alliance. Her interview with the parents raised more questions than it answered. They appeared to love their daughter and mourned her passing. At the same time, their answers to her questions were vague. They avoided certain subjects.

During college, Candace confided she assisted her parents with their finances. The strain became too great and before she completed undergraduate school, she told them not to contact her again if they needed money. Myaisha had asked Mrs. Jones if her daughter could have owed anyone money. Mrs. Jones had answered Candace never owed anyone money—they always owed her.

The comment struck her as strange, and unkind. She could understand Candace's resentment at having to help support her family. She paid her way through college, never requesting a cent from her parents. In addition, Candace said she often sent money home to help her parents *and* her siblings.

When during her interview with the mother, she had requested the phone numbers for Candace's siblings the interview soured. Mrs. Jones hustled her off the phone.

Among the people at the Greensboro Black Professionals Alliance she managed to contact, all refused to comment on Candace's work within the organization. They asserted restrictions against divulging operational information. How sharing information on Candace jeopardized their business interests, she failed to understand. They stonewalled further inquiries. Thus far, her detective work had been subpar, but even a bookshelf detective like herself recognized something amiss.

Speaking with Adán on the day of his wife's funeral about her murder would be improper. She wouldn't permit her eagerness to solve the homicide to overshadow her sense of propriety.

Frustrated, she sighed, decided to visit the mausoleum and pay her respects to her beloved. On Sammy's birthday and their wedding day, she visited the site, alone. It remained their special time together.

On her way to the mausoleum, she noticed someone off to the side. It appeared to be a woman, standing alone near a grove of trees at the end of the cemetery. Her location suggested she had not been a participant in the service, also she wore a ball cap, jeans and a jacket—not clothing appropriate for a funeral.

Myaisha detected either nervousness or anxiety as the person's leg jostled up and down. The person could be paying their respect privately, *but why?*

The individual watched the parking lot.

Curious, Myaisha forgot the mausoleum and observed the person watch the departing congregation.

After several minutes, the person left the security of the trees. When they removed their hoodie, she recognized the box braids and connected them with the woman who smacked Adán in the face. Intrigued, she trod through the damp grass, careful to maintain the element of surprise while not slipping on the slick sod.

Unaware of her approach, the woman stepped onto the asphalt and placed her hands in her pockets. If the she wanted to speak with Adán, she'd be disappointed.

A limousine chauffeured him away. Another line of cars formed, this time destined for the Pastor Matthew's house. The cemetery emptied.

The woman started chewing on her fingernails.

Myaisha hurried. She wanted to confirm if this woman assaulted Adán, and if she did, why. Good thing she wore flats. She jogged toward the lot. Once on the asphalt, she raced to catch up with the woman.

Reaching forward, she tapped the woman on the right shoulder. "Hello. I know you," she said.

As she turned around, the woman's face looked more annoyed than startled. She said, "I don't think so. Excuse me."

Myaisha continued to walk next to her. "I don't mean to be rude, but I do know you. I saw you at Adán's house."

The woman's body stiffened. Her eyes enlarged, her lips slightly parted. The words sank in. Her mouth opened as if to speak, but then shut. She strode away, averting her gaze. "You're mistaken."

"No, I'm not." Holding up her palms, she gestured for the woman to stop. "I watched you smack him in the face and accuse him of wanting to murder his wife."

The woman's face paled, her eyes narrowed. "What do you want? Are you a reporter?"

"No. I'm a friend of Candace. I'm trying to figure out who murdered her."

Arms crossed over her chest, the woman's left leg jerked up and down. "Well, it wasn't me. If you want to know who had the best motive, go ask Adán."

"I will. But right now, I need to speak with you."

The woman shook her head. "No."

"Just a few questions. I promise."

Giving her a once over, the woman unwound her arms. "Fine."

They fell in step together and proceeded towards what she presumed to be the woman's car. She noticed the woman's fingernails gnawed to the cuticles.

"Thank you. By the way, my name's Myaisha." She paused. When the woman failed to take the hint, she asked, "And your name is?"

The woman swallowed hard. "Kelley." After they shook hands, she quickly stuffed the disfigured nails into her pockets.

Myaisha said, "Nice to meet you. Now, what can you tell me about Candace? And don't hold back. I want the truth."

Her fingers rose to her lips, but Kelley quickly stuffed them in her pockets again. "Last year, I attended a seminar in Charlotte. That's where I met Candace. She held a seminar on real estate investing. Afterward, we corresponded for months before we met in person again." She hesitated.

Myaisha couldn't be sure if she was nervous or manufacturing her story. But she waited. She'd push to get her answers, if necessary.

After a moment Kelley continued. "I told Candace I worked as a teacher. I explained that my husband and I had a lot of college debt. She said real estate was the best thing for young people like us. We had time to let our investment grow."

Kelley chewed her bottom lip, while she fought back tears. "Candace promised her investing would be a sure thing—a quick flip. All I had to do was stick to her program, and the money was guaranteed. I gave her $50,000. But she—she told me I had to get other people to join. I had to do—it didn't make sense. She said if I gave her $50,000, I would double my money. I never saw a dime back. When

I complained and insisted on my money back, Candace stopped taking my calls."

Myaisha shifted her weight to her left foot. "What did Candace expect you to do?"

With a huff, Kelley's hands flew out her pockets. "I—she wanted me to get other people to invest in her group. Said that was how I would get my money back. It sounded like some weird pyramid scheme. I refused. I told her I wanted out. She said that was the only way."

After she blew her nose, Kelley explained how she pursued Candace. Trailed her around town—to conferences, work, home. One day she accosted her after a conference, insisted on a copy of their contract and an accounting of her investment. She wanted a full refund.

Myaisha studied her body language, aware they were the only people left in the lot.

Her reddened eyes begged for sympathy. Kelley said, "Candace called me a fool. She said I should have read my contract." She sniffed back tears. Her voice strengthened. "I didn't have a copy of the contract because she never gave me one. When I asked to see it, she refused. I asked about my guarantee. She said all investments carry risk." Kelley parroted the last sentence, then gnawed on her fingernail. "Since when? She never mentioned risks before I gave her my money."

Touching the brim of her hat, Myaisha asked, "Didn't you ask about the investment? Was any property ever purchased?"

"I thought she would handle all that."

"So you thought you would make a 100% return on your investment in a few months?"

Kelley shrugged.

Between the jerking leg and fingernail biting, Myaisha sensed a kernel of deception in Kelley's story. She believed the young woman invested money with Candace, but something rang untrue. Her left eyebrow arched. Unable to pinpoint the lie, she requested Kelley continue.

"There's nothing more to say. She told me to go away, or she'd call the cops—charge me with harassment. I was desperate. I contacted Adán, and asked him to speak with her."

"Why did you hit him?"

"He lied to me. He promised he could help me."

"What did he say he could do for you?"

"Get my money back. Get my contract. I couldn't sue Candace without some proof of our arrangement. Without the contract it would be my word against hers—a successful business woman versus me." Eyes lowered, Kelley chewed on her nail.

The 'poor me' comment held no sway with her. She asked, "Did you sleep with Adán?"

"No, never. I love my husband. Besides, Adán isn't my type."

"Then why did you slap him?"

"He lied to me. He set me up."

"For what? How did he set you up?"

Hesitating, Kelley considered at her fingernails, then simply refused to respond.

There they stood, evaluating each other.

Deciding to pursue a different avenue, she asked, "If you and your husband were hard up for money, where did you get $50,000?"

A spark flashed in the teacher's eyes, before she closed down again.

"Did you shoot Candace?"

"No."

"Where were you the day of the murder, before lunch?"

"At work."

"Any witnesses?"

"Of course. I stayed on campus all day."

"You never left?"

"No."

"Not even for lunch?"

"No."

Her arms crossed over her chest. "You didn't teach classes all day. I'm sure you took a break."

With a hard glare, Kelley circumvented further questions. After refusing to give her last name or phone number, she left.

As soon as she got in her car, Myaisha also departed. In her car driving home, she considered Kelley's story about Candace—and

Adán. Distracted by what she learned, she chose not to attend the gathering at the pastor's house. She needed time to think.

Checking her mirrors—her gaze lingered over any Toyotas—she realized she proceeded too fast and too hard questioning Kelley. She believed the teacher had been less than candid, *but about what? And did it involve the murder?*

Speaking to herself, she stated the facts she acquired up to this point in the case. Reconsidered what she knew. The murder had been committed before lunch. Kelley might have worked that day, but could have taken a break, left the school, murdered Candace, and returned to her afternoon classes. The timeline might be tight, but not impossible. On her mental to-do-list, she told herself to verify the teacher's alibi. Maybe contact someone at the school to ascertain whether Kelley left campus.

Should she call the police? Did they know about the teacher? With their resources, they could confirm the alibi. Her motive appeared strong. *Did she believe a teacher could have murdered Candace during her break and returned to school and teach children?* Possible. A young attractive teacher could be a cold blooded killer.

In retrospect, her vow to delve into the murder seemed immature. She thought she would ask a few questions and in no time deduce the answer. Every new piece of information she uncovered revealed something unsettling about Candace. Each fact, in and of itself might be insignificant, but taken in totality... Perhaps it would be prudent to leave the investigation to the police as Deniece suggested.

Straightening her back, she said out loud, "No, I owe this to Candace."

An orange sunset glowed over the tree tops as she drove down her street. The acrid smell of burning wood hung like a funk throughout the neighborhood. People burning trash behind their homes always disturbed her. Having lived all these years in the South, she still hadn't grown accustomed to it. Definitely, not something she experienced growing up in California. The absence of wind meant the odor lingered in the air. Her nose twitched.

As she neared the house, her gaze fell on a car positioned in front of her mailbox at the bottom of her yard. She glanced out the window as she hit the remote for the garage. Seated inside the vehicle, Detective Gamble's dark soulful eyes watched her. *What now?*

In the parking lot of her apartment complex, Kelley sat in her car. She thought back over her conversation with the woman at the cemetery. She almost confessed her embezzlement. This stress had her on edge. Something had to give. She chewed the corner of her thumb nail.

As treasurer for her school's sports teams, she had access to the athletic accounts. She intended to 'borrow' money, invest in real estate, and return the funds before the school conducted their annual audit. She regaled herself with fantasies of what she would do with the extra income—purchase sports equipment for her students, sponsor athletic trips, purchase new uniforms.

A delusion, she wanted the money to relieve her financial burdens. It would take her twenty years to pay off her student loans. In graduate school, her husband was working toward his doctorate. Even when he finished his degree, she wasn't sure how much he would earn with a doctorate in ethnic studies. His student loans already exceeded a hundred thousand dollars.

All she wanted was a little relief, to be able to pay all their bills and have some money left over at the end of the month. Now, that would never happen. They would have to borrow money to hire a lawyer to keep her out of jail.

Maybe she should confess her transgression to the school and repay the money over time. *How long would it take her to repay an additional $50,000 on her income?* Her husband would be furious; he might divorce her.

As the minutes passed, she grew more anxious. There were no more fingernails to bite. Her leg repeatedly bumped up against the brake pedal as she hid in the car.

Their apartment window was open. The plastic ten dollar blinds shut out the sunlight. In her mind, she imagined her husband on the couch watching sports—his books piled high on the table in front of him.

Tears streamed from her eyes. She didn't want to lose her marriage. She had made a mistake. There had to be a way to fix it.

Staring out the car window, she recalled the documents she returned to Adán. She'd made copies. Perhaps she could use them to find a way out of this mess. The documents might be valuable to someone. A stirring in the blinds of her apartment caught her attention. She started the motor and she pulled out of the lot before her husband spotted her.

Chapter 17

Myaisha deposited her Honda in the garage and waited as Detective Gamble walked up her cement driveway. She glanced over her neighborhood and saw an elderly woman sitting on a porch.

From the rocking chair, the woman waved at her.

Great. Mrs. De la Cruz saw him. She returned the wave, knowing that by the end of the day the entire neighborhood would know she had a male visitor. *At least he drove an unmarked car.* She preferred her neighbors believed she entertained a male guest than a police officer came over to interrogate her about a homicide.

As he made his way to the garage, his face held no expression. He asked, "Dr. Douglas, may I speak with you?"

Unmoved, she stood her ground, remaining silent. Her countenance mirrored his, displaying no emotion. From the other side of the door to the laundry room, she heard barking.

Boomer growled and scratched at the door.

Clearing his throat, Detective Gamble said, "Look, we got off to a bad start. I'd like to apologize."

"Thank you." Her face relaxed.

He sighed. "Look, we both want Mrs. Knight's murderer caught. We should help each other. I'd like to ask you some more questions. It won't take long."

"Come in." She led him inside.

Boomer waited right at the doorway. He snarled and barked at their new arrival.

"Down, Boomer."

His anger quieted, but the lab eyed the detective.

While she removed her hat, she directed the detective to the couch and invited him to sit. Reassuring him that Boomer dog wouldn't bite. *Not true. He would bite—at her direction.*

The house smelled of the peanut butter cookies she baked before she left for the funeral.

She changed into slippers, then placed a pitcher of lemonade with a tray of cookies on the table between the two couches. She sat on the couch facing the back yard, while he sat on the opposite sofa. The porch lights flickered on, illuminating her garden.

Standing guard beside the long table in between them, even the presence of cookies didn't deter Boomer's intense scowl at their visitor.

"Thank you," Detective Gamble said, accepting a glass of lemonade and a cookie. He placed the entire cookie in his mouth and glanced sideways.

Panting, Boomer growled and drooled.

The detective swallowed. "You sure he doesn't bite?" he asked

"He will if I order him to." She drank her lemonade, its sharp acidic flavor suited her mood.

Eyes wide, he washed down the cookie and placed his empty glass on the table. "Were you surprised someone murdered your friend?"

Choking, it took her a moment to clear her throat. "What do you mean by that?"

"I believe you understand my question. I'm learning a lot about Mrs. Knight, most of it highly objectionable."

Her voice increased several octaves. "If you came here to insult my friend, then you can leave."

He leaned forward over the table.

In concert with his movement, Boomer growled and stepped in his direction.

Retreating back against the sofa, he asked, "Could you put the dog outside, please?"

With her lips flat, her head tilted slightly to the right. "No. What have you learned about Candace?"

After he glanced at Boomer, he measured his tone. "How much did you know about her real estate business?"

"I knew she sold and managed properties. She had an extensive portfolio of rental properties. The *Greensboro Times* did an article about her business once. Candace had been very successful."

"She sold all her properties last year. Made quite a windfall." His fingers knitted together and rested on his knees.

Although she knew that, she bristled at his tone. Neither spoke. His steady eyes stayed glued on her face. She tried to read him, understand his position. Nothing about his manner divulged information.

"Did you know about the complaints made against her—that she deliberately secured mortgages for her clients they couldn't afford, pocketing hefty commissions? When her clients defaulted on their mortgages, she assisted the banks with the foreclosures. Collected an additional fee for her services. Then, through a shell company, she bought the foreclosed properties at a lower price—either reselling or converting them into rental units."

She regarded him, tried to think of something to discount what he said. Her conversation with Harriet came to mind, and Kelley's story. Her gaze wandered out the glass doors, she watched a bird fluttering around her magnolia tree. He requested her assistance, and had nothing to gain from lying. Emotionally, she felt defeated. Candace had been murdered, but Myaisha wanted to protect her memory. *Would it be possible?*

Her voice softened. "I knew Candace to be kind and generous. She gave to charities, encouraged young women of color into businesses. She mentored her sorority sisters. Donated her time to support the Greensboro Black Professionals Alliance."

Drumming his fingers along the couch, he said, "She charged her sorority speaking fees. Her alma mater removed her from their mentorship program because of complaints from students, she charged them consultation fees—sometimes involved them in her business schemes. Her first husband had criminal charges filed against her for forgery, then served her with divorce papers."

Her moon shaped eyes studied him. It had to be a lie, it couldn't be true. Candace confided in her about the divorce. She filed against Philip. *Would Candace have lied to her about something personal?*

"Heel, Boomer." She tossed him two cookies, the second of which he caught in his mouth.

While Boomer searched for the other cookie, she considered the detective. *Could she have been mistaken about Candace?* She thought—

Her hand trembled as she poured more lemonade for both of them.

"Please, call me Myaisha."

Accepting the glass, he took another cookie. "Todd."

"Thank you, Todd. I don't know what to tell you. Apparently, I didn't know Candace as well as I thought." *Or perhaps she did.* She chewed on her cookie and reflected.

He popped another cookie into his mouth. "I'll take anything you can give me."

Boomer watched him.

She tossed her lab a treat, gazing over the detective's shoulder she recalled the scene in Candace's office. Blocking pictures of Candace's body from the forefront of her mind, she started from the point when she called EMS.

"Candace owned a Rolex watch, identical to the one Adán wears. I didn't see it on her desk and it wasn't on her wrist. I noticed several other pieces of jewelry on her though."

Nodding, he waited.

Guess that wasn't good enough. She evaluated his face. Definitely younger than her, by how much she couldn't discern. As she considered his age, he cleared his throat. Brought back to the present situation, she thought some more.

Eyes closed, she pictured Candace's office. At first she tried to exclude the image of her friend sprawled across the floor. Gradually, she allowed those details into her forebrain. Her eyes popped open. "There were some strands of hair near her hand. I saw the forensic technician collect them."

Settled back into the cushions, his arms stretched along the back of the couch. "Yes. We found hairs. Forensics processed them, and the one on your pants leg. They didn't belong to the bod—Mrs. Knight. They weren't in her hand or between her fingers. There were no signs of a struggle. We don't believe the hairs belonged to the murderer either. They appear Asian in origin. None of the suspects are Asian."

She thought about what he said. Spoke more to herself than the detective. "Adán's mom is Filipino."

He shook his head. "The hair's too long to belong to Mr. Knight. These strands were chemically treated, the DNA degraded. What else can you tell me?"

What should she say—be honest or kind? With Candace dead, it wouldn't affect to her. *What about Adán, and Candace's family?* The question marinated in her mind, her attention wandered toward her built-in bookcase. Her eyes landed on an Agatha Christie book. Hercule Poirot always implored witnesses to speak the true nature of the deceased. In order to solve Candace's murder, she had to acknowledge the true character of her friend. She noticed Todd evaluated her much as she did him. She determined what to say—the truth.

"Candace—" Glassy eyed, she rubbed her legs and curled them under her on the couch, waiting for the emotion in her throat to pass. "I admired Candace even before I loved her. We became close in college. She was alone in California, and shared with me stuff about her family, and herself. Candace worked hard, harder than anyone I knew. And she was smart, but—." Her emotions were raw. She needed air. *Deep breaths.*

With an eye on Boomer, he leaned forward. "Take your time. I appreciate anything you tell me. If it isn't relevant to the case, it'll stay here between us."

A tear escaped her eyes when she nodded. Not sure she believed him, she decided to take a chance and trust him. Her investigation stalled. Maybe this information could help him. "Candace wasn't always like this. She wasn't. I—we lost touch when she left California for graduate school. We reconnected in Greensboro, but I knew she had changed. Her appearance, her attitude. By then she had married. Anyway, you don't want to know that." She inched toward the edge of the couch and tossed Boomer two cookies. "Candace approached me about an investment—a large investment, over a $100,000."

He whistled.

"Right. She took risks. From what I saw, those risks paid well. Back then, I was married with a child, and starting my own practice. I agreed to the deal, but later changed my mind—or my husband changed my mind. See, I trusted Candace. I agreed to become an investor without reviewing the—what do they call it—"

"Prospectus?"

"Right. Well, when I told Sammy about it, he reviewed the prospectus. Went over the financials and even spoke with an investor or CPA friend of his—I can't remember which. Long story short, I decided to back out of the deal, Candace became livid. Let's just say, it wasn't one of her finer moments. Words were said—on both sides—which couldn't be easily forgiven. It took years, but we finally got to a better place. Our relationship never returned to where it had been, but we were friends again."

"Was it the only time you invested—almost invested with her?"

She sank back among the cushions. "Yes. In fact, she never approached me again about making an investment. It surprised me when she asked me to become a customer in her medical supply business. We had kept our relationship completely social after that debacle."

"So, you weren't surprised to learn about her dishonest business practices?"

"I actually was surprised. I—I didn't consider Candace as being dishonest with me. I thought she had simply overlooked details in the agreement. Of course—I don't know. Maybe I tried too hard to hold on to our friendship."

Her gaze drifted away from the living room, unwilling to meet his. She wanted to believe it had been an accident, a one-time occurrence where Candace had a lapse in judgment. In truth, she made excuses for Candace because she wished to hold onto their friendship. There weren't many people she could claim as long-time friends. *Do we overlook the imperfections in the people we love to maintain our relationships? Do we lie to ourselves to make life tolerable?*

Their conversation waned. She needed a moment and appreciated his understanding.

Todd helped himself to another cookie. He asked, "Why didn't you mention being appointed executor of her estate?"

Before Boomer became upset, she tossed him one.

"You didn't ask." She noticed his smirk. She spoke rapidly. "It surprised me, okay. I didn't think Candace considered me someone good with money after what happened between us. She always said I was too cautious—didn't take risks."

"Hmm. Maybe that's why she trusted you. You didn't fall prey to any of her schemes."

Sitting up straighter, she resented his suggestion Candace did something criminal. "I didn't agree with how Candace conducted business. Her tactics weren't completely honest, but were they much different than what you would get from a Wall Street broker? You make it sound like Candace's business dealings were illegal."

Wiping crumbs from his mouth, he picked up his glass of lemonade. "This housing collapse has brought a lot of corrupt behavior to the attention of regulators. If your friend hadn't been killed, she'd probably be facing fines— civil and criminal. Her name has been mentioned by the state attorney's office in a bank fraud scheme out of Charlotte—not to mention a questionable 'investment program' she ran. Looks like she exited real estate just in time. Medical equipment and publishing were her next pet projects."

A shiver crept up her spine. The conversations with Harriet and Kelley swirled around her mind.

Tossing back his head, he swallowed the rest of his beverage and rose from the couch. "Thank you for your time doc—Myaisha."

Rising, she shook the hand he extended, but held onto it a second longer than intended.

His brows rose. "Was there something else?"

Succinctly, she recounted her conversations with Harriet and Kelley. After she finished, she asked, "Which gives Kelley a motive for killing Candace, right? She was desperate to get her money back."

A slight grin creased his face. "We know about Mrs. Wayne. Her alibi checks out."

Folding her arms across her chest, she grimaced. "She said she worked on the school campus all day, but she could have slipped out and killed Candace during her break."

"We checked. No breaks long enough for her to kill Mrs. Knight and not be missed from school. We're more thorough than you think. Sorry, but Mrs. Wayne is out."

Giving a wide berth around Boomer, Todd headed for the door.

Catching up with him, she tapped him on the back of his arm. "Wait. There's something else. I'm not sure it's important, but you should probably know."

Again with brevity, she detailed the incident between Candace and Adán at the pastor's home the Sunday before the murder, and next the argument between Lottie and Candace at the GWCWG meeting. She even conveyed what information, or lack thereof, she gained from her other interviews, including the one with Candace's parents.

"Would you wait a moment?" she asked.

Leaving him at the front door, she went to retrieve a large binder from her office. A large bark reminded her Boomer had not accompanied her.

When she returned to the front door, she found Todd standing outside and her lab on all fours with his hair raised.

At her whistle, Boomer sat but his eyes remained trained on Todd.

"Sorry about that," she said. Handing him the binder, before he could ask she explained. "I obtained this from a private detective Candace hired. The information is on a Charles Marshall."

"I'll check him out. Anything else?" He placed the binder in the crook of his arm.

"No. I'm sorry for not confiding in you earlier."

"Thanks for trusting me. If you remember anything—anything at all, please call. Oh, and stop with the interviews. I appreciate what you told me, but I don't want you getting involved. There's a killer out there, and if he's killed once, he'll kill again."

"So you think it's a man?"

"Just a figure of speech. Be safe. Call me about the contents of the will. I especially want to know how it affects Mr. Knight."

"I trust you'll find Candace's killer. I simply wanted to help. Since I knew her from college, I thought I had a better perspective on her than the police."

He placed a hand on her arm. "You helped by giving me this information. I promise, we'll find her killer."

Judging by his countenance, she actually felt a moment of pity for the murderer. Todd did not strike her as a fool or a slouch. She gave him a crisp smile. "Well, at least there's a reward. It should encourage people to come forward with information."

Worry lines deepened across his forehead. His jaw tensed. "Haven't you heard? The reward has been withdrawn. The Greensboro Black Professionals Alliance retracted their offer. In fact, I believe they've struck her off their roster. It seems they weren't immune to her schemes either."

Her hand on the door knob weakened. Her heart sank. "Thank you, Todd. I appreciate your coming by."

She locked the front door and let Boomer out back.

In the bathroom she changed her clothes, observed her reflection in the mirror. It never occurred to her Candace could be a criminal. Arrogant, self-centered—yes. But she attributed those traits to her success. *When had her deceit began? What about Philip? If she lied about her marriage, what else did she lie about?*

Deniece had been right, she needed to abandon her investigation into the murder. She wished to do something noble for her murdered friend. Now, she simply wished to be done with this entire horrid affair. Candace hurt, cheated many people. She wasn't even sure she still wanted to be executor of the estate.

Her phone vibrated. The screen read 'AJ'. She smiled. "Hello."

"Hey, how're you doing?"

"I just returned from my friend's funeral."

"Oh—hey—look, I'm so sorry. I didn't know."

"I know you didn't. It's okay."

Over the next hour, they discussed friendship, family and everything in between. Last night they spoke for over an hour. She delighted in his deep voice. As he spoke, she visualized his large smile. When she hung up the phone, she went over to the entertainment system and turned on some music. Their conversation left her relaxed.

Her phone pinged. She hoped for a good night text from AJ. Instead, she received a calendar reminder about her appointment with the estate lawyer. In an instant, her mood soured. She turned off the music, wondering what surprises the will might hold.

Chapter 18

Monday morning opened to blue skies. Myaisha stretched her stiff neck, her thoughts returned to Candace. Sitting up in bed, she reflected on their time together in college. Born and raised in California, she helped her friend adjust. As a military dependent, she empathized with the feeling of being in a foreign environment where you didn't know anyone. *Probably also the reason why she held on strongly to their friendship.*

After undergraduate school they lost contact. She journeyed to the Midwest for medical school. Candace attended graduate school in the South. Later, Sammy's fellowship brought them down South too. When they relocated to Greensboro, she reconnected with Candace.

Glancing at the clock, she hurried into the bathroom. If she didn't hustle she'd be late for work. Boomer trotted outside while she braided her hair into one large plait from the nape of her neck down her back. She threw a tunic over her head and slid into slacks. After setting out water and food out for Boomer, she reached inside the foyer closet for her jacket. Grabbing her fedora off the shelf, she decided to abandon the jacket and raced out the house.

Once she arrived at the office, she called the estate lawyer. She wanted to get a look at the will. Although she agreed she shouldn't pursue an investigation into the murder *herself*, she didn't see a problem with assisting the detectives. Todd appreciated the information she gathered and showed an interest in how the will benefited Adán—who apparently the police still suspected.

She also wanted to understand why Candace chose her as executor. They hadn't been close for years. Candace overlooked her husband, her parents—*Could she be the closest friend Candace had? A pang of sadness hit her. Should she have tried harder to mend their rift? How much time does it take to say I'm sorry and move forward?*

Wearing a shielded mask and surgical gown, Dina knocked on her office door and said, "Your patient's ready."

Biting her lip, she shook her head. With her stethoscope in hand, she headed for the exam room. In her world, medicine trumped murder.

Halfway through the morning, she noticed a familiar name on her schedule. Tapping on the exam room door, she opened it to find Lottie seated on the exam table. She meant to call her the night of Candace's homecoming. Now, she could pay her respects in person.

After closing the door, she walked up to the exam table. "Lottie. It's good to see you. I'm sorry about Candace."

She nodded, but didn't speak.

"I missed you at the memorial service."

"I stood in the back," Lottie said. "I saw you in the pew behind Mary. There were so many people there. I never saw the church at standing room only."

The sanctuary had been over capacity. Quite a few people stood in the back behind the pews. She asked, "Why didn't you sit up front with the family?"

Tension creased Lottie's face. Her temporal muscles tightened. Her voice sounded strained. "I felt more comfortable in the back. I couldn't stay long. Herman wasn't feeling well. I needed to slip out. It seemed easier to stand in the back."

Accepting the explanation, she reached around Lottie's sagging shoulders and gave her a long hug. At first, Lottie simply sat there, stiff. Gradually, she returned the embrace. Myaisha stepped back and gazed into her friend's face.

Slightly hyperteloric, Lottie's average brown eyes had large bags underneath them. Her shoulders were rounded as she hunched forward.

"What's wrong?" she asked.

Chin trembling, Lottie used the pencil weaved between her locks to scratch her scalp. Dry flakes fell onto her shoulders.

A whiff of dandruff shampoo floated by Myaisha's nose.

It took a few seconds for Lottie to regain control. "It's—It's been a hard time."

"I'm sorry. What can I do to help?"

Sniffling, she drew herself up straight. "Nothin'. Herman and I'll be alright."

Her brows knitted. She missed something. They seemed to be talking at cross purposes. Lottie didn't appear to be referring to Candace's death. *Back up and refocus.* She asked, "How is Herman doing?"

A grin cracked through Lottie's hard exterior. Animated, a large grin pulled her eyes even farther apart. "Better. Thank you for asking. The new wheelchair really helps." She picked at a plaque on the back on her hand.

Myaisha had arranged for the insurance company to cover a motorized chair for Herman. Since his construction injury left him disabled, Lottie assumed a lot of his maintenance and personal care. Perhaps the strain had become too much for her.

"Good. I'm glad. Let me know if you need anything else. I can arrange for in-home nursing care if you need assistance. They can help with his personal care and meals."

"No. We don't need any help. Herman's fine."

The statement ended that topic of conversation, at least for now. Pulling up Lottie's chart on the EHR, she steered their conversation to the present issue. Listening to her explanation about her psoriasis had become aggravated, Myaisha suggested trying a different therapy since the topical creams weren't helping.

After a brief discussion, she performed an examination. Pinpoints of blood dotted the scaly dry plaques on Lottie's hands. She pulled aside the braids to examine her irritated scalp. In the EHR, she completed and printed out an electronic prescription, handing it to Lottie.

Washing her hands, she spoke over her shoulder. "Let me know how the Dovonex works. Next week, we should get the biologics in. You should be able to get your first injection before the end of the month."

Lottie's eyes glistened. "I hope it works."

"I've read good results with biologics for psoriasis. I also consulted a dermatologist I know in Charlotte. I'll have my staff call you when the medication arrives." Prepared to leave, Myaisha's hand hovered over the knob. A thought occurred to her. Stepping toward the table, she asked, "How's work at the bank?"

Her face wrinkled. Loose skin around Lottie's neck jiggled. Her placid countenance transformed to consternation. Again, she applied the pencil to her scalp. "I left that job. Actually, I was let go. The entire bank loan department shut down."

"I'm sorry. Where are you working now?"

"I got an office job."

"I had no idea."

Lips puckered, she scratched her head. Pulled her purse strap tight around her shoulder and climbed down off the exam table. "You were too busy with your own problems." She exited the room.

With her head slanted to the right, Myaisha stood in the hallway and watched her friend depart. The comment left her feeling upbraided. *Had she neglected her friends?* Since Sammy died she had to raise Josiah alone. Between work and home, she had her hands full. *Understandable, right?* Her son had only one parent. *Didn't his welfare warrant all her time?* Of course, he didn't request her complete attention, she simply gave it.

Lottie's comment struck her deep. She *had* retreated into being a widow, wore it like a badge of honor. Much had changed since Sammy died, to her friends, her community, the world. Perhaps she had neglected the needs of those around her—failed to appreciate the changes in the lives of her friends. Candace may not have been a saint, but she had been her friend. No one should be allowed to take another person's life. As Hercule Poirot would say, "I don't approve of murder".

Hearing a cry from her next patient reminded her she had other duties to attend to at the moment.

After speaking with the lawyer, she managed to call the Greensboro Black Professionals Alliance and the Greensboro Association of Realtors. Candace had been a member of both organization for years. Myaisha hoped someone there might offer clues pertinent to the homicide. She hadn't gained much information, but she had left messages for several of Candace's associates.

Didn't Todd tell her to stop with the interviews? Her mother called her hard-headed for a reason.

It was late in the afternoon before she could attend to her patient messages. With the phone angled into the curve between her shoulder and neck, she tried to converse with Mrs. Carston while she completed her notes. She couldn't remember where she had placed her headphones. Because she hated clutter, she always put away her materials. Unfortunately, she put them away and then forgot where.

"Are you listening to me?" Mrs. Carston asked.

She had not. "Yes, Mrs. Carston," she said. "I understand you're worried about the mammogram results but I personally spoke to the radiologist. She said everything looked good."

A shrill voice shouted through the phone. She moved the device away from her ear.

"I don't care what the radiologist said. I know I have cancer. I can feel it in my chest."

She typed up her notes, tried to soothe Mrs. Carston. From the base of her skull, she felt a headache creep up and settle between her eyes. For a second the computer screen blurred. Multicolored lights blinked before her eyes. *Great, a migraine.* She saved the patient note. Closed her eyes and focused on listening to her patient.

When her patient took a breath, she used the opportunity to speak.

"Mrs. Carston, I have examined you twice in the past month. I do not believe you have breast cancer. The pain you are feeling may be something else. Respiratory, gastric, maybe muscular. I want you to document every time you experience any pain—when it happens and where. We are going to sit down together and discuss your symptoms in detail."

"Thank you, doctor. I just want someone to listen to me. I know my body. I know when something is wrong."

Massaging her temples, she forwarded the call to the front desk. Instructed her staff to schedule an appointment.

Her cell phone rang.

"Hello. Is this Dr. Douglas?" the voice asked.

"Yes, it is. Who am I speaking with?"

"I prefer not to give my name. I heard you've been asking around about Candace Knight."

Her migraine felt worse. She sipped water to stave off her nausea. Opening her desk drawer, she searched for some medicine for her head. "I have. Are you a member?"

"Look, I don't have much time. I thought you'd like to know what's going on."

"Yes. Anything. Please."

"I see what they're doing to your friend, and its wrong. Mrs. Knight wasn't the only person involved in that real estate crap, but they've decided to make her the sacrificial lamb. She's dead already, so why not. Right?"

Myaisha winced. Her throat burned and she tasted bile in the back of her throat. "I understand what you mean."

The voice on the line whispered. "There are spies all over this place. I attended the Alliance meeting last week—the week before the murder. When I came out, I saw this woman approach Mrs. Knight. Some young thing, with box braids. Mrs. Knight pulled a gun on her. I almost called the police, but I saw they recognized each other. Mrs. Knight put away her gun and they talked for a while. Anyway, you don't care about that. Listen, your friend is being framed."

"What's going on at the Alliance? Why won't anyone speak with me?"

"This housing stuff. People knew what Mrs. Knight was up to. Hell, they suggested it. They all made money off it. Now the shit's hit the fan, and the law is involved—someone has to take the blame."

She heard something in the background over the phone.

The voice lowered further. "Look, I gotta go. If you're gonna keep asking questions, watch your back."

"Do you know who killed Candace? Is there a way I can contact you?"

"No. I can't get involved. Check out the Alliance."

Click. The screen went blank.

Her eyes closed, she laid her head on the desk. When the nausea subsided and her vision cleared, she reached into her side drawer for some acetaminophen. Before she could pop the pills into her mouth, someone knocked on the door. Without waiting for a reply, the person pushed through. She exhaled when she recognized Deniece.

"Oh, good. It's just you," she said.

Shutting the door, Deniece sat down. "Who were you worried about?" she asked.

"Anyone." Fingers tightly gripped her water bottle as she swallowed the pills, she then chased them down with a chug of water.

Walking around the desk, Deniece bent down and gave her a hug. She tilted her head back and gave her a long, hard stare.

Once she emptied her water bottle, she asked, "What?"

"You looked like you needed a hug."

"I did. Thank you. It's been a long day."

"Sorry, lady. Anything I can do?"

"No. I'll be fine."

"Why don't we grab something to eat? I know you aren't cooking anything. I'll drive."

Prepared to challenge her friend's assertion, she surrendered. It was true. She rarely cooked anymore since Josiah left for college. Occasionally she baked something for her office staff or church family. Usually she ate a salad or sandwich while she read a book or worked on her manuscripts. Her stomach growled.

She hated Deniece for knowing her so well, and loved her for the same reason. Time for a well-deserved break. She earned a treat.

She waved to her staff as they exited the office from the back, discussing Candace's death.

As they crossed the parking lot, she said, "I'll follow you. Where are we going?"

Coming to a dead stop, Deniece gaped over her right shoulder.

Curious, she spun around to see what captured her attention. To her surprise, and dismay, AJ proceeded in their direction. Tall, dark, and handsome, he clutched a small box in his large hands. It purported to be a gift according to the wrapping.

Presented her with a dilemma, her heart raced. Her fingers touched the brim of her hat. Though happy to see him, her problem was AJ had become her sinful secret. She hadn't told anyone about him, not even Deniece. Well, now her friend would know, and Deniece would not be happy she hadn't mentioned him. She felt her migraine inch up her brainstem. Flushed, she struggled with how to handle the situation.

Unaware of her consternation, AJ strode up to them with a large smile on his face. He said, "Hello. I hope I didn't come at a bad time."

Frozen with uncertainty, she didn't respond.

Stepping in front of her, Deniece held her hand out toward AJ. "Hi," she said, "I'm Deniece. Myaisha's best friend and her translator when she forgets how to talk. What's your name?"

Smacking Deniece in the shoulder, released from her daze, Myaisha made introductions. "Deniece, this is AJ. AJ, this is my best friend, Deniece."

They shook hands.

"Nice to meet you." He turned toward her. "Is this a bad time?"

In unison, she said "yes" while Deniece said "no".

He laughed. "Sorry. I just came by to see how you were doing. I brought you a gift."

Because she hesitated, Deniece smiled up at AJ and relieved him of the package. Removing the wrapping, she opened the box. Winked and tilted the box in her direction to display the sweets inside. She murmured. "Mmm. Dark chocolates. Myaisha's favorites."

"Are you a doctor too?" he asked.

"I'm a nurse. I teach at the nursing college in Winston-Salem." Her friend closed the container and placed it in her purse.

Not wanting them to get too chummy, she took control of the conversation. "We're on our way to dinner, AJ. Maybe..."

While they spoke, Deniece circled around behind him. Gave him a thorough once over, and nodded her head approvingly. She looked at her, suggestively lifting her eyebrows. Biting the corner of her lip, Deniece mouthed the words 'Nice'.

Suppressing a grin, she felt herself blush. To signal her to cut it out, she bent her brow severely in a non-verbal gesture.

"I'm sorry, AJ," she said. "I hope you understand, but we already made plans." She wanted to depart before Deniece's machinations moved her fledgling relationship with AJ on a faster trajectory than she desired.

"May I join you ladies?" he asked.

Simultaneously, she said "no" and Deniece said "yes".

With a stern squint directed at her friend, she said, "I'm sorry, not this time. We made plans for two."

"No we didn't."

Her nostrils flared. She eyed her. "Yes we did." Softening her countenance, she pivoted toward him. "Maybe some other time."

"How 'bout I call you later?" He smiled.

Relieved, she exhaled. "Yes. That would be great. Thank you for the gift."

After he told them good night, he returned to his vehicle.

They stood side by side and watched his double wide truck pull out of the lot.

Once he departed, she swiveled toward her office and caught her staff gawking out the windows. They shut the blinds in a failed attempt to hide their snooping. Her head throbbed. Embarrassed, she felt tired.

"D, how about a rain check on dinner? I don't feel well."

"What? No way." She strode away.

Raising her voice, Myaisha followed. "My head hurts. I have a migraine."

"Take some medicine."

"I did."

"See. You'll be fine. I'm hungry." She slid into the passenger seat.

Settling in behind the steering wheel, Myaisha drove away.

A long thin ribbon of caramel dripped down Deniece's chin as she ate a piece of candy.

With her eyes on the road, she addressed the unspoken. "I'm not ready to date. It's too soon."

"Too soon? Sammy died five years ago, Mya."

Her shoulders sagged. Her voice lowered. "I know."

Once she turned onto the main street, she chanced a glance at Deniece. She watched as her friend consumed the candy the good-looking man brought for her. During the drive, her mouth watered for the chocolates. "I thought we were taking both cars," she said.

"Um hmm. We were. But I can't drive and eat."

From the corner of her eye, she saw her devour another piece of chocolate.

"I thought those were mine." Her stomach grumbled. Rich scents of chocolate and the buttery aroma of caramel filled her vehicle.

After Deniece consumed another piece, her mouth full of chocolate, she said, "I thought you didn't want them."

Stopped at a red light, she couldn't resist. She reached over and grabbed a piece. Popped the candy in her mouth before the light turned green. Sucking on the candy, she let the warmth of the cocoa bean coat her tongue. Creamy passion fruit burst into her mouth and dripped down her throat. *Delicious.* She licked her lips, sensed Deniece watched her. "What?" she asked.

"Mya, have y'all gone out yet?"

"No."

"Why not?"

Her back straightened. "I told you. I'm not ready. Besides, he's not my type."

She rolled her eyes. "Yeah right. No woman likes a tall handsome man who brings them gifts. That gets real old."

Parked in front of her favorite restaurant, she pivoted in the seat to face her friend. "D, I'm not... I'm not ready. Not yet."

"You'll never be ready, girl. It's just a date. Someone to talk to." She held her gaze.

After a deep breath, she confessed. "We've been talking for a few days. I met him at the hospital."

"You're attracted to him, aren't you? Who wouldn't be—he's hot. If you didn't like him, you wouldn't be talking to him." She patted her hand.

Tears threatened to spill over her eyelids. "I know. I do like him. But I'm afraid of what happens next?"

Holding her hand, Deniece rubbed her fingers. "Whatever you want to happen. Look, you're attracted to this guy. He's the first man you've been interested in since Sammy. Go on, girl, and get you some."

After her stomach growled again, she retrieved her purse and exited the vehicle. "You're married."

"Married, not dead."

They entered the restaurant. Scents of spices and fried foods greeted them.

While they waited to be seated, she read the menu. "I don't know," she said. "It feels—"

"Different. It feels different because it is. AJ isn't Sammy, and that's okay."

They followed the server to a table in the back of the restaurant.

Once the server took their order and left, Deniece looked her in the eye. "Not living won't bring Sammy back, and being happy isn't dishonoring your love for him."

Misty eyed, she gave her friend a slight grin. The edge on her migraine a miniscule lighter.

Chapter 19

Tall, stately trees shaded the car. Down the street from the Knight residence in the driver's seat of their police vehicle, Todd listened to his partner crunching on potato chips. Since Mr. Knight refused to help them confirm his alibi, he remained their number one suspect. Pain pulsed across Todd's forehead, he closed his eyes and rubbed his head. He inhaled the humid, woody air, trying to relax amid the crisis.

Only Monday morning, and he'd already had the chief upset. Their homicide investigation stalled. Tomorrow, the chief had to deliver a report to the mayor and city council. They hadn't solved the crime, and their suspects included the victim's spouse and several residents of the Triad.

In the car, he drummed his finger along the steering wheel. He gritted his teeth and continued to observe the house. "Ian, want to give the chips a break?" he asked.

"Fine." He shook salt from his fingers and picked up the wrist ball.

"For a fitness buff, you eat a lot of crap."

"Only at work. It's hard to eat healthy sitting in a car. I make up for it at the gym." He flexed his biceps.

He eyed Ian's grin, and pointed out the chips on his chin. Reaching under his seat, he picked up pocket sized binoculars and looked around the neighborhood.

An hour later, his partner tapped his leg and woke him up. He had dozed off watching squirrels race up and down the trees aligning the street.

Stammering, he wiped his face. "What?" His eyes followed Ian's pointing chin toward the Knight house.

"Looks like the widower has company," Ian said.

Struggling to remove the binoculars from around his neck, Todd strained to focus his vision on the images. He regained his perception and viewed Adán Knight at the front door. The widower's face was animated face, and his body blocked a lady from entering the house. For her part, the woman attempted to bypass him, her fingers directed at his face as they argued.

Recognizing the woman as Mrs. Wayne, he knew she had assaulted Mr. Knight before.

Too far away to hear the discussion from their car, they exchanged glances. Ian threw his bag of chips in the back as Todd placed the car in gear. Careful not to alert the couple, their vehicle inched closer to the house. He hoped they'd catch snippets of the conversation.

Wide eyed and gesticulating, Mrs. Wayne said, "You owe me, Adán. Just give me back my money and I won't go to the police."

A crooked grin crossed Mr. Knight's dimpled face. "The police? With what?"

She took a step toward him. "About how much you wanted your wife dead. How you discussed getting rid of her. You were afraid of the prenup. With her dead, there's no prenup to worry about *now* is there. How much do you expect to inherit Adán?"

Todd noticed Mr. Knight glance in their direction. He made them, but she had not.

Their car crawled up the driveway, as the widower reached out his hand to touch her arm.

Mr. Knight said, "Uh, Kelley—"

Smack.

She slapped his hand away. "Don't touch me you jerk. I'm gonna tell the police everything."

Through his clenched jaw he said, "Kelley, shut up."

Her eyes followed his, she turned around. Her jaw fell.

Todd and Ian stepped out of their vehicle and approached the front door.

"No, please," Todd said, "continue." He waited in vain.

Neither Mr. Knight nor Mrs. Wayne spoke.

Closing her mouth, she stepped away from the door and tried to leave.

From his periphery, he saw Ian stride in front of her, blocking her escape.

"Where're you going?" Ian asked.

"Home—I mean work," she said.

His gaze pivoted from Mr. Knight to Mrs. Wayne. "Why don't you both accompany us down to the station?" he asked. "You can finish your discussion there, and then we have a few questions of our own."

Retreating back over the threshold of the home, Mr. Knight said, "Not without my attorney"

"Absolutely. We want your attorney present when we discuss why this woman threatened to tell us about how you wanted to kill your wife."

Extending his arm toward their unmarked vehicle, Ian asked, "Would you like to drive with us, ma'am?"

Her leg trembled. Unable or unwilling to move, she gawked at his partner, who led her away from the home.

He heard tidbits of their conversation, watched Ian lead her toward their vehicle. His gaze reverted toward Mr. Knight. "Do you need to get anything, sir, before we go?"

"I don't need to go downtown. I didn't do anything." Twisting his Rolex around his wrist, Mr. Knight slipped inside the home.

Making a mental note to ask about the watch, Todd came into the foyer.

"Mrs. Wayne's accusations are serious. With her allegations—" He shrugged. "I bet it would qualify for grounds for an arrest, but I think you'd rather come downtown of your own volition."

Rubbing his head, Mr. Knight stumbled into the living room. "I can't believe this is happening."

Discretely shutting the door, he brought up the rear. A quick glance around the house showed the widower had finished grieving and started to pack. *Where did he plan to go? And why immediately after Candace's murder?*

"What was Mrs. Wayne doing here?" he asked.

Face vacant, Mr. Knight plopped onto the couch. "I don't know."

He stood there. *More would come. Be patient.*

After a moment, Mr. Knight looked up at him, speaking slow and with emphasis. "She's a friend, just a friend. She wanted—asked for my help."

Perched on the arm of the couch, he gazed down at him. "Then why did she threaten you? Doesn't sound like she's your friend—not a good friend at least."

Leaned forward, elbows on his thighs, he said, "She invested money with my wife. Now, she wants it back."

His eyes narrowed as he sized him up, not sure he believed the story—or at least that there wasn't more. Mr. Knight wouldn't be the first homicide suspect to commit adultery. An affair would be another motive for murder. He recalled what Dr. Douglas told him about her conversation with Mrs. Wayne. He sat on the couch feet wide apart. He asked, "Why did she come to you? Why now?"

"I don't know. I guess she thought I had money."

"Why would she think that?"

"She wasn't the first client of my wife's to approach me about money." Avoiding eye contact, he rubbed his hands on his thighs. Twisted his wedding ring around his finger.

Mental note, follow up on the financial audit.

"Where were you the morning your wife died? And don't give me any crap about client privilege. You're a life couch, privilege doesn't apply. With the threats from Mrs. Wayne, and your reluctance to provide an alibi, I promise you, I can find a judge who'll grant me a warrant to search this house and haul your ass downtown. So, talk."

"Okay, okay. I was with a client."

Unmoved, his eyes bore into the suspect. He smelled fear—and cologne. He grimaced.

Sweat beaded on Mr. Knight's forehead. He stood, gesticulating with his arms as his voice elevated. "Fine, she's more than just a client, but it's not what you think. We've been seeing each other for a few weeks. I found her online. We meet in Statesville, where no one knows us. I kept negotiations between us secret because—because I worried it would get back to my wife. After her murder—I didn't want anything to screw up my plans. I'm telling the truth."

Over the next half hour, he recounted how he planned to enter into an arrangement to take his life coaching business to the next level. He didn't want his wife to know about it because he feared she'd quash the negotiations. "Candace had connections all over the South. Our marriage was ending and I prepared my parachute. You know, to soften the blow."

Todd obtained the details of the mysterious 'business partner'—name, number and address. Back at the station, he would confirm the information. "Were you involved in your wife's businesses?"

"No."

Knight's voice wobbled. Wary, Todd leaned back on the couch. "This is off the record. Tell me the truth. Did you know about your wife's real estate scams?"

"Yes—no. Some of it."

Fingering his watch, Mr. Knight explained how he started to hear rumors around town, bits of information from friends about his wife's businesses. After a while, people approached him. Some requested help, asked him to intercede on their behalf with his wife. At first, he figured they were simple misunderstandings. Things escalated to threats. He learned Candace had been less than upfront with her clients. Over time, he learned she was committing fraud.

Pacing around the couch, he said, "But I never got involved in her schemes. I even kicked her out of my business when I learned what she was doing. It's why our marriage fell apart. I insisted we keep our business and finances separate."

Knitting his fingers to rest on his knee, Todd said, "I find that hard to believe. She made considerably more money than you."

"If it's illegal money, what good is it to me?"

"You didn't seem to have a problem spending it."

"All I cared about was it being traced back to me. I don't believe there's anything illegal about spending it."

"Your alibi for the day of the murder, why were you secret about it?"

"The woman I'm working with is married. I didn't want her husband to get the wrong idea, and she doesn't want him to know about our business deal."

"Do you know what happened to your wife's watch? It wasn't on her body at the time of the murder."

"No, no idea."

With permission, Todd inspected the deceased's jewelry box. He recorded the pieces present in the box to check against the list of the deceased's personal items located at the crime scene. Everything appeared accounted for, but the watch. *Could the motive for the murder be robbery?* No, he already ruled it out. *Why would the murderer take the watch but leave the other valuables?* It didn't make sense—unless it was a decoy to throw suspicion away from the real motive for the murder.

He questioned Mr. Knight about whether any other personal items belonging to his wife might be mislaid, even asking about the laptop. The widower continued to deny any knowledge of anything missing. Before he left, he cautioned him about leaving town.

———

Outside, Todd decided he and Ian should—he stared at an empty car. *Where were his partner and Mrs. Wayne?* The vehicle parked at the end of the driveway also disappeared. He checked his phone and read a text from Ian.

Want 2 b here 4 interview

Ian must have accompanied Mrs. Wayne downtown in her vehicle.

Texting him to proceed, he hopped in the car and took off. There were more alibis to verify. If Mr. Knight's alibi held, he had to find another number one suspect.

Before he returned to the station, he remembered he had a video to check out. A security guard at the Courthouse mentioned seeing someone resembling the deceased arguing with another woman. This other woman struck the victim and escaped before security arrived. Depending upon what the video revealed, he might have his next suspect.

Crammed into the small Courthouse security room, Todd and Ian watched the video over the guard's shoulder. On his way downtown, his partner called to inform him the interview with Mrs. Wayne ended before it started. The teacher refused to answer questions after they arrived downtown.

He swung by the station, picked up Ian, and together they drove to the Courthouse.

Young and skinny with a goatee, the security guard loaded the video into a classic VHS player. A second guard stood by the door, arms rested on his potbelly.

Although grainy, the images showed two women arguing in the parking lot adjacent to the building. Depite the poor quality video, having stared at her picture for the past five days, he identified Mrs. Knight. At the bottom of the screen, he watched as she pointed her finger at a smaller darker woman. He didn't recognize the other woman as someone they interviewed in the course of their investigation.

Seconds ticked by. The unidentified woman smacked the finger aside. Mrs. Knight appeared to say something else. Short and stout, the second woman reared her right arm back and punched their victim in the face. Mrs. Knight fell on her knees to the ground, her hand covered her nose. After she pummeled their victim over the head with her handbag several times, the other woman fled. Before security arrived to assist their victim, a car could be seen speeding out the parking lot.

He tried and failed to read the license plate. He asked the guard, "Can you increase the magnification? I missed the plate. "

"Give me a sec," the guard replied."

Enlarging the video destroyed any definition in the blurred photo. On the tape, security guards could be seen helping the victim to her feet. Mrs. Knight conversed with them for several minutes before she exited the parking lot in her signature red sports car.

He wondered if the widower now drove the Cadillac.

The remainder of the tape proved uninformative.

Standing up straight, he stretched his back. Questioned the skinny guard with the goatee. "Mrs. Knight didn't file a complaint?" he asked.

Goatee guard swiveled around in his chair, chewing on the end of a straw. "Nope. She refused."

Pad in hand, Ian asked, "Did you get the name of the other woman?"

"Nope. We asked what happened, the lady wouldn't say. She refused to file a complaint, so we went back to work."

Todd shared a look with his partner.

The guard at the door said, "I called when I heard about the murder. I looked through the tapes until I found the video with your victim."

He thanked the guards. "Good job guys. We appreciate the help. Can we get a copy of the tape?"

"Sure thing," said goatee guard. He turned around in his chair and copied the tape.

Once they exited Courthouse with the tape, Todd said, "We need to find out who assaulted our victim."

Ian crunched on a candy bar. "It's a good thing they caught the footage. In another week, it would have been recorded over."

Settling under the steering wheel, he placed the tape on the console. "We need to identify the woman on the recording. I can think of two avenues to obtain the license plate number."

"I'm listening."

"Both women were at the Courthouse. We can search for traces of the mystery woman on other surveillance cameras around the building. Find out what department she visited and check the visitor log. Or, we can canvass other shops in the area. Find a camera pointed at the parking lot."

Crumbling his candy wrapper into a ball, Ian tossed it into the cup holder. "The second sounds more promising. Do you think this woman could be involved in the murder?"

He started the engine. "I don't know. From the way she beat up the victim, she probably would have killed her with a blunt object instead of a gun."

"What do we have on our 'to do list' after this?"

"Did we get anything on Mr. Washington?" He drove into a gas station across the street.

"Kevin Washington? No, not yet. He cleared out. His family hasn't heard from him since the murder. I asked one of the officers to check with his military buddies."

"There's no record of him owning a gun," he said. "Besides, Mrs. Knight had two guns, one in her desk and one in her purse. If he came in to the office, she would've had her weapon out."

Ian unbuckled his seat belt. "Not to mention leaving both doors open for him."

He exited his vehicle, spoke across the hood of the car. "Exactly. She had a confrontation with Washington the week before. If he came by her office, she would have had her gun front and center."

As they strode up to the station to speak with the attendant, they continued to discuss the case.

With his hands on the door, Ian asked, "You think we'll have a suspect for the chief this week?"

He rubbed his forehead to the back of his neck. "Not sure. Something tells me this case is about as convoluted as Knight Enterprises. Let's go in. The cameras from this station point directly at the parking lot next to Courthouse. The solution to our case might be inside."

Chapter 20

Darkness surrounded her. With a start, Myaisha sprang up in her bed. Pushed aside her comforter and rubbed the sleep from her eyes.

Boomer's barking woke her up. He snarled and circled the bed. Her California king bed was positioned between two windows facing the back yard. Boomer continued to bark as he ran to each window in turn

Another squirrel, she figured. She hoped it wasn't a raccoon—they terrified her. She slid into her slippers and opened the bedroom door.

Boomer shot out the room like a rocket. He pawed at the sliding glasses doors leading out back.

She didn't want to let him outside if a raccoon created the disturbance—it could hurt him. Peering through the shades into the early morning light, she tried to distinguish shadow from— Scared, she shut the blinds. A person—a man—ran across her yard. She turned off the living room lights and went to the kitchen for a knife.

His barking escalated as Boomer hurled himself at the doors. His nose fogged up the glass.

As she dialed 911, she released him loose outside.

<hr>

Noises from her staff cleaning the exam rooms were interrupted by her cell phone ringing. Her typing stopped as she answered the call. "Yes?"

"Dr. Douglas, its Detective Gamble."

Exhaling, she resumed typing even as she spoke with him. "Hello, Todd. Have you made any progress in the investigation?"

"I actually called about the attempted break in at your place."

Again, she stopped typing. "You believe it was an attempted robbery? The patrol officers thought some kid ran through the yard, perhaps as a prank. Several of the neighbors reported someone running through their backyards too."

"With your connection to Mrs. Knight's murder, I'm concerned it's more than a mere neighborhood prank."

"But why would anyone break into my house? What could they expect to find?"

"Maybe they weren't looking for something, but someone. I can't be sure, but I heard you've been asking questions about the Greensboro Alliance."

Hesitating, she considered how to reply. She couldn't lie, he already knew the truth.

He asked, "Dr. Douglas—Myaisha, are you still there?"

Sheepish, she said, "Yes."

"Good. Listen to me, stop asking questions, and stay away from the Greensboro Alliance."

"Why?"

His sighed audibly over the phone line. "Please, let me do my job. And, I can't do my job if I have to worry about you. Understand?"

"Yes, I understand."

He hung up.

Now she had a prowler around her home and the lead homicide detective angry with her. *Good job, girl.*

Patient charts didn't concern her at the moment. Closing her browser, she made a call of her own. "Hello, Grace? This is Myaisha Douglas."

Grace said, "Yeah. What can I do for you?"

"I have a job for you. Can you drop by my office?"

"No problem. What did you have in mind?"

Dina poked her head through the doorway wearing another face mask with splatter guard.

She needed to lock those masks in her office. After taking several deep breaths, she cupped her hand over the phone. "Dina, we talked about—"

"Dr. Douglas, you have a walk in patient. Do you want to see them?"

She spoke into the phone. "I have to go. I'll explain when you get here. How long will it take?"

"I'm in High Point. Be there in 20."

Deferring her discussion with Dina about the face masks, she went to see her patient.

———

As soon as she finished meeting with Grace, Myaisha steered her car toward Jamestown. Adán texted her. He wrote urgent.

This would provide her an opportunity to get her questions answered. Yes, she had told herself not to pursue an investigation, but she remained curious. As executor of the estate she had license to question potential suspects. *If she told herself that lie often enough, she might actually believe it.* Truth be told, she simply wanted to know who killed Candace, and didn't have the patience to wait for the police to solve the crime.

Sunset saw her driving west away from Greensboro. Spindly trees cast long shadows along the road, adding suspense to the atmosphere surrounding Adán's neighborhood—thick with foreboding.

At the house, she rang the doorbell, squinting through the blinds of the large picture window. Boxes of varied sizes were scattered around the living room. *Someone planned a trip, or a remodel.* Seconds passed, tired and hungry, she rang the bell again.

Three rings brought Adán to the door.

Peeking through the chain, he inquired whether she stood there alone.

Once she satisfied him that she stood there alone, he unlatched the door.

"Myaisha, thank you for coming," he said, stepping aside so she could enter. "I really appreciate it."

The living room resembled a life-sized obstacle course. Preceding him into the living room, she maneuvered around boxes and debris like it a minefield. She rearranged items on the couch to create a sitting area.

On the opposite couch, he removed stuff, placing them on the ground and created himself a seating area. "Sorry about the mess. I'm trying to get things in order." For a few minutes he worked to straighten up the space, shuffling boxes around.

Miscellaneous objects kept sliding up against her on the couch, so she decided to sit in a winged back chair.

"What's wrong, Adán?" she asked. "You texted urgent."

Removing a pile of packing material, he abandoned his attempt to clear away the clutter, and sat on the couch surrounded by half-filled boxed. "Can I get you something to drink?"

"No, thank you." Exhausted, legs crossed, she wanted to get at her questions and leave. "What's wrong?"

On the couch, he sat holding a shoe box. He looked lost. "You hate me, I get it. But you're Candace's executor, so we're gonna have to talk."

With a deep breath, she regarded him. Deniece's statement about him being eye candy seemed appropriate. As far as brains, she wasn't sure. "I don't hate you. I just don't understand why you stayed with Candace if you didn't love her."

"What makes you think I didn't love her? Candace was my everything. I loved her with all my heart."

Her raised left eyebrow raised. She didn't answer him.

A tiny grin gathered at the corner of his lips. He placed the box on the floor beside his feet. "Too much?"

Her head nodded.

"Sorry, but I did love her—once. You never heard my side of the story, Myaisha. Everything wasn't my fault. Candace had as much responsibility for our marriage ending as I did. It takes two to destroy a relationship."

Her head slanted to the right. She wondered what fault Candace had in her death. She stretched her legs. "You're right. I'm sorry. But that's not important now. I just want to know who killed her."

"I didn't. I swear. Why would I?"

"To get her life insurance. To inherit her estate. To be with your girlfriend, Kelley."

He chuckled. "Maybe for the money—not to be free of her. I didn't have to kill Candace to be with another woman. And for the record, Kelley isn't my girlfriend. She's married." He stood up and sauntered around the living room. "Besides, if you saw her husband you'd understand why I had no intention of messing with her. Dude looks like a line-backer. *And*, she not my type." He stopped circling the room and looked directly at her. "Kelley got sucked into one of

Candace's schemes. She came crying to me for help to get her money back."

From her seat, she scrutinized him—his demeanor, his tone. He twisted his watch around his wrist, anxious. Doing nothing to reassure him, she waited to see what his nervousness produced.

"Would you believe me if I told you Candace orchestrated a real estate scam for over ten years, and an investment scheme?"

She recoiled from his accusation. Her eyes narrowed. "You're lying."

Solemn, he shook his head. "No. I'm not. Candace and I lived together for two years before we married. Her schemes started before we met. Our relationship ended when I refused her assistance with my business."

"What's wrong with that? Candace had accomplished a lot. I'd think you'd appreciate her help with your business." She heard her voice, realized she answered too quickly to be objective.

He looked at her more seriously than she'd ever seen before. "Sure. If her business wasn't illegal."

"Are you saying every business transaction she conducted had been illegal?"

"No, of course not. She got involved with some shady people through the Greensboro Alliance."

Her eyes opened wide. She slid to the edge of the chair.

"I see you've heard about the Alliance. They're worse than—" He paused, appeared to reconsider something.

Her hands clenched the sides of the chair. She didn't interrupt him.

Turning his body away from her, he changed topics. "If Candace set her mind on obtaining a goal, she had to accomplish it. No matter what, no matter how—and no matter who it affected. She decided to become a player in business politics of Greensboro and Charlotte. She wouldn't accept being left out. It had something to do with her ex-husband, like she was still competing with him."

His gaze shifted to the darkness of the backyard, which prevented him from viewing the astonishment on her face.

She fought back tears. Saddened by the length of Candace's illegal activities. *When had she lost her Candace, in California?* The young woman she knew—hardworking ambitious—morphed into someone else when she returned to the Tar Heel State. She mourned the death of her Candace, this second Candace disgusted her. Lost in her thoughts, she hadn't noticed he had been watching her.

"Surprised, huh? Me too. Candace wanted to use my business—exploit it like she did everything else. She wanted my contacts for her investment scheme. When I refused—" He stared back outside. "Let's just say, I became nothing to her. Everything ended. Don't get me wrong, I didn't refuse because I'm such an honest person. I refused because I worried. She handled some shady stuff, dealt with serious people—people with money and influence. In the last six months, I started getting threats. Former clients demanding their money back, or else."

To the detriment of his ego, he admitted to distancing himself from her professionally out of self-preservation. He feared what would happen if the authorities looked too closely at her business enterprises, or if her clients came in search of retribution.

Frown lines crept across her forehead. "It doesn't make sense. Community leaders respected her. People admired her, awarded her for her work."

His laugh sent a chill through her body. She hugged herself for comfort. Perhaps he heard how disturbing his laughter sounded because he apologized.

"I'm sorry, Myaisha. These business *leaders* were idiots. They had no idea what Candace was up to—some of them. Others, she paid handsomely not to see, or they were involved in the schemes too. Some people—when they found out buried her secrets to protect their own reputations. Either way, with the housing market crashing soon everyone would know what she did. That's why she got into the medical supply stuff. She knew real estate was drying up. You heard about Lottie's job right?"

Too many thoughts filled her head, like a band tightening around her skull. She struggled to accept her dear friend had not been the person she knew and loved. Her college friend Candace, died years ago. *When had the transformation occurred?* She believed her experience with Candace had been an unfortunate circumstance, not a systemic behavior her friend used to take advantage of her clients. *Had Candace deliberately tried to deceive her?*

As he spoke, he fiddled with one of the boxes. He said, "I stayed with Candace because—because I had to. Financially, I depended on her. After we married, I let a lot of my businesses go at her insistence. With my poor credit and limited earnings— she provided me with a comfortable life."

"Candace consented to the arrangement?"

"Appearances mattered to her. She told me my job was to behave as a loving supportive husband—in public. Privately, I no longer enjoyed the benefits of a loving marriage."

She winced—TMI.

"She just wanted her adoring public to see us as a model couple. A lie I became very good at. We lived separate lives for the past six months. Then, all of a sudden, Candace said she didn't need me anymore. She wanted a divorce. She hired someone to follow me around town, trying to dig up dirt on me. When she couldn't get evidence I committed adultery, she hired people to make up crap."

"So, you never had an affair?"

"No. I didn't have time. I made some contacts down in Charlotte. I intend to take my business to the next level. I already secured an investor."

"May I ask who?"

His stroll around the room continued. With a crooked grin on his face, he said, "I already informed the police. They know all about my alibi for the day of the murder. I drove down to Statesville, at least 70 miles from Greensboro."

Extending her legs forward, she removed her hat. "So you were prepared to just walk away from the marriage, with nothing?"

"No way. After all those years, dealing with threats from her angry clients—no chance. Candace owed me. I knew she would pay me to go away."

Leaning forward, she asked, "Why?"

He grinned. "When I realized what Candace was up to, I started collecting information of my own—for *my* protection. I have information on her—" He stopped.

What did he plan to say? Everyone seemed to have a hidden agenda. This mystery started to seem like an onion—the more she peeled away, the more there was underneath.

In front of the fireplace he stopped pacing. "With everything going on with this mortgage fraud stuff—Candace would have given me what I wanted just to shut me up. She would've paid me in the end. She valued her reputation. Appearances mattered to her—too much."

She felt wounded. His story confirmed what she had heard from Harriet and Kelley. *How could someone she considered a dear friend be such a cheat?* Candace had intended to defraud people—to defraud her. *What happened to their friendship? Was there ever any trust?* Fatigued, she placed her hat on her head. It was past time for her to leave. She desired a hot shower and some tea.

"I'm sorry, Adán. I didn't know about your—situation. Why did you call me?"

He collapsed onto the couch. Several items fell on the floor. He made no attempt to pick them up. "When do you think I'll get the life insurance money?"

She grimaced, making no attempt to hide her disgust. His text read urgent. Worried, she rushed over after work—no dinner, no rest. She wanted to help the husband of her murdered friend. Her fists clenched. "I don't know. It depends on when the authorities complete their investigation."

"It could take months. I can't wait that long."

His expensive cologne peppered the air. Dressed in acid washed jeans and a designer t-shirt, his hair nicely coiffed with manicured nails. She didn't think he suffered from lack of anything. "There's nothing I can do. Surely, you and Candace have money in the bank."

For a second his eyes deviated to the hard wood floors. He avoided her gaze. "We had separate bank accounts. I have some money, but with expenses, Candace's office overhead, I don't know what to do."

Her mouth opened to reply, but she snapped it shut—unsure how much she cared to delve into his personal affairs—Candace's personal affairs. This evening she learned more than she had expected, more than she wished she knew. Her shoulders slouched. She sighed and stood. "Go to the bank. They should grant you access to—"

With a raised voice, he interrupted her. "I tried. You think I'm an idiot. I already tried the bank, *and* the lawyer. They won't help."

Her eyes flashed on him—an idiot, a murderer, or both. *What did she know?* Adán admitted to living off Candace. He had planned an exit strategy out of his loveless marriage. Usually more empathetic, whether from fatigue or disgust, she wanted to leave—get away from Adán, Candace, their house. She needed to rest her brain and her body, wash away the deceit. They had deserved each other.

He fidgeted, twisted the Rolex repeatedly around his wrist.

Reminded about the office, she recalled the crime scene but still couldn't remember seeing the watch. *What happened to Candace's watch, and did it matter?* Her head ached.

Adán, it'll work out. Call the creditors. Ask for extensions on the payments. Given the circumstances, they'll grant you leniency. Once the police solve the murder, you stand to inherit the life insurance. Pastor Matthew will be by to check on you. If I hear anything, I'll let you know."

Thanking her, he escorted her out.

Inside her car, she rolled down the windows. As she drove away, the wind whipped her face—slapped her out of the world of the Knights. She thought she knew Adán, thought she knew Candace. It begged the question of whether you could ever really know anyone.

This murder exposed information about her friends she didn't want to know. She couldn't stop from learning the truth now even if she wanted. *What did she want?* Right now a hug from Boomer and a long hot shower. Suddenly, she remembered she'd forgotten to mention the contents of the will. Probably a good thing. Let the lawyer inform him Candace left the entire estate to her.

Feeling impotent, she turned on the radio. Her mind needed to be cleansed. She didn't believe things could get worse after she discovered Candace murdered. But every new revelation felt like killing her Candace all over again.

A feeling of foreboding sent shivers up her back. She rolled up the windows. A premonition that the worst waited in front of her trembled her body. Shaking off her fears, she steeled her resolve. The answer to who killed Candace still remained elusive. At least she had learned the worst about her friend. No more lies.

Adán secured the door behind her, attaching the chain and deadbolt. He rested his back against the frame and contemplated his next move. The police suspected him of killing Candace. He had an alibi, but using it might backfire. *Would his witness confirm his story?* She hadn't told her husband about their business arrangement. If she changed her mind about their deal, she might deny ever meeting him. *What if the police didn't believe him, or her?* He had no way to prove they had met the day of the murder.

Twisting his Rolex around his wrist calmed his nerves. He knew if things became desperate he could always pawn the watch—and Candace's jewelry. *Wait, did he get the jewelry in the will?* He couldn't remember. After the lawyer mentioned the five-million-dollar life insurance policy, his mind blanked on everything else.

With his mind on his money problems, he banged into a large box and stubbed his toe.

"Shit!" Hobbling to the couch, he slid items on the floor so he could sit down.

The bank froze Candace's accounts. The safe in their study had been emptied. *She must have moved everything to a safety deposit box at the bank.* Another expletive poured from his mouth. The estate lawyer explained the life insurance company controlled the money from the policy. Although Myaisha had been assigned executor, she had no influence over the life insurance company.

Considered a pariah in town, he could hardly leave home. Reporters or cops followed his every step. He needed to escape Jamestown, get out of North Carolina. Myaisha was right, nothing would change until the cops caught the killer.

Like a moth to a light, he wandered toward the large glass sliding doors, gazed out into the back yard. Night hid the trees, but he still stared into the night. He had some thoughts on who could have murdered his wife. He really could care less, except that person stood between him and millions of dollars.

Should he call the police with the information? They might think he was trying to shift suspicion to someone else. Before he stepped away from the sliding doors he double checked the locks then shut the curtains, tight.

Frustrated, he walked over to the wet bar and prepared himself a drink. The police wouldn't believe him unless he had proof. Ice cubes clanked in the tumbler as he poured himself some brandy.

After a long draught, he decided to play a lone hand, see if his suspect would take the bait. Maybe even collect some money from the information.

With a smile, he slid his phone from his back pocket and hit send. "Hey, we need to talk."

Chapter 21

Last night, Myaisha forgot to set her alarm.

Boomer pawed her awake to serve him breakfast.

Afterward, she barely had time to shower and dress, which left her no time to round on patients in the hospital before morning clinic started. Three babies in the hospital waited to be discharged home. Generally, she would have seen them before going to the office, however, she woke up late. She arrived at the office as Dina roomed her first patient. Yvette called the hospital and notified her patients she would be there around noon.

Wednesday morning, hump day, and she felt like she was running up a hill. Most of last night involved completing patient charts after she visited Jamestown to speak with Adán. She hurried between exam rooms. The morning passed by in a blur.

She arrived at the hospital a few minutes after twelve, and managed to complete patient rounds with one more baby to discharge when her cell phone rang. Assuming it to be from her office, she muted the phone. Once she completed the final discharge note, she gave the families their new baby packages and left. *No lunch again.*

As soon as she returned to the office, she booted up her laptop and started seeing patients.

Opening the exam room door, a smile sprang to her face. She said, "Hello, Dequan. How are you doing today, young man?"

"I'm five," he said, dressed in a gown too long for his five-year-old body.

She glanced over at the empty chair next to his grandmother and spied dollar bills clipped to the front of his shirt with a safety pin.

"Well, happy birthday." She would have to get a bill out of her purse to add to his cache for the day. She addressed his grandmother. "How are you today, Mrs. Kent?"

Her wig slightly askew, his grandmother wore thick lenses. "How you doin' doctor? Dequan needs his physical. He's a big boy now. Going to school and everythang."

Beaming with pride, he tried to sit up straighter. His paper gown tore. "I go to school."

"He goin' in the fall."

"I go to school like Josiah." When he squirmed, the table paper crinkled.

Seated on her stool, she asked Mrs. Kent for the school form. Josiah occasionally babysat Dequan. She assured him, her son would be home for the summer, plenty of time for them to hang out together before school started. The family were members of her church. Dequan missed Josiah almost as much as she did. *Almost.*

Exam completed, she explained to Mrs. Kent about the vaccinations Dequan needed for school. Exiting the room, she detoured to her office to get money for the birthday boy. Her office manager intercepted her.

Yvette waited in the hallway next to her office door. She said, "Mrs. Doctor, you have a call from a lawyer."

Confused, she stopped to regard Yvette.

The office manager's face appeared placid, but her eyebrows questioned why a lawyer called.

In her office, she retrieved her purse and removed several bills. "Who is it? Did they say what they wanted?"

Rolling up her sleeves, Yvette said, "A Ms. Tran. She says it's private, and important."

After asking Yvette to give the money to Dequan, she closed the door. It took a moment for her to collect herself before she picked up the line. "Hello. This is Dr. Douglas."

On the line, a lawyer spoke in brisk short clips. "Dr. Douglas. We need to meet. Tomorrow's best. Any day's fine. I can accommodate."

The calendar on her computer listed her date with AJ tonight, followed by her writing club meeting tomorrow evening. Each day had a full roster of patients. "I have patient appointments all day tomorrow," she said.

Ms. Tran didn't hesitate. "Friday? We need to meet. This week."

"What is this about?" Ideas circled her mind. *Could a patient have made a complaint? Did someone plan to sue her?* Those thoughts impeded her from hearing what the lawyer said. She asked, "Excuse me, could you repeat that?"

"Lunch. We can do lunch. If you prefer."

Did she prefer? She wished the lawyer would explain the nature of her business. Door, she heard her staff and patients. She became impatient. "Mrs., excuse me, Ms. Tran, what is this about?"

"Mrs. Knight. You're the executor, correct?"

"Yes."

"My client lost money. She has a claim, against the estate." Over several minutes, Ms. Tran's detailed how her client lost money in a business venture Candace represented. The woman suffered significant losses, which she intended to recover from the estate.

Irritated, she directed the lawyer to contact the firm handling the estate and hung up. *What other surprises awaited her as executor?* Candace entrusted her to manage her affairs, but the assignment might turn out to be a curse rather than a compliment.

No one seemed to require her attention at the moment, so she made a call. "Hello, Grace? You have a moment?"

"Yeah," Grace said. "I take it; this is not a social call."

"Sorry, too soon?"

"I got what you asked about Mrs. Knight's first husband, Philip Scott. According to the Guilford County Courthouse, she had been arrested but never formally charged with forgery."

The line went quiet. She needed a moment to digest the information. Candace had lied to her. *Why? What purpose could she have had for lying about the divorce?*

"Myaisha? You still there?"

"Yes. Sorry. I needed a moment."

"You still want me to get information for you about Charles Marshall's whereabouts?"

Seconds passed as she gave it some thought. "Yes—no. From the information you already collected for Candace, he has a great motive. But, I already shared the information about him with the police."

A knock at the door reminded her about the patients.

Through the door, Yvette said, "You have two patients waiting, Mrs. Doctor."

"Thanks. I'll be right there."

She spoke into the phone. "Grace, do you know anything about the Greensboro Black Professional Alliance?"

"Yeah, Why?"

"Their name has come up a few times."

"I'm not surprised. You know they're having an open house tonight."

"No I didn't. Did Candace ask you to do any other work for her?"

This time Grace paused. After half a minute, she said, "Let's talk about it later, when I get the other information together for you."

As she ended the call, she had a feeling she wasn't going to like what Grace had to tell her. *What did Candace get herself into?*

Her phone beeped a reminder about her date with AJ tonight. She thought about the evening ahead. Last night, he sent her a text. Dress casual.

What did he mean? One person's casual might be formal to someone else. It drove her crazy trying to figure out what to wear. At home, she packed three different outfits into a suitcase. Busy rooming patients, her staff didn't see her haul it into the office that morning.

Yvette called her attention back to her patients.

She grabbed her stethoscope and rushed to the next patient room.

Having dismissed her last patient, she holed up in her office. Locked her door and removed her suitcase from under a side table. She evaluated each outfit. On the other side of the door, her staff joked and moved about the office straightening up before they departed.

She waited, hoping they would leave soon. Shutting the blinds, she heard the noises from the office diminish. Kicking off her shoes, she slipped out of her exam coat and shimmied out of her slacks. A dress and a pair of jeans lay on her desk, out of the suitcase. *Which one to try on first?* In her office clad only in her underwear and a bra, a knock on her door almost caused her to urinate on herself.

Trembling, she hurried to pull up her slacks. "Yes?"

"We're leaving, Mrs. Doctor. Do you need anything?" Yvette asked.

"No." *Did she answer too loudly?* Unsure, she said, "Thank you. Good night."

With her ear against the door, she listened. She cracked open the door and called out for Yvette. No response. Holding her breath, she rushed over to the window and watched her staff exit the lot. She closed the blinds, tight.

Skipping down to the bathroom, she brushed her teeth and rinsed the sweat off her face. She combed her thick curly black hair, inserting silver combs on both sides of her head. Her hat wouldn't fit over the combs, so she ditched it. She applied extra deodorant and coated her arms and legs in shea butter. Her mahogany brown limbs shined. A light blue wrap dress flowed over her head and snuggled against her frame.

Her office clock read two minutes until six. He should be there any moment—probably already arrived. She locked up the office and hurried out back to her car. Tonight, she had more to worry about than a date with a handsome man.

Between patient appointments, she sent AJ a text, asked if they could stop by the Greensboro Black Professionals Alliance offices on their way to dinner. Since no one at the Alliance would answer her questions, she planned to drop in on their meeting.

Outside, the cool evening air refreshed her senses. It calmed her racing heart. Traffic and insects were the only audible noises. Her Honda crawled around to the front of the office where she spotted a large pickup truck parked at the edge of the lot. AJ.

He stood beside his double wide truck, flowers in hand. He wore boots, jeans and a button down shirt with a sports jacket. They agreed to take his truck to dinner.

Fear and bile rose up inside her. She swallowed, the acid burning her throat. Her hands clenched and unclenched the steering wheel.

After a moment, the nausea subsided. *Breathe deep.* She set the brake and cut the engine. *Just nerves, girl. Calm down.*

His slow approach gave her a moment to collect herself. She chewed her lip, remembered she had applied lip gloss in the restroom and stopped. *Did she get anything on her teeth?* A quick glance in the side mirror confirmed she looked fine. Her tongue tasted strawberry.

His wide grin proceeded him. "Are you ready?" he asked.

"Yes." Embarrassed by her squeaky voice, she admonished herself for acting like a fool. *He's just a man.*

A short trip brought them to his truck. Although he hadn't touched her, she felt heat emanating from his body. His presence sent her senses on high alert. Avoiding eye contact, she used his arm as leverage to climb inside the truck. She reconsidered her outfit. A knee length dress with low heeled mules made climbing into his truck complicated, at least to do with elegance.

They exchanged light conversation on their drive downtown. For her part, she responded in monosyllables. Her mind focused on confronting the Greensboro Alliance, she gave him little attention.

"So, tell me about this meeting," he said.

Time to confess. She hadn't been upfront with him about her motives. She looked across the seat at him, took a deep breath. "I don't actually belong to the Greensboro Alliance."

His wrinkled brow side glanced her. "What do you mean?"

After they parked and entered the building where the Alliance met, she realized the murder case had escalated. She entered the property of the enemy. "I'm trying to find out about the organization. I believe they're involved in Candace's murder."

He stopped mid-stride. She did likewise.

"Are you saying—what are you saying? Why are we here?"

"I apologize. I didn't mean to get you involved, AJ. It just happened their meeting fell on the same day as our date."

Without responding to her statement, he approached the gathering. She walked next to him, the tension between them palpable, further straining her nerves.

Glancing through the open office doors, the area looked like any routine business lobby. People ambled about, conversations peppered the room. A few chairs were assembled along the walls of the wide open central area. Piped in elevator music could be heard when the conversations lapsed. Surveying the area, she evaluated the people in attendance, weighed who could provide the answers she sought.

From her left, a woman with a big smile and an even bigger clipboard walked up to her and extended her hand. She said, "Hello. I'm Terri. I haven't met you before. Are you a member?"

"No. I want to learn more about the group. I'm interested in joining. Is there someone in charge I could speak with?"

Her smile grew larger. "Yes, absolutely. Let me see if I can find the president." Terri walked off.

From the corner of her eye, she noticed AJ side-eye her. Returning his gaze, she asked, "What?"

"Nothing. I'm just watching you in action." He grinned.

Not wanting to become distracted by his flirting, she observed Terri speaking with a large man next to a refreshment table. The gentleman turned toward her, an unsmiling hardened expression on his face.

Her body tensed as the man hurried in her direction. She braced herself. Her arm felt AJ come closer to her side. Her skin tingled. When the man stood a foot away, she held out her hand. "Hello, I'm—"

The man did not accept her handshake.

Rude.

He glanced at her, then eyed AJ, who stood a foot taller than him. His gaze floated back toward her. He said, "I know who you are Dr. Douglas. Why are you here?"

"I had some questions and no one will return my calls."

He advanced in her direction. "Dr. Douglas—"

AJ stepped forward. "Who are you?" he asked.

After he sized up AJ, he retreated a step. "I'm Derrick Jenkins. This is my organization. My offices. And you two aren't members."

She interceded between the two men. "I only want to understand Candace's relationship with the Alliance."

Derrick said, "She was a member. Nothing more to say."

"Why did you withdraw the offer of a reward for information on her murderer?"

Looking aside, he motioned to someone. Two large men in non-descript suits headed in their direction.

Sensing AJ come closer to her side again, he brushed up against her arm.

"What we do," Derrick said, "is none of your business. Now, if you'll excuse me, I have members to attend to—and you *both* need to leave."

Ignoring the security men, she said, "Did you have anything to do with Candace's murder?"

His back straightened, he leaned toward her.

When AJ started in his direction, she touched his arm. "It's fine."

He stopped beside her.

Derrick spoke through his teeth. "Watch what you say doctor. I'm sure you're familiar with libel."

"I think you mean slander."

He strode away. The two guards barred her and AJ from following him.

Angling her head around them, she observed Derrick engage a group of business people on the other side of the room. With a nod toward AJ, she said, "I'm ready to go."

In the parking lot, he assisted her up into his truck. He said, "Well, that was fun."

She grinned at his smirk.

———————

AJ drove them to a nearby Indian restaurant.

Myaisha loved Indian food, and wondered if it was a lucky guess or did Deniece give him a hint. Either way, she didn't care. Her stomach churned and confirmed its delight.

The smell of curry greeted them as they entered the establishment. Thick red carpet with a wall mural added to the '70s flashback ambiance. Only the food mattered. With the restaurant half empty, they were immediately seated.

After placing their entrée orders, she took a long drink from her mango lassi. Gazing up at him from under her lashes, she watched him eat samosas. His large full lips munched on the brown spicy triangles. He had a perpetual smile. When he noticed her watching him, she choked on her drink.

"Sorry." She took a sip of water.

He pushed the tray of samosas toward her. "You feeling better?"

Accepting a samosa, she hesitated. "Yes, thank you. I'm sorry about the Greensboro Alliance. When we scheduled our date, I didn't know about their meeting. I—I had to see for myself. I apologize for getting you involved."

"Don't worry about it. I'm accustomed to women using me for my body."

She smiled.

"This is about your murdered friend, right?"

"Yes. I've never been an executor before. I want to do the right thing by Candace, but—"

"What's wrong?"

"I don't know. Maybe I'm going about this the wrong way. Deniece says I should stop investigating the murder."

"Why *are* you investigating her murder?"

"She was my friend."

"Someone murdered her, Myaisha. Leave it alone. Let the cops do their job."

"Why does everyone keep saying that?"

"Because we care about you. A murderer is dangerous. You can act as executor without becoming involved in the investigation."

Part of her wanted to argue. She hated to leave something incomplete. Not only had Todd warned her to stop her inquiries, but the prowler outside the house frightened her. She allowed the noises of the restaurant to place some space between them.

After eating a few samosas, she asked, "So, have you always wanted to be a firefighter?"

"No. After I completed my degree in history, I searched for a job. There wasn't much available for a history major. Eventually, I applied and became a firefighter. Let's talk about you." He smiled.

She liked his smile. A lot. *Was she moving too fast?*

He asked, "How's the food?"

"It's alright. My favorite Indian food restaurant is in Charlotte, but this is okay in a pinch."

"I'll take you there on our next date."

She laughed. His smiled radiated just as big as he did. Embolden, she asked, "How tall are you?"

He sat up straighter. "Six feet, seven inches. Is that a problem?"

"Sorry, just curious. I'm sure people ask you about your height all the time."

"That and did I play basketball. Like every tall black man dreams of playing sports."

"You don't like sports?"

Finishing his tandoori, he wiped his mouth. "I love sports. I just hate the assumption."

"I know what you mean. Everyone kept telling me to put Josiah in sports. Like every black child should aspire to be an athlete."

They shared their experiences with societal expectations. She explained although she worked at the same hospital for over ten years, people still called her nurse. Even patients assumed she had to be the nurse and asked when the doctor would arrive. At church, people questioned why she worked at all when she was married to a physician—as if women only married for financial security.

She and AJ even talked about plans in Greensboro to build a civil rights memorial.

Sometime during the evening, she began to relax and enjoy herself. She discovered him to be an avid reader. He preferred non-fiction, mostly history or an occasional memoir. He didn't like mysteries—*no man was perfect*. She listened to his discussion of his current book on the presidents of the Civil War.

Chiding herself for associating him with the term eye candy, she blamed Deniece for putting the term in her mind. She found AJ interesting and intelligent. A brain controlled all that muscle. For the first time since they met, she found herself more than physically attracted to the firefighter.

"I remember my school counselor kept trying to get me to play a sport—any sport. He didn't believe I could get accepted to college on merit. I'd choose classical literature or a museum over a ball field any day.

"A black male as an intellectual is foreign to most people."

Glass lifted, he gave a toast. "Here's to breaking stereotypes."

She duplicated his gesture. "To breaking stereotypes. Cheers."

Their glasses clinked. She looked into his eyes. As he held her gaze, she breathed him in. His scent, his smile, his voice. Neither spoke. They simply enjoyed each other's company.

The server delicately placed the check on the table. Before she could reach forward, he palmed the tray holding the bill. She offered to split the tab.

He removed several bills from his wallet, placed them on the tray and helped her from her seat. They left.

As they drove to her office, he asked, "Are you busy this weekend? There's an exhibit in Charlotte I'd like to see. I'd enjoy some company."

"My office is open on alternate Saturdays. Maybe another time."

"Sure."

He pulled into the parking lot of her office, and parked beside her car.

Turning his frame toward her, he said, "I'm sorry about your friend, Myaisha, but please, leave the investigating to the police."

With the ignition on he walked around the truck and assisted her out of the cab.

They walked in silence toward her vehicle.

She scrutinized his face. *Handsome.* Different than Sammy, but the same. At her car, she stared into the night as her thoughts drifted over the evening. She perceived something approaching and noticed AJ's face coming nearer. Surprised, she held her hands up onto his chest.

"I'm—I can't AJ. I'm sorry. I'm not ready," she said.

He smiled. "I understand. I didn't mean to rush you."

Once she settled inside her car, he returned to his truck and followed her onto the main street. He continued driving behind her all the way to her house. There, he circled the cul de sac, and departed.

<hr>

From the garage, Myaisha entered the house. While Boomer went outside to relieve himself, she slipped out of her heels. Then she made a beeline for the stereo, inserting her favorite tape. Sammy bought her the entertainment system for her thirtieth birthday. A reel to reel, record player, eight track player, the works. He recorded a special tape for her. Turning on the tape player, she listened to her favorite songs.

Music started and Stevie Wonder's *I Was Made to Love Her* sang through the speakers. She retrieved picture albums from the built-in cabinets and sat on the couch. Scanning through photos of her and Sammy, she found old photos of Josiah as a baby.

Her feet curled underneath her, she sighed. Gazing out toward the yard, she thought back, tried to remember what Sammy looked like that last morning before he went to work. *Did he kiss her goodbye? Had she told him she loved him?*

For months after he died those last moments replayed continuously in her mind. In time, other images replaced them—the day they married, vacations, Josiah's birth. So many moments, too many memories. She wanted to keep them all fresh in her mind.

Tears trickled down her cheeks as she looked at pictures of Sammy in scrubs rounding in the hospital during his fellowship. She loved him so much. With his family history of diabetes and high blood pressure, they should have worried more about his health. As a neurologist, he knew all about strokes. When he had started to slur his words at work that day, he alerted his staff to call 911, then he directed them to call her.

Her lips quivered, wet with tears. To no one, she said, "You knew so much, except how to save yourself."

Frankie Valli's *My Eyes Adored You* played while she viewed their wedding album. Unable to afford a formal affair, their ceremony took place in a family friend's backyard. A younger Sammy looked healthy and happy. By the time Peabo Bryson's *I'm So into You* started, sobs prevented her from seeing the pictures.

Switching the tape deck switched off, she stepped over Boomer and locked the back door. She inserted a broom stick in the window track as a preventive measure.

In the bathroom, she examined herself. Makeup smeared around her eyes like a raccoon. Her face looked splotchy and bloated. She splashed water on her face and gazed into the mirror again. Her appearance worsened.

Still dressed, she staggered into the bedroom. Snot and tears poured down her face as she face-planted onto the bed. Curled into a ball, she hugged the pillows.

A whining Boomer pawed her and tore at her dress. She pushed him away. Through tears she told him to stop.

His whine increased, he pawed her harder.

Frustrated, she sat up. "Stop it."

A short bark followed more pawing and whining. He persisted.

Grabbing a pillow and blanket, she gave up and settled on the floor.

Boomer sniffed and licked her face and head. Making repeated circles around her body, he finally rested in the small of her back. Head down, he slept.

In a few minutes, she did too. For the first time since Candace was killed, she dreamed of something other than the murder.

Chapter 22

Adán adjusted to the darkness as he waited. His pinpoint pupils reacted as the harsh headlights slammed onto his face. The car stopped yards away.

Traffic on Interstate 85 hummed around them on both sides of the median. In the late evening commuters were sparse, most of the vehicles were semi-trucks. The median sat between the north and south bound interstates nestled between a grove of trees. The highway patrol used it to ambush unsuspecting speeders. It also provided a great place for a clandestine rendezvous.

His guest exited their vehicle, but remained beside it. Head lamps illuminated.

Since he arranged the meeting, he took the initiative and left his SUV to approach the other car. Careful to step around the debris on the dirt road, he minimized the distance between them. As he advanced, the driver extinguished the head lights. He slowed his approach. Plunged abruptly into darkness, his pupils required time to dilate.

Walking forward he said, "Thanks for coming. I thought you'd prefer to discuss what I found in my wife's safe in person. You know, instead of me taking the information to the police."

Cloud cover obscured the moon light. No sounds were audible except the semis and the car engine of his guest. The grin on his face faded the closer he got to the other car. As his vision improved, his dimples retracted. The quiet unnerved him. His guest made no attempt to speak.

He detected the outline of his companion, and could make out a cap and jacket. No facial features were clear though. Becoming impatient, he took a few more steps forward. He'd almost reached the other car when he asked, "What's with you? Are we gonna talk or not? If you don't want the cops to know about—"

Even in the dark, he could make out the object extended in his direction. The distinctive shape of a gun pointed in his direction. He threw up his hands. "Wait. We can work this out. I don't want a lot. Just enough to get away. Please."

The individual remained behind the car door without responding. The revolver didn't waver.

Straining to make out the face, he lowered his arms. "You? What are you doing here? You can't do this. How are you—"

Bam. Bam.

Possum scurried further into the woods. An 18 wheeler roared down the road kicking up debris and leaves.

The figure bent down over Adán, removing the Rolex and searching his body. The pockets held a wallet, keys, and a cell phone.

Wait. There were two cell phones. Placing one phone back into the pocket of Adán's slacks, the individual returned to their vehicle.

Driving past the body, they stopped beside the SUV. Less than a minute later, the car rolled onto the black top and headed north up the interstate for Greensboro.

Chapter 23

S lamming his desk drawer closed, Todd ignored the glances from his fellow officers. He blew out the air in his lungs then inhaled deeply and did it again. Scents of coffee and pastry flooded his nostrils. He watched his colleagues watching him. After a moment, he powered up his desk top computer. Glanced across the desks at his partner.

"What?" he asked.

Ian grinned. "Bad news?"

His eyes narrowed, he tried not to project his anger. The difficult morning couldn't be blamed on anyone—except his boss. The chief fumed about his perceived lack of progress on the investigation. Yesterday, they verified alibis, spoke with the forensic accountant, and tracked down the Adán Knight's 'friend'. None of which had satisfied the chief.

Answering Ian's question while he typed, he said, "Knight's alibi held up. I talked to the woman he met in Statesville."

Swoosh. Ian popped open his soda can and took a drink. "What? Some chick he scammed off the internet?"

"No, she's married. Like he said, they met at one of his empowerment seminars. Her interest in him is only professional. I talked with the local police department. The place Knight mentioned checked out too. Other witnesses corroborated his alibi."

"What's the different between a class and a seminar?"

"$500."

Soda spit out Ian's mouth and nose. "You've got to be kidding."

"Nope." He continued to type.

Returned from cleaning himself up, Ian tossed him a soda can.

Catching it, he said, "Watch it. Now it's gonna explode."

"No it won't. Just give it a minute." He sat down. "Remember when I mentioned a possible suspect in Charlotte?"

"No."

"Sure you do."

His fingers hovered over the keyboard as he glanced up. "You stated our victim had connections in Charlotte, you didn't mention a possible suspect there."

Staring him down with a frown, he asked, "What, are you man-struating? Don't be pedantic."

"Sorry, it's the English major in me. Go on." He grinned.

Ian pitched a pencil at him, striking his hand.

The pencil bounced off his hand and fell on the floor. "Hey." He picked it up off the ground.

"Listen," Ian said, "last night I spoke with a friend of mine in the Charlotte DA's office. He mentioned a case about a bank executive wanted for embezzlement. We got to talking and I dropped the name of our vic. As it turns out, Mrs. Knight associated with the guy."

"What are you waiting for? What's his name?"

"Charles Marshall. Word is, he got our vic started in real estate."

"I know. The doctor gave me a dossier Mrs. Knight paid a private detective to compile on Charles Marshall."

Shooting him a mean glare, Ian slammed his hand on the desk. "How long have you known, and when did you plan on telling me?"

"Dr. Douglas provided me with the information late Sunday evening. I handed it over to the forensic accounting department since it involved financial fraud. Seems Mrs. Knight was concerned about Mr. Marshall, and had the PI look into his business operations and assets."

Pulling out his note pad, Ian scanned through the pages. "He's being investigated for mortgage fraud and misappropriation of client funds. He was arraigned and released on bail. When Charlotte authorities discovered he'd committed other indiscretions they revoked his bail. Their attempts to contact Mr. Marshall at work and home failed. His family and associates haven't seen him in weeks."

In unison, they said, 'fingerprints'. Both picked up their respective desk phones.

"I'll call forensics," Todd said. "Get them to check the database and run his prints against those at the crime scene."

"I'll check for priors. See if this guy registered any weapons."

An hour later, they compared notes.

Reviewing the crime scene photos, Todd re-evaluated their case. "Any ideas?" he asked.

"The husband's out. The mistress, Mrs. Wayne, is out. Time to look at business associates. Charles Marshall is rising on the list of suspects." Taking a long drink of soda, Ian covered his mouth then burped. "Excuse me. Did we get the license plate of the woman who assaulted our vic in the parking lot?"

He searched among the stack of papers on his desk. "I saw a list of the plate owners somewhere. I remember glancing at it earlier. I asked one of the desk officers to compare the plates from the gas station with the courthouse recording."

"Cool. Any interviews today?" Ian opened a bag of chips.

"Not yet. I have to get my report to the chief. Today makes one week since the murder and we're no closer to identifying the killer."

"This may be bigger than Greensboro. Maybe it's associated with the mortgage fraud out of Charlotte. Should we chase down that angle?"

Before he could reply his desk phone rang. With a finger, he signaled his partner to wait. He lifted the receiver. "Detective Gamble." He looked across the desks as he listened to the caller. His brows creased, his jaw tightened. Scribbling information obtained from the caller, he observed his partner's demeanor change in response to his.

Speaking into the phone, he said, "Thanks for the information." Ending the call, he paused and considered what he'd been told.

"What? What is it?" Ian asked.

Wiping his forehead, he fingered his soda can. "You're not gonna believe this."

Myaisha rushed from exam room two. The toddler at the weight scale screamed his objection to being undressed. His mother struggled to remove his shoes. The waiting area was full of patients. Noise from the television blared between the outbursts. The day had only begun, and it promised to be another exhausting day.

Running into her private office, she searched the desk for a business card with the urologist's information. She recalled bringing there, but couldn't remember what she did with it. Her patient needed to be seen immediately, and she wanted to send the referral to Cathy, the new urologist in town. Eventually, she found the card underneath a pediatric magazine. Her office manager entered at the same time she picked up the phone.

"Mrs. Doctor, you have a call on line four," Yvette said.

Dialing the number, she didn't look up. "Take a message. I have to call the urologist for Keith. His mom pulled his foreskin back behind the head of his penis and now he has a phimosis. I don't understand why American parents can't deal with foreskin. Most males in the world aren't circumcised, but no matter how often we tell them to leave the foreskin alone—"

"Mrs. Doctor, it's the police."

Glancing up, her eyes widened. Yvette nodded.

The card was given to Yvette with instructions on how to handle the referral. As her office manager left her office, she picked up the line. "Yes."

Her chin cradled the phone against her shoulder. Giving the phone conversation half her attention, she completed a note in Keith's chart to send to the specialist.

"Dr. Douglas, we'd like to come by your office. We need to speak with you this morning if possible."

Recognizing Todd's voice, she continued with her note. Her patient list, not only long, included several complicated patients. *Another day without lunch.* She resolved to leave the office at a reasonable hour this evening. "I don't have time this afternoon. Can we—"

"Mr. Knight's dead. Shot in the chest, just like his wife."

Her mouth dropped. She froze. Her mind switched to autopilot. "I'll make time. Come over."

Twenty minutes later, she sat in the back seat of the detectives' car as they questioned her about the last time she spoke with Adán. She requested they conduct the interview in their vehicle. Her staff were competent, but gossiped. Until she understood what occurred, she wanted to limit the dispersal of information.

Answering the detective's questions, her gaze shifted between them trying to read their faces. She wanted to understand what occurred, glean as much information as possible. "I spoke with Adán on Tuesday," she said.

Making a note in his book, Detective de Jesus asked, "How did he seem to you?"

Her gaze drifted back toward the office. The blinds in her room window twitched. The staff watched them.

He called her attention back to their conversation. "Doctor?"

"He didn't look like he was about to be murdered."

His body twisted around in the seat to get a better look at her. With his large size, she knew he couldn't be comfortable. "Please just answer the question."

She looked him in the eye. "I'm sorry. He asked me about the life insurance policy. The company held up the payout pending the criminal investigation. Candace's bank accounts were frozen. Bills were due. The lawyer informed him it would be weeks, if not months before he received any money from the estate."

Her gaze encompassed both detectives, probing their faces for information. She peppered them with questions. "Where did you find Adán? Why would anyone kill him? Did the same person kill him and Candace?" Each question rapidly followed the other, and each remained unanswered. The detectives refused to give her any details.

Detective Gamble asked, "Was he worried about anyone in particular? You said he mentioned threats?"

"No. He didn't mention anyone by name." She sighed. *Why hadn't she paid more attention to Adán?* It never occurred to her to worry about his welfare. And now he'd been murdered—shot like Candace. *But why? Why would anyone kill him?* He was...The words which came to mind were helpless and useless. Cruel perhaps, but not wrong. Apparently she had been wrong. Someone viewed Adán a big enough threat to kill him. "Did you look into Charles Marshall?"

"Dr. Douglas, stop trying to do our work for us," Detective de Jesus said. "Is there anything else you can remember? Anything at all? No matter how insignificant."

"No."

"Well, thank you for your time," Detective Gamble said. "Call if you remember something later."

"I will." Her hand reached for the door knob when she saw Yvette fly out the back door headed in their direction.

Rushing out the car, she ran toward Yvette, who was yelling.

"Mrs. Doctor, we have an emergency! A baby with a fever and a rash."

Detective Gamble also got out.

As she sprinted for her office, she heard Detective Gamble say they'd be in contact. For some reason, she stopped mid-stride—almost tripping on the asphalt. She spun around and asked, "What about Kelley?"

Standing there for a second, Detective Gamble frowned. "What does she have to do with it? You think she killed him?" he asked.

"I just thought you'd want to speak with her." *Why did she ask?*

Detective de Jesus exited the vehicle, his writing pad in hand. "Just focus on answering our questions, Dr. Douglas. We'll do the investigating."

Stung by his retort, she had to admit it had merit. She wouldn't expect them to understand the management for neonates with necrotizing enterocolitis, so should she defer to their knowledge about homicides.

In tandem, she and Yvette returned inside the office. She hurried into the patient room with the ill, crying infant. Dina and the parents simultaneously provided the history. Directing the medical assistant to deliver antipyretics, the nurse assisted her with undressing the child. One look at the baby's chest and she told the nurse to call 911. Her gloved fingers palpated the erythematous macular papular rash and palpated the crusted pustules. She recalled 'dew drops on a rose petal' from medical school as signs of varicella—chicken pox.

The coughing baby appeared uncomfortable. The infant's rapid breathing reminded her bacterial pneumonia could be a complication of varicella.

She listened to her chest—scattered wheezes, oxygenation at 90%. The nurse helped her apply a face mask to deliver oxygen to her tiny patient. Saturations increased to 98%. Respiratory rate decreased. She brought up Cindi's medical chart on the EHR, and saw the baby had never been immunized. Her shoulders shrank.

Addressing the parents, she asked, "Does Cindi go to childcare? Has she been out the country recently? Attended any parties?"

The parents conferred with each other and shared a worried look.

The mother said, "We attended a chickenpox party last weekend, but Cindi didn't go. Her sister went, but she's fine."

In her mind, Myaisha counted to five before she spoke. "Cindi has chickenpox."

Further explanation had to wait. The ambulance arrived. Helping to settle the baby into the carrier on the stretcher, she gave EMS the infant's vital signs. The front staff provided a summary of the visit and vaccine records—or lack thereof.

After telling the parents she would come to the hospital as soon as possible, she gave a quick call to the ER for isolation precautions and returned to her regular patient schedule.

Not until later in the evening did her thoughts return to Adán. She hadn't known him long. *Should she contact his family or leave it to the authorities?* She called their pastor then turned on her tea kettle.

An uncomfortable feeling coalesced in her mind. If she wasn't careful... Adán's death confirmed the seriousness of the murder investigation. She needed to abandon her inquiries, avoid the Greensboro Alliance, and purchase a home security system.

Chapter 24

Automatic doors swished open, Myaisha entered the library. She walked around the circulation desk and passed the shelf of new additions. The hush of the library relaxed her stressed mind. Juggling a busy medical practice, her assignment as executor, and the police investigation into a double homicide, overtaxed her mental faculties.

The only reason she came out to the meetup was to support her writing group, but she desperately wanted to go home and rest.

In the downstairs conference room, she found a circle of women conversing about recent events. The authorities must have made the second murder public. Circumventing the group, she overheard the discussion. It revolved around Candace and Adán. She didn't want to answer any more questions about the murder, so settled on the side of the room near the windows.

Placing her bag on the table, she considered the turnout. The writing group meetup more than doubled the number of people from last week. A morbid thought crossed her mind that more people attended due to the groups association with the murders. Gruesome, but not unheard of. People pretended to be shocked by violence, but they often relished it. *Ghoulish.* With the increase in membership her absence would not have been missed. She should have gone home after work like she wished.

In the opposite corner of the room, she identified a familiar face. Waving to the urologist, she gathered together her personal items and approached Cathy's table.

"Hello. May I join you?" she asked.

Smiling, Cathy said, "Of course, Myaisha. Have a seat. How are you doing?"

Setting her items on the table, she sat down. "Fine. Are you liking Greensboro, how's business?"

"Getting better. It's picking up. Oh, by the way, thanks for the referral."

She recalled her little guy with the phimosis. "Thanks for taking care of him. Mom says he's doing better, but he won't leave the dressing alone."

Cathy chuckled. "Children always remove their bandages. It won't impede healing."

They discussed work, while she arranged her bags on the table. Sharing their observations about the hospital, their talk ceased when a bell rang.

Holding a tiny bell, Lottie encouraged people to take their seat. "Take a seat, ladies. It's time to get started."

After giving her a quick hug, Mary plopped down in a chair at her table.

Myaisha whispered introductions between Cathy and Mary.

"Goodness, it's been a long week, hasn't it?" Mary asked.

Repositioning her purse to the back of her chair, she said, "I know. I still can't believe—"

Standing before the wall adjacent to the entrance, Lottie explained the rules of 'Think it, Ink it'. "Try to write for the full hour. No talking. I do want to make one quick announcement. Green Pastures is offering a discount to all members of GWCWG. We will be issuing cards to our members. You must show your card at the time of purchase."

Several women looked toward the door.

Curious, Myaisha followed suit.

Inside the doorway stood Detectives de Jesus and Gamble.

They attracted Lottie's attention. She frowned. "Gentlemen, we're having a meeting—for women *only*. Please shut the door on your way out. We need to get started."

She realized Lottie had no idea who the detectives were.

All eyes observed the men enter the room.

The detectives surveyed the women, scanning the room.

Rising, she made her way to the exit. She assumed they sought her out for more questions. Her attempt to make eye contact with Detective Gamble failed. His gaze passed over her.

Holding something in his hand, which she believed to be his badge, he addressed the group. "We'd like to speak with Mrs. Mary Thompkins," he said.

Her feet halted.

The women searched amongst themselves for Mary. She—and those who knew her—immediately transferred their gaze from the detectives to the soft-spoken stay-at-home mother. She noticed Mary appeared to shrink into herself.

In increments, Mary raised her hand. "I'm Mary Thompkins," she said, her voice quivering.

Striding up to the table, Detective Gamble loomed over her. Detective de Jesus maintained his position at the door.

"Mrs. Thompkins, would you please come with us. It would be better to speak outside," Detective Gamble said.

Her face blanched. Mary glanced at her before she rose. As she marched toward the door, Detective Gamble followed close behind. Everyone watched the procession. After he exited the room, Detective Gamble reached back to shut the door. On his heels, Myaisha brought up the rear.

He bumped into her. "Excuse me," he said.

"No problem," she said.

His lips pressed together into a thin line. "We'd like to speak with Mrs. Thompkins alone, if you don't mind."

"I do mind." Making no attempt to move, she glanced around him and caught Mary's eye. "Unless you object?"

Her eyes filled with tears. "No," Mary said. "I want you to stay with me."

The four of them exited the library. Traffic outside was minimal. The sun had begun its descent. Street lights hadn't come on yet. Despite the cool air Mary began to sweat.

She rubbed Mary's arm. Together, they faced the detectives, and braced for the interrogation.

"Our vehicle is over there Mrs. Thompkins," Detective Gamble said. "We'll give you a ride downtown where you can answer some questions."

Detective de Jesus walked toward the vehicle, and took up a stance beside the open rear door.

As if in a trance, Mary floated toward the car.

When she realized Mary prepared to accompany them to the police station, she grabbed her arm, and pulled her friend to her side. "Wait, Mary. What's this about detective?" she asked.

Grimacing, Detective Gamble said, "Dr. Douglas, if you wish to accompany us downtown too that's fine, but this is police business. Please step aside." He lifted his brows and flicked his head slightly to the right.

If he attempted to relay a message to her, she ignored it, refusing to surrender her friend to the police. She couldn't fathom what information her friend could possess pertaining to the murders. "Is Mary under arrest?"

She felt Mary beside her, trembling but quiet.

Striding forward Detective de Jesus fingered the shiny silver handcuffs hanging on his belt. "Doctor, you're interfering in official police business. We could take you in too."

"Unless you have an arrest warrant, you're not taking anyone anywhere." Her left eyebrow arched. She glared at him. Her head snapped back to encompass Detective Gamble. "Do you have a warrant?" she asked.

He scowled, stepped away from her and approached Mary. "Mrs. Thompkins, we know about the incident at Courthouse. If you want to come to the station and make a statement it will go easier for you." A card flicked between his fingers, which he extended toward Mary.

Her tremulous fingers accepted it.

Sending another intense glare at Myaisha, he headed for his vehicle.

Before he walked away, his partner gave her a similar look. Once they got in their vehicle, they departed.

Uttering a gasp, Mary squeezed her hand and almost collapsed in her arms.

She pulled her in for a tight hug, and held her until her shaking subsided. When she gazed up, Myaisha noticed a bunch of eyeballs watching them between the window blinds of the library. Arm in arm, she guided her friend toward the parking garage. She wanted to get her away from there. They needed to talk. There had to be a reason the authorities wanted to question Mary about the murder.

How could this mild-mannered Sunday school teacher be involved in Candace's death? Preposterous.

Out of earshot of the library, she asked, "What's going on?"

Tears trekked down Mary's cheeks. "Oh, Myaisha, I didn't do it. I said I would. I even thought I could. But I didn't. Lord as my witness. I didn't kill Candace."

———

The drive to her home was quick and quiet.

Myaisha placed a cup of tea in front of Mary and took the adjacent seat.

Her friend sat at the kitchen table, staring into her mug.

Her cell phone vibrated, and she checked the screen. A text from AJ. After sending a short message in reply, she set her phone down on the table. Romance would have to wait. Right now, she had no time for anyone but Mary.

Preparing a snack for them, and replenishing Boomer's water bowl, she figured gave Mary time to compose herself.

Washing her hands, she returned to the table. After a sip of tea, she spooned in more sugar. "Are you ready to talk?" she asked.

Red-rimmed eyes looked up at her. Mary hadn't tasted her tea, but held onto the cup with both hands. "Yes, I suppose. Thank you, Myaisha. I—I don't know what would have happened if they got me downtown."

"Why would the police want to speak with you? What happened at Courthouse?"

"I'm so embarrassed. I can't believe this is happening," Mary said. She lifted the mug to her lips, but placed it back on the table without drinking. Small hands covered her heart-shaped face. She cried softly, using a napkin to wipe her tears.

A puzzled frown creased her forehead. "What happened?"

"I hit Candace."

Her mouth opened to reply, but she restrained herself. Folded hands rested on the table as she waited. She correctly anticipated an explanation would follow.

"I didn't hit her just once, I kind of smacked her around. I left before the police arrived." Slowly, she stirred the warm, inky fluid. Her eyes directed down at the table. "I jumped in my car and left before I could be arrested."

"Why? What did Candace do to you? Why would you assault her?" Laying her hand on Mary's, she felt them tremble.

Pushing back her chair, her friend abandoned her embrace and jumped up from the table. Walking around Boomer, she sauntered out onto the porch.

Joining her at the sliding glass doors, Myaisha found her gazing across the yard.

Boomer crawled off the floor and followed. He trotted outside. Crickets chirped in the night.

Mary didn't directly address her, instead she spoke into the night. "How can I explain this to you so you can understand? You're financially independent. If you need money you can see more patients, moonlight at a clinic, maybe take out a personal loan. You're a physician. You can't appreciate how desperate I was, and how limited my options were."

She lightly rubbed Mary's back. Her shoulder's relaxed

"It doesn't matter if I understand," she said. "I have to know. If I'm going to help you, I need to know what happened. Tell me."

The wild eyed woman who turned in her direction startled her. Troubled, her voice wavered. "Mary, are you okay?"

The voice which replied sounded harsh and bitter. "Candace always talked about her real estate deals—about how successful she was. She kept after us to invest—to leverage the equity in our home. *Use the money for investments.* She promised we couldn't lose."

Stepping out onto the stone patio, Mary's shoulders slumped. When she turned around, worry lines multiplied across her forehead. With measured breaths, her tone calmed. "I'd heard the rumors. People said Candace took advantage of them, stole their money. I didn't believe them. Candace was our friend, our sister in Christ. I never knew that part of Candace. In church, she always seemed so nice. She donated to the church building fund, to Dorcas." Sobs shook her friend's small body.

Her hands guided Mary by the shoulders inside the house. Sitting her down on the couch, she waited. Helping to dry the tears, she comforted her. Gradually, the crying subsided.

"Candace lied to us," Mary said. "She took our money and did nothing to help us with our investment. She expected us to find other investors, dupe them like she deceived us. I never realized how Machiavellian she could be."

Sympathizing, Myaisha understood what Mary meant. Until her fractured investment with Candace, she too only saw the kind honest character of the successful business woman. But she thought the episode had been an accident—an oversight. She didn't believe Candace ever had the intent to deceive her. But she'd been wrong. All the time and love they shared—had it ever meant anything to Candace? Her heart broke, as did her pride. She had invested so much emotional capital into their friendship. *How did she not see that part of Candace's character?* Biting the inside of her lip, she walled off her feelings. Right now, Mary needed her attention.

Sniffling, Mary said, "Greg didn't believe her. He thought it was too risky, but I felt we were missing out. His friends at the hospital took out home loans and invested their money. They were taking vacations, buying timeshares, second cars. I thought we should at least hear what Candace had to say."

With a side hug, she encouraged Mary to continue. Sorrowful eyes reflected back at her.

"You know Greg. So cautious. He didn't care about a larger home or fancy trips. He likes security. But I argued, pleaded. I told him we should at least try. We could pay off our small home and upgrade. With Candace' help, how could we fail."

Boomer returned inside and settled beside Mary. She leaned over to scratch him behind his ears.

"Of course, she collected a hefty commission after we closed on our rental properties. Then I heard the housing market was collapsing. I called Candace. She said we needed to get with the program before the bottom fell out of the market. Well, you know the rest. Later, I found out she had sold her investment properties at the same time she encouraged us to *leverage our home's potential*. She knew about the pending housing market collapse and she still encouraged us to invest. She sold her properties for a profit but never sold one of ours—not one."

"I'm sorry."

Mary squeezed her hand. Twirled Boomer's hair between her fingers. "Fortunately, Greg works at the hospital, but with reimbursements down he may have to take a pay cut. We owe more on the house now than it's worth. We also have to pay the mortgages on the investment properties Candace never sold."

Bringing Mary closer to her side, she allowed her friend to cry on her shoulder.

Boomer stood between both women, watchful and guarded.

Between sniffles, she said, "We could lose our home. The place we lived in since our wedding, where we brought our children home from the hospital."

She wiped her friend's damp face with her sleeve. "Mary, you should have told me. I could've helped."

"Myaisha, it's not your job to help us. We're adults. We should have known better. I should've known better. Greg feels horrible, like he can't provide for us. But I—I feel even worse. This is all my fault. I should have listened to him. I never believed Candace would do this to us."

"If the hospital job isn't enough, I can help Greg get another position."

"It's fine. Greg got a part-time job teaching at the college." Mary patted her shoulder, stood up and strolled over toward the bookcase.

From the couch, she observed her friend pace around the living room. She asked, "Is that why he resigned as deacon?"

Looking at the pictures on the bookshelf, Mary nodded. "He's too busy trying to keep us solvent. The extra money will take some of the pressure off. I still may have to get a job though, it depends. Candace arranged an adjustable rate mortgage for us. Next year, when the mortgage payments increase... I don't know."

She joined Mary. "I'm not going to let my goddaughter lose her home."

Eyes filled with tears, Mary choked up. "We made a terrible mistake. I'll probably have to get a job. Put my children in daycare."

"That's not going to happen. We're going to figure something out, and I'm going to help you. Right now, I'm more concerned about the police."

She detected a retraction in Mary's demeanor as her friend pulled away from her. *What was she hiding?* Given what she discovered in the past week, she doubted anything would surprise her—but she needed the complete truth.

Her hands rose to her hips. "Mary, the police aren't going to charge you with assaulting Candace a week prior to her death. What aren't you telling me?"

Sauntering away from her, Mary hid her face and mumbled. "I threatened to kill Candace. On a couple of occasions—in front of witnesses."

Not being shocked stood as a testament to the events of the past week she had to endure. Each day brought new revelations about the people she thought she knew.

As Mary turned away from the cabinet, her speech increased in speed and volume. "I needed Candace's help to get us out of the second mortgage. She had documents which proved the bank exaggerated our assets—inflated Greg's income where we would qualify for a higher loan amount. When I requested the information she refused. I told her we could lose our home. She had the gall to blame us. Said we should've followed her directions and unloaded our properties onto some other unsuspecting victim. They commit bank fraud, but we get rebuked."

"They who?"

"Candace and her banker friend in Charlotte."

"Do you know his name?"

"No. We mostly dealt with her."

Assault, threats, she understood the authorities position. Her behavior landed Mary at the top of the police suspect list. Frowning, she beheld her friend, one of her first friends in Greensboro. Josiah babysat her children. Their families attended mutual family gatherings. She and Sammy accompanied Mary and Greg on an anniversary vacation trip. She was godmother to their youngest daughter. She considered Mary—short with her round full cheeks—not the face of a killer. *Or could she be mistaken about another friend?*

Her left eyebrow arched. "Did you tell me everything? Is there anything else the police might have against you? Tell me. Otherwise, I can't help you." Years spent working with children and adolescents—she recognized the look of guilt spreading across her friend's face.

Throwing back her shoulders, Mary faced her. "I went to Candace's office to get my loan papers. If I had the originals—"

"When did you go to her office?"

"The day she died—was killed. I went that morning. She was supposed to be out of the office."

Her teeth gritted. "What *time* did you go there?"

"I'm not sure what time, maybe around eleven." Her forehead creased, she paused a moment, appearing to consider her words. "I went into her office and found her lying on the floor."

"You found Candace lying on the floor and you did nothing?"

Stumbling over her words Mary stammered. "She was dead. I—I didn't know what to do. I panicked."

"How could you be sure? Did you check?"

"I saw her eyes. No question, she was dead."

"You should've called 911. You could've explained to the police you came there to retrieve some papers."

Plopping down into a chair near the entertainment center, Mary stared at her feet. Squirmed in the seat, her voice soft. "I brought a gun with me. I couldn't call the police with a gun on me."

Her hand smacked her forehead. Staring at Mary without seeing her, she thought it couldn't get much worse.

The doorbell rang.

Barking, Boomer raced toward the front door. He continued to bark and circle in front of the entrance.

Her thoughts interrupted, she put aside what she wanted to say to Mary and answered the door. Before she got there, the knob jostled and Deniece entered.

Whining, Boomer circled around her legs.

"Hello, Boomer," Deniece said, leaning down to pet him.

Tired, she sighed and looked at Deniece with confused brows. "Why are you—" Before she could finish her question, Deniece held up a bag displaying the name 'M. Douglas'.

Placing it down on the coffee table, Deniece said, "You left it at the meetup. I thought you might want it. When I got to the library Cathy told me what happened." Her head bent around Myaisha to where Mary sat in a wing back chair cradling her face in her hands. "Hey, Mary. I heard about the police. Everything okay?"

She addressed Deniece. "No. Thanks for retrieving my bag." She pivoted to face Mary. "Don't tell anyone what we spoke about tonight. Understand? We need to get you a lawyer."

Climbing out of the chair, Mary said, "Myaisha, we can't afford a lawyer."

Plopping down onto the couch, Deniece said, "You can't afford *not* to have an attorney."

She agreed to make the arrangements and headed for the kitchen. "Come on. I'll make us something to eat."

Smiling, Deniece scooped up her purse and hurried into the foyer. "Can't. I have a date."

Both she and Mary stopped to regard Deniece.

She asked, "With whom?"

"With my husband, of course. It's good to keep the marriage alive." Deniece laughed and winked.

"I should go too." Mary followed behind her.

Unable to convince Mary to stay, she placed the food back into the refrigerator.

Running in circles around them, Boomer yelped.

She recognized his typical antics when he wanted an invitation to go for a drive. She picked up her purse. "I'll drive you downtown to get your car."

"Since she's a free person, I'll drive her back to her car," Deniece said. "No need for you to leave home. Come on, Mary." On her way to the door, she asked, "Speaking about keeping the romance alive, how did it go with AJ?"

She smacked Deniece's arm. "D, this isn't the time."

Mary asked, "Who's AJ?"

Simultaneously, she said, "no one" as Deniece said, "her boyfriend".

She said, "He's not my boyfriend."

"Umm hm. Who is he then?" Deniece grinned.

Mary looked from her to Deniece. "Who is he?"

Her arm hooked around Mary's elbow, Deniece led her outside. She said, "I'll explain in the car."

They exited.

With a large smile, Deniece leaned her head back inside the doorway and said, "I want to hear all about the date later."

As they walked away, she picked up trails of their conversation.

Deniece spoke to Mary. She said, "He's a fireman—a very sexy fireman."

She shook her head, and shut the door.

Boomer gave a short bark of disappointment. He trod out to the back yard after realizing he wasn't going for a drive.

In the kitchen, she prepared a salad. Crunching on lettuce as she thought over what Mary had said. *Damn.* She forgot to ask about the gun. The police could perform a ballistics test and compare the bullet markings from Mary's weapon to the bullet that killed Candace proving Mary's innocence. She should call her.

As if on cue, her phone hummed. Wiping her hands, she picked up the phone from the countertop and read the text.

Dinner Friday? Indian food n Charlotte. AJ

She smiled and sent a text back. The insane week had not diminished her desire to see him again. The first man who interested her since Sammy died, the closest she had come in years to a personal life—a romance. Candace's death showed her how temporary life could be. Focused on grief, she neglected life. AJ seemed like the type of man worth her time.

In an act of impulsivity, she texted him back, inviting him over to her house for dinner. Instead of a drive to Charlotte in weekend traffic, she would prepare them a nice meal. A glance at her watch alerted her to the late hour. She cleared away the dishes and locked up. The broom handle went into the sliding glass door for extra security. Tomorrow, she would speak with Grace.

As she undressed, she again considered what Mary had said. Candace was not supposed to be in the office. *If Candace had an appointment, why didn't she go? And how did Mary know?* Questions swirled in her head. Caught in a real life mystery, unlike the sleuths in her books, she had no ideas. If Candace did have a meeting, LaDonna would know.

Was it too late to call? What were considered good manners when trying to get information in a homicide? She tossed her phone aside. It didn't matter anyway; she didn't have LaDonna's personal number. She'd call Candace's office tomorrow.

With her computer on her lap, she snuggled into bed. Writing mysteries suddenly became a lot easier than solving them, which didn't say a lot because writing them could be murder—pun absolutely intended. After she stared at her manuscript for fifteen minutes, she powered down the computer. Clicked off the lamp on her side table and tried to sleep.

Jolting upright in bed, a disturbing thought woke her up. If Mary hadn't been involved in the murder, then her gun wasn't used in the crime. Forensics could easily prove her innocence. But her friend worried. *Why?*

There would be no sleeping tonight. She had a disturbing feeling proving Mary's innocence would be harder than a simple forensics test.

Her ears picked up a movement outside.

Boomer sprang off the ground and barked at the windows facing the back yard. A low growl emanated from his gut, then just as quickly he lay down again and settled at the foot of her bed.

Between the insects chirping she listened for larger pests. She reached under her mattress for her machete. Her dad brought it back from Vietnam. Old and rusted, it served as a perfect weapon. If the cut didn't kill her attacker, tetanus would.

Several minutes passed with nothing other than nature sounds. Her head reclined against the headboard. Minutes later, her eyes closed. Her brain remained alert.

Chapter 25

Instead of attending Friday morning Grand Rounds at the hospital, Myaisha decided to drop by the Bradley Building to speak with LaDonna. When Candace purchased the building she re-named it after Dr. Josephine Ophelia Boyd Bradley, the first African American student to integrate a whites only North Carolina high school. The memory reminded her of the Candace she knew in college—a role model for women of color.

She thought returning to the scene of the murder would conjure up disturbing visions of Candace lying on the floor, she was wrong. She entered into a new and remodeled office—she didn't recognize it. The only thing consistent with the previous office was LaDonna sitting at the reception window.

She handed a gift box through the window. A small gesture of kindness for the receptionist. "Hello, LaDonna," she said. "How are you feeling?"

Accepting the gift, LaDonna left her desk, came out into the waiting area and gave her a hug.

"Thank you, Dr. Douglas," she said. "I guess I'm doing all right. How do you like the new office?"

Gazing around the office, Myaisha said, "It looks nice. Who authorized this?"

Inviting her to be seated in the new plush leather chairs, LaDonna explained that the building manager leased the space to a new tenant. Grimacing, she said, "He didn't even have the decency to wait until her body was at peace in her grave."

She doubted Candace rested in peace. She asked, "What will you do?"

"Glen wants to relocate to Atlanta. He has family there."

She grinned. Like Gladys Knight sang, LaDonna would be right by his side. Not exactly on a midnight train to Georgia, but she would follow her man. She said, "LaDonna, I apologize for asking you to think back on the day of the murder, but do you remember Candace having an appointment that morning?"

"Yes. She had an appointment with a client for a medical equipment order. A cardiologist in High Point, I think." LaDonna returned to her desk and searched her for the information in her computer.

"What time?" she asked.

Tapping her well-manicured nail on the desk, LaDonna said, "Umm. The calendar says 11:30."

"What time would she usually leave for an 11:30 appointment?"

"Oh, Mrs. Knight was very strict about being on time for appointments. Sometimes she would leave early and wait in the parking lot. She said it was unprofessional to be late."

Myaisha remembered her dad always said, "If you're on time, you're late". She asked, "Did she say anything to you about altering her plans?"

"No, not that I remember." She pressed her lips together.

She noticed the lack of furrows or wrinkles on her forehead and wondered if LaDonna received Botox injections.

"Oh, wait. She planned to meet with the cardiologist at the restaurant. She told me she wouldn't be back until after lunch. Late. She had other errands to run, I remember."

"Would she have rescheduled the appointment? Held it here instead?"

"I don't think so—not without telling me. Otherwise, she wouldn't have let me leave early for lunch. Why? Is it important?"

"Why would Candace still be in the office? She should have been on her way to High Point."

Tears welled up in LaDonna's eyes.

She felt bad for bringing up painful memories, but she needed answers.

"I thought she had been murdered before she could leave for the appointment." She dabbed at her eyes to prevent her mascara from running.

"What time was the appointment again?"

"I scheduled the reservation for 11:30."

Candace would probably want to leave by eleven—earlier if she had to pick the doctor up from the office. If she arranged to meet with someone in her office, it would have to be brief or she would be late. Mary had said she arrived around eleven.

LaDonna provided her with the name of the cardiologist. She could call to see if Candace had cancelled or altered their appointment. The murderer must have arrived before Mary, meaning the crime occurred before eleven. Unless Mary was mistaken—or lied.

Myaisha arrived at her office and worked hard to complete her patient charts. She felt giddy, excited about the evening ahead. Having AJ in her home—this was something new for her. *Was she moving too fast, inviting a man she barely knew to her home?* Maybe she hadn't thought this through, goodness knows she had a lot on her mind.

She heard vacuuming, her staff were closing down the office. It had been a long week. Pastor Matthew informed her Adán's parents wanted his funerals services held in Florida where they lived. The church intended to hold a memorial for him, but hadn't yet settled on a date.

Walking into her office, Yvette asked, "Mrs. Doctor, do you need anything before I go?"

She sighed deep and long. "No, Yvette, thank you. Who will be working with me tomorrow?"

"No one. There are no patient appointments."

"None?"

"No."

Narrowing her gaze, she stared at her office manager with suspicion.

Rolling up her sleeves, Yvette said, "Okay. We had one patient on the schedule, but it wasn't urgent so I rescheduled them for Monday. You need to rest. First your friend was murdered and then her husband. Do the police know anything?"

"No." She noticed all movement and noise in the office ceased. Peeking around Yvette, she saw her staff looking toward her office. Her staff were all competent at their jobs, but they enjoyed gossip. She didn't want to complicate Todd's job with innuendos and fabrications.

Projecting her voice so everyone could hear, she said, "I don't know anything about the murder investigation."

A second later, sounds of industrious labor again reached her ears.

"Do you think the murders are related?"

"I have no idea."

Her receptionist approached her office door.

After wishing her a restful weekend, Yvette departed.

The receptionist said, "Dr. Douglas, there's a Grace Jones here to see you. She says she's not a patient."

"Thank you. Bring her back, please."

Her eyes opened wide, but the receptionist didn't move.

If she expected an explanation about who Grace Jones was, she would not be satisfied. She looked up. "Is there a problem?"

"No, doctor."

After escorting the private detective into the office, the receptionist left.

Before Grace could speak, Myaisha placed a finger to her lips, signaling Grace to remain silent. They sat there looking at each other until all the staff departed.

Glancing through the shades to view the lot behind the office, she watched as her employees drove away. "Sorry about that," she said. "I love my staff, but they gossip."

Stretching her legs forward, Grace removed a notebook from her purse. "That could be useful."

"It can, sometimes, but not in this situation. What have you got for me?"

She skimmed through her notes and said, "First, I don't think your prowler was Charles Marshall."

She frowned. "Why not?"

"My sources put him in Florida. He bought a yacht a few months back. The prevailing theory is he plans to skip town on it."

"How do you know that?"

"Hey, you pay for the information, not the sources."

She shook her head. "Fine. Whatever. Who else would try to break into my place?"

"Maybe it has nothing to do with the case. Robberies in your neighborhood are rare, but not unheard of. I'd say it was a coincidence—unrelated to the murders."

Her head tilted to the right as she gave it some thought. Someone had been outside her home. She remembered how Boomer went ballistic. He knew a raccoon from a burglar. A prowler could be a coincidence. *What were the odds?*

"Let's move on. What about Candace? What other projects did she hire you to perform?"

She noticed Grace shifted her position in the seat. Something unspoken descended between them. Confused, she leaned forward. "Grace?"

Clearing her throat, Grace said, "I'm trying to figure out your angle. Is it idle curiosity or something else?"

"I want to know if it concerns the murder."

"Fine. I don't want to offend you. I know you cared for Mrs. Knight."

Flattening her palms on the top of her desk, she braced herself for more unsavory information. "What did Candace ask you to do?"

Sliding her chair forward, Grace placed her notebook into her purse. "I told you before, Mrs. Knight hired me for a reason. She was tight with money. Not cheap—but she got her money's worth." She paused. "She also knew my background—retired military. Sometimes clients think ex-soldiers are willing to performing certain tasks another PI would not. She asked me to *find* incriminating information on her husband and a member of the Greensboro Alliance—actually several members."

Her brows knitted into a question. she asked, "Isn't that what you do?"

"No. I surveille people, do background research. I don't *dig up dirt* on people to incriminate them."

Her eyes widened. She understood the emphasis on those last words. "She wanted you to manufacture information?"

With a smirk, Grace said, "I like that. I'm gonna use it. Yes, she did. Mrs. Knight wasn't particular about whether the information turned out to be true or false. It only had to be incriminating."

"I understand her divorce with Adán. But what is going on at the Greensboro Alliance?"

"Don't know. I turned her down. I didn't start looking into the group until you asked me. I don't have much yet. From what I have gathered, they were complicit in the real estate scam."

"Really?" Myaisha leaned back in her chair.

"Well, when I say they, I mean a few of the members. I can't get a lot of information because everyone has lawyered up. The major mortgage fraud out of Charlotte extended up into the Triad. I can't lean too hard on anyone without attracting attention—which I don't want. The authorities are conducting their own investigation."

"Do you think Charles Marshall could have killed Candace?"

"Could he, yes, why not. He's desperate to flee the jurisdiction—in fact he's under investigation and the police can't locate him. He pressured Mrs. Knight for money."

Speaking more to herself than Grace, she said, "And Marshall could have approached Adán, believing he could access Candace's funds."

"Exactly."

She sighed and looked across the desk. "Makes sense, except—"

This time, Grace frowned. "Except what? Charles Marshall seems like a good suspect to me. Just because he wasn't your prowler doesn't mean he couldn't have committed double homicide."

Her thoughts flowed back to Mary. She remembered the look of determination on Todd's face. "Except, it wouldn't explain why the police want to speak with a housewife about the murder."

Before the garage door closed, Myaisha rushed into the house and started dinner. She assembled fish on a baking tray, seasoned the filets and returned them to the refrigerator. With Boomer outside, she took a quick shower.

AJ sent her a text, he should arrive at 6:30pm.

She brushed her hair into obedience and dabbed perfume on her neck. In the kitchen, she finished preparations.

Thirty minutes later, he arrived—right on time. His knock sent electricity down her spine. *Excitement, fear? Both.* Her heart fluttered. Smoothing down the sides of her dress, she took a deep breath before she opened the door.

With a bottle of wine and a box of chocolates in hand, AJ greeted her.

Her grin paled in comparison to his large smile. She enjoyed his smile—all teeth and full lips. She felt herself staring at his lips. *Stop it.* Inviting him inside, she accepted his gifts.

Once in the kitchen, she detected his absence. Turning around, she noticed Boomer stood at the door.

On all fours, his hair raised, his belly growled. Teeth bared, his tail pointed straight back.

Her tongue clicked, calling Boomer to her side. It took more than a few commands before he stopped sneering at their visitor. With her reassurance, AJ entered the living room.

"Nice neighborhood. How long have you lived here?" he asked.

"Since Sammy—" Stopped mid-sentence, she blushed. "I've lived here for over twelve years."

He came to her side. "Myaisha, I don't mind if you want to talk about your husband. He was an important part of your life. I get that."

His sentiment touched her heart. But her memories of Sammy were hers, not to be shared with anyone. In the kitchen, she gathered supplies. As soon as she stepped away from AJ, Boomer moseyed over, growling and baring his teeth again. Attuned to the sound, she called him to her side.

The chocolates were placed on the countertop. "I'll leave these here. Foods ready, we can eat outside." She picked up the dinnerware and led him outside.

After a few minutes, she got them situated on the porch—over Boomer's objections. The night air flowed around them, crisp and dry. A quarter moon hung high in the clear sky. The porch lights illuminated the bead board blue ceiling. She could finally breath.

He poured her some wine, but declined any for himself. "I have to work tonight."

"You should have told me. We could've rescheduled."

"It's not a problem. A couple hours ago, one of the guys asked me to switch with him—family emergency. I wanted to see you. The guys can hold the fort down for a few hours." He caressed her hand.

Boomer bounded over to her side.

Chastened by the dog, he released her hand.

Sitting, Boomer didn't move from the table.

He cast his eyes at the lab. "Someone doesn't want me here."

Rubbing Boomer's coat, she said, "No, you're fine. He has to get used to you."

"Have you dated since your husband died?" He drank his lemonade.

Her gaze sought the safety of the large magnolia tree in the corner of the yard. "No. You're the first man I've gone out with since Sammy died."

"What happened? An accident?"

Feeling his eyes on her, sweat trailed down her back. At first, telling him about Sammy seemed awkward, uncomfortable. In time, she found him to be an attentive listener, patient. He let her tell her story in her way.

"How long has it been?"

"Five years."

"I'm sorry."

"Thank you."

After a brief pause, he asked, "You weren't interested in dating, or too busy?"

"Both. I never dated much before I married, so I didn't miss it."

"Yeah. Dating's changed a lot. I remember back before I got married when dating didn't require an internet connection. I had never even heard of speed dating."

"Since my husband died, I hadn't wanted to date anyone until I met you." She gazed into his eyes, wanted him to understand her sincerity.

He smiled, sat up straighter. "I never felt this way before either. Not that it stopped me from dating."

She laughed. "Why did you divorce?"

"Not my choice. She found someone who made more money and had more time." His smiled deflated.

Watching the metamorphosis in his countenance from gay to grave, she felt a heaviness in him. Her hand found his and gave it a tender squeeze. His strong fingers contrasted with his gentle nature. She said, "I'm sorry."

"Don't be. No one wants to be with someone who doesn't want to be with them. No marriage is better than a bad marriage." He picked at the edges of his cake.

She would have to take his word for it. She had a great marriage, couldn't imagine being stuck in a bad relationship. Their conversation drifted to lighter topics. Relaxed, she warmed to his company. Delighted in the warm scent of his cologne.

He tried to feed a piece of cake to Boomer.

Staring at him, Boomer let the cake fall to the ground. He gave him a look which said, 'No way buddy. I still hate you.'

The food remained on the ground, neglected.

"I guess I should pick that up. He doesn't seem hungry."

"Don't worry about it. He'll eat it as soon as you leave."

"Is he always this mean?"

She avoided his gaze. "You're the first man in the house since his daddy died."

"Of course." He smiled and reached for her hand again.

When Boomer growled this time she sent him away.

He took a few steps back. Laying on the ground with his head on his front paws, he surveilled AJ under bushy brows.

"He's a fat dog. Do you take him for runs?"

"We go for walks every day, but we don't run." Placing a piece of the lemon pound cake on her fork, she savored the sharp lemon against the sweet sugary icing.

"He needs to run. He's really fat."

Raising his eyebrows, one after the other in turn, Boomer lumbered to his feet. Directed his hind end toward AJ and farted.

He pinched up his face, attempted to wave away the funk. "Did he just fart in my face?"

She laughed and moved to another area of the porch. "Don't call him fat."

Abandoning AJ to the malodorous miasma, Boomer relocated near his mom.

———

At the end of the evening, Myaisha accompanied AJ to the door. "Thank you for coming. Oh, and thank you for the wine and chocolates."

"You're welcome." He smiled down into her eyes.

She watched him scan the area behind her. His eyes locked on Boomer, not a foot behind her.

"I'd kiss you goodnight, but I'm afraid Cujo would go for my throat," he said,

On her tiptoes, she leaned up into his face. He reciprocated her actions in reverse. Their lips brushed against each other, soft and light. They held the position for a few seconds. As if trying to read her, he waited before pressing his lips tighter against her mouth. An emotion stronger than herself melted into him. A part of her desired such a moment for a long time. His firm kiss sent a warmth throughout her body.

Growling and barking hastened their romantic interlude, as Boomer voiced his objection.

Tilting his head in Boomer's direction, AJ said, "Next time, we'll meet somewhere else."

Not appreciating the snide remark, Boomer barked again and advanced on AJ's position.

With a precipitous goodbye, he didn't give the lab an opportunity to further express his displeasure. He left.

Securing the door after his departure, she was careful to apply the chain and deadbolt. She sauntered out onto the porch and collected their dishes. Reflecting upon the evening, she ran her tongue along her lips, reliving his kiss. *Why did this guy excite her so much?*

He was nothing like Sammy. Being with AJ had nothing to do with Sammy. It would take a while for her to accept these new feelings. Fortunately, AJ seemed patient—allowing her to move forward at her own pace.

Pots and dishware needed to be cleaned. First a stop in the living room to turn on some music. ELO's *It's a Living Thing* played as she danced around cleaning. She started to close the sliding glass doors, as Boomer ate the cake AJ dropped on the stone patio. Van Morrison's *Brown Eyed Girl* began. After Boomer bounced back inside, she secured the doors and loaded the dishwasher.

Her cell phone twirled. Smiling, she expected to find a message from AJ.

Instead, Deniece sent her a text.

Tina cant get son 2 talk.

Like a sudden summer rain storm, her mood shifted. She ambled over to the entertainment center, turned off the music and sank back into reality. Tina de Jesus was Deniece's friend and the mother of Detective de Jesus. Her hope was Tina could provide a backdoor into the police investigation. Unfortunately, Tina couldn't obtain information from the police either.

Her working assumption was Candace and Adán had been killed by the same person. In news reports, the police refused to confirm the murders were linked. Without Tina as a back door into the police investigation, she didn't know how to proceed.

None of this mattered if the investigation into Mary evaporated. She hoped to divorce herself from the investigation, but she couldn't leave her friend to the whims of the police.

In her bedroom, she undressed. A good night's sleep should help. She needed more information. Preoccupied with other aspects of the murder, she forgot to call Mary about the gun. For now, her friend remained free. As long as she stayed out of jail, Myaisha didn't have to fret over the homicides. Nothing untoward should happened before she spoke with Mary again—she prayed.

Chapter 26

Unlike most mornings since Candace was murdered, Myaisha's thoughts did not immediately return to the homicide. Sporting her fedora, she pushed a heavy grocery cart down the aisles of the big box store. Smells from the roasting meats made her hungry. Looking at grocery displays, she wondered what to make for dinner.

Since her office manager rescheduled her Saturday patient, she intended to spend the rest of the day on her new manuscript. She abandoned her attempt at young adult sci-fi. Her heart belonged to mysteries. Perhaps she should try romance—now she had some fresh insight courtesy of AJ.

The industrial lighting highlighted the multitude of food options. She could bring home a roast chicken to share with Boomer. With her head bent over her cell phone, she read items off her grocery list. Distracted, she rammed her cart into another shopper's cart. Apologies poured forth. She steered her cart around the collision. One thing remained on her list, dog food.

The person who controlled the cart she hit cleared their throat.

When she stopped to view who she struck, she beheld her pastor's face. Rushing to his side, she said, "I'm so sorry, Pastor Matthew. Are you okay?" She scanned his body, checking for any injuries.

Grinning, he patted her hand. "I'm fine, Sister Myaisha. I see you're out early too." He glimpsed inside her basket.

Returning to her cart, she moved it from the middle of the aisle and maneuvered closer to the pastor. "I got up to walk Boomer early because it looked like it might rain. Since I was already up, I decided to do some shopping. What got you out on Saturday morning?"

Together they strolled down the aisle.

He said, "I got a call from Greg this morning. The police arrested Mary, so I had to go downtown with him while Angela watched the kids."

As soon as the words left his mouth, she abandoned her cart and ran from the store.

Yelling after her, Pastor Matthew stated Mary might not be allowed visitors.

Nonetheless, she hurried from the store, intending to speak with Mary.

———

With one eye watching for patrol cars, she raced toward the downtown police station. She didn't want a ticket, but drove modestly above the speed limit. On the drive, she considered what led the authorities to arrest Mary. They must have obtained some new evidence. She shuddered to think what else they discovered.

Parking in the lot across the street, with a fast gait she strode into the police station. She overlooked the obnoxious odors of cigarettes, sweat and funk. Marching up to the plexiglass window, she addressed the officer seated at the desk. "I'm here to speak with Mrs. Mary Thompkins," she said.

Without answering, the officer looked down at the papers on his desk. Middle aged with a freckled face, he moved as slow as molasses in February she thought. Apparently not finding what he sought, he turned aside to the computer. His lips mumbled as he typed. He deserted the computer for the phone, speaking in the slowest southern drawl she'd ever heard. She hoped he didn't also work at the 911 call center.

Out of the officer's line of sight, her foot tapped on the tiled floor. She watched him converse over the phone.

Avoiding her gaze, he ended the call, addressing her through the speaker inserted inside the plexiglass window positioned between them. "She's with the detectives, ma'am. Are you her lawyer?" he asked.

"No, I am not. Please tell Mrs. Thompkins I'm here. She needs to speak with me."

Hound dog eyes looked up at her through the window. The thought of Opie from Mayberry came to her mind. "I can't do that ma'am." His attention returned to the papers. Conversation ended.

Staring at the top of his head, she wanted to ask, 'Why the hell not' at the top of her lungs. Making a scene in a police station would not be a good idea. *Walk away.* She abandoned the window and considered what to do next. Removing her cell phone from her purse, she placed a call to Mary. No answer. Immediately after leaving a voice message, she sent a text to Mary and then called Greg.

The door leading inside the station opened. Greg walked out, audible ringing emanating from his pocket.

Rushing up to him, she asked, "Greg, where's Mary? What happened?"

Eyes bloodshot, clothes wrinkled, a weary Greg hugged her. "Myaisha, they came to the house this morning. We barely had time to call the lawyer when the police hauled us down here."

Holding onto Greg's arm, she pulled him closer to her side. "Where's Mary?"

He gripped her hand. "Back there with the lawyer. They made me leave when her attorney arrived."

Arm in arm, they walked toward the exit. She lowered her voice. "Did Mary say anything?"

He whispered into her ear. "No. She didn't mention—"

With intense purpose, she lifted her eyes up toward the camera, squeezed his arm and cut off further talk. Her head inclined toward the exit. "Let's go."

Outside, sunlight shone on them like a spot light. It rays provided her no warmth. Not until they walked several yards away from the station did they resume their conversation.

With her back toward the entrance to the police station, she asked, "Did you speak with the lawyer yesterday?"

Greg explained that on Friday he and Mary visited the attorney, who agreed to represent Mary. After the appointment, they returned home. This morning they awoke to police officers pounding on their door. His body shook as he related the events that transpired. Toward the end of his tale, his voice increased.

He said, "I couldn't believe it. Police officers. On our doorstep, in the early morning. What will our neighbors think?"

She could care less what his neighbors thought. She needed to know what the police thought. She asked, "Did they have a warrant?"

Removing his glasses, he wiped his face with a handkerchief. His shaking subsided, but the right side of his face twitched. "They had an arrest warrant and a warrant to search our home." His voiced climbed another octave. "Our home. With our children asleep inside." His body shakes returned.

Police officers circulating outside the station glanced in their direction. The last thing they needed was Greg detained on a charge of disturbing the peace. She escorted him further away from the station.

"They handcuffed her, in front of our children," he said, tears pooling in his eyes.

She gave him a side hug and asked about the kids. Angela, the pastor's wife, removed them from the home while the pastor accompanied him downtown.

"Myaisha, I don't know what to do. The kids are at the pastor's home, but they can't stay there. My sister is on her way from Greenville. I'm not sure if I should send them there, or keep them with me."

Cogitating, she recalled the events of the past week, thought over his situation, wondering what she could do to help. She felt helpless. He looked defeated. She tried to rally him. "Don't worry, Greg. We'll get Mary home. Angela and Pastor Matthew can help with the children. If they can't, I can."

"What about your job?"

"I can shut down my office for a few days if necessary. We can work out a schedule with Angela and Pastor Matthew to care for the children."

His eyes strayed over her shoulder.

She turned to see an African American woman exit the building. Recognizing Mary's lawyer, together, she and Greg hurried back to the station. His long strides carried him to the lawyer first. With rapid fire questions he peppered the lawyer, inquiring about his wife.

The attorney led them away from the station answering his questions. She stopped when they reached the parking lot across the street. Palm up, she signaled him to stop. The attorney said, "Mr. Thompkins, this isn't the place to have this conversation. Let's find somewhere to talk and we'll discuss how to proceed."

"Okay. Thank you, Mrs. Lawrence. Thank you."

Part of the trio, Myaisha asked, "Where's Mary? Why is she still at the station?"

Mrs. Lawrence eyed her through designer glasses. "Dr. Douglas, I know you're paying my bill, but Mrs. Thompkins is my client. I can't discuss her case with you."

Shifting her weight to her left leg, hands sat on her hips, she said, "Keisha."

"Fine," Keisha said with a sigh, "Mrs. Thompkins has been formally charged with the murder of Candace Knight."

Greg cursed. Balled fists, punched the air, and covered his face as he cried.

Rubbing his shoulder, Myaisha asked, "How? What evidence do they have?"

"It's not what they have but what Mrs. Thompkins doesn't."

"The gun."

Keisha nodded.

Wiping his face, Greg said, "She explained that. She got rid of it. She was afraid to keep it in the house with the kids."

Tall, dark skinned with extensions draped down her back, Keisha gave Greg a polite smile. "Ballistics matched the bullet that killed Candace to the one in Adán's chest. They were killed with the same revolver. Mrs. Thompkins bought a Smith and Wesson, but she didn't get a receipt."

"Can't they check with the seller?"

A palpable tension rose. Heavy gray clouds in the sky above added gloom to the atmosphere. A breeze blew between them.

He regarded the lawyer, bags under his red streaked eyes. His body sagged in apparent defeat. "She bought it second hand—from some guy on the internet. They met at a shopping center."

In an aside toward her, the lawyer rolled her eyes and said, "To make matters worse, she disposed of the weapon."

Myaisha sighed.

Greg moaned.

"We informed the police where Mrs. Thompkins stated she discarded of the gun," Keisha said. "Law enforcement will attempt to locate it. If they're successful, the police will conduct ballistics tests."

"And if they can't locate the weapon?" Myaisha asked. She and the lawyer exchanged a knowing glance.

Greg's face fell.

Squinting, Myaisha scrutinized the attorney. "How did the police know Mary purchased the gun?" she asked.

"They wouldn't tell me. Probably a tip from a concerned citizen."

As her brain mulled over the information, Greg pivoted toward her.

Wide-eyed, looking helpless, Greg asked, "Myaisha, can you think of anything—anything to help Mary?"

Her heart broke for him. She, in turn, turned toward Keisha. "What about bail?"

Shifting her briefcase to the other arm, the lawyer proceeded toward her car. "I'm heading back to my office right now—see if I can locate a judge. If I can't, Mrs. Thompkins will remain incarcerated until Monday. They arrested her today on purpose to keep her detained over the weekend—make her languish in a cell to break her resolve."

"Did Mary say anything which might help her case?" She fell in steep with Keisha, Greg brought up the rear.

The lawyer explained their conversation had been brief. She cautioned her client not to speak to anyone. Keep her mouth closed. No statements. No phone calls. Keisha asked Greg, "Can you cover bail?"

His expression went from worried to terrified. His entire body caved. His facial tic returned. A single tear slid down his face, joined by a succulent rain drop. "We don't have any money. The flip houses sucked us dry."

Myaisha said, "Don't worry Greg, I can cover bail. We'll get Mary home. You take care of the kids" Pelted by rain she gave his hand a squeeze. "Mary isn't guilty. We'll get her out."

Lips firm, his chin trembled. She offered to drive him home. He declined, stating he needed time to himself before he spoke with his children. Greg thanked her before he headed toward his car, zombie walking.

She and Keisha remained side by side, watching him drive off. When he left, they stood there a moment. Showered by more raindrops, they headed for their vehicles.

Her keys jingled in her hand. "Keisha, how does it look?"

"Not good. How deep are those pockets of yours?" she asked.

Swallowing, Myaisha said, "Whatever you need to get Mary home."

Keisha removed her blazer and placed it on the passenger seat. "Getting her home isn't the problem. We can get her out, temporarily. The problem is keeping her home for good."

"What can I do? Find the killer?"

Rain drizzled around them.

Her engine started, Keisha settled into her SUV. The lawyer shook her head. "Post her bail then go home. There's nothing you can do. The authorities are searching for the weapon. I'll work on her defense. Everyone does their part."

She stood there in the rain, observed Keisha exit the lot. *What else could she do?*

Green Pastures café was located a couple blocks from the police station. She decided to pay Harriet a visit. If nothing else, she'd get out of the rain. Maybe she'd get some inspiration about how to proceed.

Once there, she noticed the coffee shop sat mostly empty. Aromas tickled her nose, enticing her appetite. At the counter, she searched for any signs of Harriet as the cashier took her order.

A metal stand displayed her order number, which she placed on a table in the far corner of the café beside the window. She stared outside for a few minutes, then pulled out her cell phone and located a number, considering whether to make the call. A server placed her order on the table—chai tea latte and a cranberry muffin. Huddled in the corner of the café, she drank her tea. Her eyes focused on her phone, but she detected someone's presence nearby. Twisting her head to the side, she viewed Harriet's humble face smiling down upon her. They exchanged greetings.

Harriet took a seat at the small table. Her jaw clicked as she wrung a cloth towel in her hands.

"How are you doing" Myaisha asked.

"Not bad—yet," Harriet said, her eyes twinkling as she wiped her hands on the dish towel. The older woman took a deep breath.

She appreciated Harriet's outlook. It summed up Mary's situation as well—not bad yet. Sliding to the edge of her chair, she leaned forward. "Harriet, you mentioned a deal you made with Candace about the purchase of this café. Did you and Candace ever exchange any money?"

"No. Mrs. Knight arranged the sale of my old place. The bank deposited the money in her account 'cause I signed some papers. She didn't give me no money." Paper crinkled as Harriet unwrapped a piece of candy. Placing a Tootsie roll in her mouth, she sucked slowly on the chocolate confection.

"So you were to make your money back from renting out the conference room?"

"Yeah, and get a cut of the money she made off her book."

Manuscripts, query letters, synopses. Myaisha thought about all the aspects of writing a book. At each step writers could be charged consulting fees, pay for critiques. As a published author, Candace would have gained credibility. It seemed she planned to sell her expertise and use their writing group as her platform. She felt another stab to her heart.

Every step forward brought to light another unfavorable aspect of her friend's character. Like dawn cresting over the horizon, her eyes opened wide. Realizing her mouth gaped open, she shut it.

She had approached this case all wrong. Instead of viewing Candace as a victim, if she considered her as being complicit in her own death… Eyes raised, she noticed Harriet watched her with concern. With a tight grin, she placed her hand over Harriet's.

"I apologize. I know you're struggling. I haven't forgotten my promise to help you. I've been trying to figure out who murdered Candace, and why."

"I know, sugah. It's just awful." Harriet placed her hands over hers and smiled. "First, Mrs. Knight, now her husband. Somebody really didn't like those two. They must've known something' they shouldn't."

"We'll get you through this. I'll figure something out." She squeezed her hands.

Traffic in the café picked up. Harriet left to attend to customers.

Considering her phone again, Myaisha made a call then finished her tea and muffin. A half hour later, Grace ambled over to her table. With a smile, she invited the private detective to be seated. "Thanks for coming. Would you like anything?" she asked.

For a moment, Grace studied the penciled menu on the wall above the cash register. "I'll order something in a minute. By the way, this is going on your expense report." Her large teeth smiled.

Myaisha chuckled. "Understood. I need your help." After detailing what she required, she excused herself. When she returned from the restroom, Grace had a large plate of food in front of her.

"This stuff's not half bad," Grace said between bites. "I thought it was gonna be some sort of earthy unflavored health food. It's actually pretty good."

"The café looks like a bohemian refuge from the outside, but it's all comfort soul food inside—with a touch of gentrification." Her phone buzzed and she quickly checked it. Deniece. She let it go to voice mail. She asked Grace, "So, do you think you can help? I need to get Mary out of jail. The best way to do that is to find out who committed the murder."

Holding a fork in her hand, Grace said, "You realize this person has already killed twice. Someone walking outside your house scared you—what do you think will happen when you go up against a murderer?' Grace wiped her mouth with her napkin.

Myaisha frowned across the small table at Grace. "I'll deal with that later. Mary needs me—I have to help her." Even as the words escaped her lips, she considered if it would ever come to her having to confront a murderer. Her jaw clenched as she re-evaluated her previous comment.

Saturday night and Todd was stuck at the station writing reports. The din in the station dropped off around 5 o'clock when most of the officers left. Todd poured creamer into his mug to mask its bitterness. He had to stop drinking the nasty police station coffee. He glanced up as his partner approached. He asked, "What happened?"

Placing a bag of chips and soda on the desk, Ian said, "The judge granted $500,000 bail. The doctor posted the bond."

"What are we missing?" Closing his eyes, Todd considered what he knew about the murder. He gazed vacantly over at the computer.

"Nothing," Ian said, chomping on his chips. "Both Knights were shot with the same caliber gun. This Thompkins woman bought a revolver a month before the murder. Now it has *conveniently* disappeared. We're supposed to believe she threw it away because she worried about her kids. She didn't just get these kids. If she worried about her children, why did she buy a gun in the first place? She bought it to kill the Knights."

Rubbing the stubble on his chin, Todd didn't speak. Several minutes passed as he stared up at the ceiling, and thought over their investigation. He side eyed his partner. "She doesn't fit. I don't believe that woman murdered anyone. The captain ordered us to arrest her, but I'm not buying it."

"She smacked the woman around in front of witnesses, *and* threatened to kill her," Ian said. "What more do you want?" He took a long swallow of his soda.

Todd slammed his hands down on the desk. His mug wobbled. "Evidence. The facts fit, but I can't see her as a murderer. Without the revolver, it's all conjecture."

"So what, now you're a lawyer?"

Drumming his fingers along the desk top, Todd shot his partner a blistering glare.

"The best killers don't look the part," Ian said. "She doesn't have an alibi for the first vic's murder, and her children are her alibi for the second murder. Her husband had a class at the college that night. And don't forget her motive. Knight screwed her over."

Extending her arms behind his head, Todd said, "Mrs. Knight suggested she use the equity in her home to invest in real estate. It's not illegal. Not all her clients were scammed. Some people tried to play the market and lost."

"You don't believe she had a motive?"

"It's weak. What about how Mr. Knight died?"

"What about it? One shot to the chest—easy as pie."

Leaned across the desk, Todd asked, "Do you think a woman—who knows nothing about guns—could take down a man with one shot to the chest?"

Ian shrugged. "We don't know she doesn't know anything about guns. That's her story. She knew enough to buy a gun. Besides, it could've been beginners luck."

"Possible, not likely." He opened his side drawer and got out a file. "Let's go over the evidence again." Todd spread papers around the desk and pointed at a photo of the office crime scene. "In Mrs. Knight's murder three bullets were fired. One lodged in our victim, another in the desk. The third bullet struck the wall behind the desk."

Examining the pictures, Ian picked up a stack of papers. He read the forensic report, then tossed it back onto the desk. "It shows rage, or an amateur killer. That's consistent with Mrs. Thompkins."

"But Mr. Knight's murder doesn't. One shot, straight into his heart."

Gathering the photos together, Ian scrutinized the crime scene again.

Todd asked, "How about the rest of the evidence? DNA? Fingerprints."

Reading the forensics report out loud, Ian said, "Nothing. Chemicals degraded the DNA from the hair. We can't test it against our suspect."

Tapping his pen against the desk, Todd picked up his mug. He considered the dark slurry liquid then grimaced, placing the cup as far away on his desk as possible. He asked, "Finger prints?"

"Consistent with the assistant, husband, victim. Some unidentified. From our suspect, nothing."

"Not even a partial?"

"Nope."

"Did we check Mrs. Knight clients against the other prints?" Todd asked.

Crunch, crunch. Ian finished his bag of chips, shook the crumbs from his hands. He shuffled papers around. "The ones who consented to be printed or had prints on file. Still a couple unknowns. We never got Kevin what's his name to come in, but we checked out his alibi. He was in Asheville with a fellow vet. Where's my notebook? The guy's name is in there somewhere."

Tidying up his desk, Todd gathered the documents together and returned them to a folder. "Wipe your mouth. Let's run through her client list again, business associates. If Mrs. Thompkins didn't kill our victim, we need to figure out who did. By the way, did we locate Mrs. Wayne?"

"Who?"

"Wayne, the teacher who smacked Mr. Knight around."

"Do you think she had something to do with the murders or you just bothered by what the doctor said?"

Irritated, Todd snapped back. "Did we question the teacher after Mr. Knight's murder?"

"No."

"Why not?"

Looking for something Ian said, "I'd have to ask Roberts. I assigned him to look into it."

Todd rose and collected the folder. "We need to find her."

"You think she's the killer or a victim?"

"Yes."

Before he could leave, Todd's phone rang. After several minutes on the phone, he hung up. He answered the question in his partner's eyes. "The lab. They matched a print from the chair in Mrs. Knight's office to Charles Marshall." His hand rested on the phone as he thought about the significance of the information. As he pondered over the facts, another phone call interrupted him. He ended the second call and powered down his computer. "Let's go."

"What's the hurry?" Ian swallowed the rest of his soda and chucked the can into the trashcan.

"I'm pretty sure we arrested an innocent woman."

Outside, Ian jogged to keep up with him.

Turning on the ignition, his partner jumped inside the vehicle and secured his seatbelt, as Todd sped out the lot.

Bracing against the dashboard, Ian asked, "What's the hurry?"

Droplets pelted the front window. He frowned. "I thought about what the doctor said?"

"The forensic guy?" Ian removed a candy bar from his jacket.

Rain drops poured from the slate gray sky, increasing in frequency as they popped off the windshield.

He adjusted the wipers. "No, the lady doctor. The internist."

"Uh huh. What about her?" Ian asked, munching on a candy bar.

"Remember her comment about the teacher."

"Yeah, so."

Facing forward, he gave Ian a side glance. "Dude, chew with your mouth closed."

"Dude, concentrate on driving and you won't see my mouth open."

His jaw tightened. "On Thursday, I tried to reach Mrs. Wayne. No answer. Her husband stated she left home Wednesday morning for work and never returned. They'd been having marital problems, so when she didn't return home he thought she wanted time to cool off."

"So." Ian tossed the empty candy wrapper into the cup holder.

"Just now, one of the patrol officers called. She thought we'd like to know about a missing person report filed by Mr. Wayne. His wife's been missing for two days." He could feel Ian's eyes on him.

"The day Adán died."

"No," Todd said, "the day we found his body."

"So, she could have killed Adán. The patrol officer witnessed her assault Mr. Knight at the house. She knew she'd be a suspect. Maybe she's on the run."

Behind a slow moving truck, Todd took his eyes off the road to glance over at his partner. "She's alibied for Mrs. Knight's murder."

"Who said the homicides were committed by the same killer?"

They locked eyes. An understanding passed between them. Todd focused back on the road.

Chapter 27

Opening the sliding glass door, Myaisha inclined her head toward the lush, wet back yard.

The labrador gazed over the yard, but refused to move.

Looking down at him, she asked, "You don't want to go outside? It's just a little rain."

Angling his head up toward her, he raised one eyebrow at a time. After a large yawn, he turned and settled on the floor, watching the rain.

"Fine." She shut the door and reclined on the couch. Pulling out her phone, she stared at a number in her phone. Hesitating, she spoke to herself. "Just do it." She pressed the call button. The phone rang three times before he answered.

A male voice asked, "Hello? Who's this?"

Sitting up straight, she ignored his tone. "Philip? Philip Scott? This is Myaisha Douglas, a friend of your ex-wife, Candace." Noises in the background prevented her from hearing him clearly, but she thought he cursed.

"Myaisha, the doctor?"

"Yes."

"Why are you calling me?"

A little taken aback by his attitude, she understood from his perspective her call would seem odd. It had been years since they spoke. After Candace's divorce, there was no reason for her to ever speak with him again. Their relationship began and ended with Candace. What little she remembered about him wasn't positive. It appeared his disposition hadn't changed over time.

"I'm sorry to bother you, Philip," she said, speaking quickly. "I won't take much of your time. It has to do with Candace. I'm sure you heard about her murder."

He snorted. "Yes, I heard. I'm surprised no one killed her sooner."

Her teeth clenched. His attitude grated on her nerves. Reminding herself she did this for Mary, she said, "I know it may be uncomfortable, but were you aware of Candace's business—"

"Scams."

Deep breaths. Perhaps this conversation had been a mistake. "Are you saying, she had been committing fraud during your marriage?"

"Candace was competitive. She had to succeed at everything, beat everyone—especially me."

"None of her businesses were legitimate?" she asked.

"Her first businesses were genuine, then someone invited her to join the Greensboro Alliance. It went to her head. I told her it wasn't a good idea, but she thought I was trying to hold her back. She became involved with some unscrupulous people."

"Is that why she forged your signature on the loan papers?"

"You know about that. She tried to play in the big leagues, but didn't have the cash. She asked me to cosign on a business loan for her. I said no, and told her to stay away from the Alliance. She was doing fine on her own, but she was impatient. She wanted to be successful overnight. Next thing I know she hooked up with Marshall."

"You know Charles Marshall?"

"Knew. Nothing but a hoodlum in a suit. I thought he wanted to get Candace in bed. I was wrong. He was pruning her for a partnership. The joke was on him, Candace learned and surpassed him."

"What happened with the forgery?"

He released an audible sigh. "I insisted the police file charges, but it did no good. The district attorney refused to prosecute."

"Why?" Her voice sounded immature even to her.

"I don't know. Probably involved in the scheme too—or profited from it. Maybe someone from the Greensboro Alliance called in some favors."

"How did you feel when you heard about her murder?"

He laughed. "You were her college friend right—the one from California? If you're upset about her death, I'm happy for you."

Shocked, she raised her voice. "Happy?"

"Yes, happy she died while you still considered her a friend. Look, I don't have time for this. Candace was a lying thief. I'm not surprised someone killed her. Good riddance."

The line went dead. She gaped at the phone.

Once Myaisha received notification that Mary's bond had been secured, she drove downtown to pick her up. Greg wanted to get the children from Pastor Matthew's home, so when Mary arrived the children would be at the house.

Making her way through the dark, rainy streets, Myaisha waited in the car for Mary to finish speaking with Keisha. The thought of Mary languishing in a jail cell all weekend, to her seemed intolerable. Myaisha only gave a passing thought to the money required to secure her freedom.

As her fingers clenched the steering wheel, Myaisha realized it would be temporary if the authorities didn't identify the real killer. *How many innocent people languish in prisons?* Shaking away the negativity, she cracked the car window to allow in cool air without the rain.

Once Mary settled into the car, Myaisha waved good-bye to Keisha and drove off. After giving Mary a moment to decompress, she used the drive home to get answers to her questions.

Her gaze remained focused on the road. She asked, "Are you feeling better?"

Shivering, Mary said, "Yes. Do you mind if I turn up the heater?"

"No, not at all," she said, because she was about to turn up the heat too, so to speak. While she waited at a red light, she side glanced at Mary. "Tell me what happened in Candace's office. Start from the beginning, and don't leave anything out." She turned to look her friend directly in the eye when she made the last statement.

Rubbing her arms, Mary said, "I called the office the day before on the pretense of scheduling an appointment. LaDonna mentioned Candace had appointment in High Point. I already knew LaDonna lunched with her boyfriend on Wednesdays, so I thought I would have plenty of time to search for my documents."

"Think, Mary. What time did you showed up?"

"I... Close to eleven. When I made it back to my car, the clock said 11:20."

"Could it have been earlier?"

Shaking her head, Mary warmed her hands in front of the vents. "No, maybe after, but not before."

Cursing as her tire sank into a pothole, she asked, "Did you find what you were looking for?"

"No. Seeing Candace there on the floor. I—I lost it. Her eyes fluttered and I almost wet myself."

Frustrated, she stopped the car and eyed Mary. "Think. Can't you remember anything to help your case? Did anything appear strange to you at the time? Out of place? Did you notice anyone in the building you knew?"

Pounding against the car seat, Mary screamed. "I can't! Don't you think I've tried? I was frightened. I'd been bad-mouthing Candace all over town—not to mention assaulting her. There I was, standing in her office with a gun in my purse. I only thought about getting out of there."

"Fine. What did you do after you left?"

"I had to slip out the back of the building because people were standing around the entrance. When I got in my car, I thought about where could I dispose of the gun."

"Why didn't you just keep it? You knew you didn't shoot her."

Mary pivoted toward her with a scowl on her face. "If I was capable of rational thinking, I wouldn't have been there in the first place. Goodness, if I had any brains at all, I wouldn't have fallen for Candace's scheme."

She couldn't argue with Mary's comment, having almost become a victim herself. *How would she have felt if she had lost a $100,000? Would she have been able to forgive; would she have held a grudge?* She tried to imagine being enraged to the point where she wanted to commit murder, but she couldn't. Her fingers clenched the wheel. She bit her lip, fighting back tears.

Her relationship with Candace had moved beyond the fiasco with the investment because she believed Candace had made an innocent mistake. Now she discovered it had been Candace's modus operandi. Philip said Candace's initial business operations had been legitimate. *What about the Greensboro Alliance led her astray?*

Nothing Mary said provided Myaisha with any new information toward identifying the murderer. After speaking with Greg and the children, she made the slow soggy drive back home.

Unable to sleep, Myaisha had been reading Candace's novel. Now, she placed the book on her side table. Careful not to step on a sleeping Boomer, she slung her legs over the side of the bed and went into the bathroom.

While she braided her hair, she meditated on the story about an African American girl escaping the racially charged small town she grew up in only to struggle with racism in the big city out west. The protagonist epitomized Candace.

Lathered in cocoa butter Myaisha returned to bed, glancing at the book. The engraved reflex-hammer she used as a bookmarker protruded from the top. A gift she gave to Sammy when he completed his neurology fellowship. Tears welled up in her eyes as she read the engraving. She reached past the book and retrieved her cell phone. Trembling fingers sent a quick text to Josiah, her son.

Love you. So proud.

Within two minutes she received a text back.

Love u 2.

Switching off the light, she listened to Boomer snore as she curled up in bed around her pillow. Sleep proved elusive. Twisting and turning, she lay on her back. Stared through the darkness up at the ceiling. She heard Boomer sniff and wine. Throwing aside the sheets, she checked the time—almost dawn.

She opened the sliding glass door leading to the backyard. Boomer trotted outside.

Shivering against the cold, she smelled the delicate scents of her gardenias. She shook away the drowsiness. As Boomer did his business, she thought about Candace's book. The premise wasn't original, but the writing was clean and the characters relatable. She'd known Candace for over twenty years. *How did she not know Candace could write?*

Jealous much. Becoming a published author had been her dream since forever. Candace seemed to succeed in everything.

As Myaisha sat on her darkened porch, crickets chirped in the background. Closing her eyes, she sent up a short prayer. Thankful for her son, she committed to being a better friend—and asked for help to complete one of her manuscripts and become a published author. Amen.

Chapter 28

Outside her office window, the cloudy, rainy day suited a Monday. Myaisha, however, felt upbeat. Her light patient schedule served as the first positive sign of summer. A calm Monday, such an oxymoron.

On impulse, she called Todd. His phone rang. When the voicemail clicked on, she left a message. "Hello. This is Myaisha Douglas. Please give me a call. I needed to discuss Candace Knight's case with you." After leaving her cell phone number, she hung up. She didn't have any new information for him, but she hoped he might share some with her. Also, she wanted to ask him if he truly believed Mary guilty.

Rain battered the windows of her medical office. Her staff left an hour ago. The storm accentuated the emptiness of the office. She could still taste the peanut butter sandwich she had for lunch. Maybe she should switch it up a little—bring a salad for lunch instead.

Sitting at her desk, she removed her bookmark from Candace's book and read the first few pages of the next chapter. Her intention had been to wait until the rain lessened before she drove home, but it continued unabated. Using the reflex hammer to mark her page, she placed the book in her purse. Time to go home and rest. Saturated, her mind begged for nourishment.

After locking up the office, she sprinted for her Honda, bypassing puddles, careful not to fall. She arrived at her car and jumped inside. As she closed the door, she happened to glance down. *Damn!* A flat. Rain pattered her hat as she surveyed the tire.

Resigned to being wet, she walked toward the trunk and slipped into a puddle. *Great, muddy shoes.* Pushing aside the latch for the trunk, she lifted the cover off the spare tire. It fought back, and she struggled to lift it over the lip of the trunk. Annoyed, she released the tire and let it fall back inside. *Dammit!* Another flat—no spare tire.

Exhausted and wet, she sat in the car. For a moment, she watched the rain beat steadily upon her windshield. Alright, plan B. She didn't have a car service plan. *Why not?* She would sign up for one when she got home. Revised plan B—Deniece. Her friend answered on the second ring.

Myaisha said, "Hey, lady. I need a ride. My tire's flat and so is the spare."

"Don't worry. I got you. Help's on the way," Deniece said.

Nowhere to go, she pulled out Candace's book and read some more. A chapter later, the sound of an approaching truck aroused her attention. *Did Deniece send a tow truck?* That's what she wanted to avoid. Her eyes strained to view the vehicle through the steamy water-soaked windows. A large grey double wide truck crept around the corner. *AJ?*

Setting the book down on the passenger seat, she remained in her car and watched as he brought his truck adjacent to her driver's side.

The window scrolled down. His large smile beamed down upon her, his charm infectious.

Rolling down her window, she grinned. "Well, hello."

He tipped his cap. "Hello, ma'am. I heard you were in need of assistance."

Shutting off his engine, he hopped out the cab and disappeared around the back of his truck. In under a minute, he rolled up with a tire.

Exiting her vehicle, she held an umbrella open over his head as he exchanged the tires. While trying to keep him dry, she admired his physique as he labored over the wheel. Large strong hands. Sinewy biceps. Full brown lips. Reminiscing over their first kiss, she felt her skin flush. Smells of wet grass faded as the scent of his cologne reached her nose, not too strong, enticing.

Minutes later the rain had stopped. In short time, he had the tire changed.

She tore her attention away from his biceps to her evaluate her vehicle.

He placed the flat tire in her trunk along with the spare. Wiping his hands on his jeans, he gave her an even bigger smile.

Her eyes drank in those lips. "Thank you. What do I owe you?"

Eyes soft, he sauntered over to her. Raised his eye brows and bit his bottom lip.

She laughed. "I meant, for the tire."

With his finger and thumb, he brought her chin up toward him and kissed her lips. "I got the tire from a friend. Don't worry about it."

Then she wouldn't. Hands on his chest, she tiptoed upward and returned his kiss.

His hands found her waist, and he wrapped her in his arms.

Quite a few minutes later, she broke their embrace. "Thank you, again," she said.

"For the tire or the kiss?"

"Both."

He squinted and examined her chin. "I think I got some dirt on you." He rubbed the spot. "Sorry. I'm making it worse."

"Don't worry about it. We're both drenched and dirty. AJ, I appreciate your help. I'm sorry Deniece called you."

"Myaisha, I told you, call me anytime. I meant it." He opened her car door.

Once she secured her seat belt, he closed the door. "Drive safely. I'll call you later. I have to get back to work." With a wave, he climbed into his truck and followed her out onto Elm Street. He drove south.

She turned north. Steering the Honda with one hand, she used the other to search for a napkin in her purse. She scrubbed her chin and evaluated the substance. *What was that?* It looked too black to be mud. She brought the fabric under her nose. It smelled like—oil?

It made sense. AJ smeared oil on her face when he touched her chin. She crumpled up the napkin and started to set it in the door handle receptacle when she recalled something. The odor triggered a memory. *Where had she smelled oil recently?*

Realizing she had stopped in the middle of the intersection, she cautiously navigated the car to the side of the road before she caused an accident. Her head rested against the steering wheel as she reflected upon what memory the scent triggered. It took a moment, but she remembered a similar odor in Candace's office on the day of the murder.

The odor had also been on her pants leg with the stray hair. When she got home she used stain remover and vinegar to eliminate the substance. *What would oil be doing on someone's hair?*

Not oil, tar. Coal tar shampoo. But Candace relaxed her hair. *Why would she use coal tar?* The stuff tore up your hair. She doubted her friend even did her own hair. Candace definitely had a stylist.

Rain drummed on the roof of the car, pounding in her ears. She strained to block it out. *Focus.* An idea started to coalesce in her mind. At first, she perceived a tenuous connection. An answer teased at the base of her brain. If she pushed too hard, it would go dormant. *Relax.* It would come to her. Seconds ticked by in rhythm with the rain drops pinging on her car. Her hands clenched the steering wheel.

Her body bolted upright in her seat. "Got it. I know who murdered Candace." She placed the car in gear and pulled away from the curb.

Everything made sense. All the pieces fell into place. Suddenly in a hurry, she navigated onto the main road, executed a U-turn and headed west. On the drive, she played out the scenario in her mind as she believed it occurred. Her fingers tapped the steering wheel as she recreated the crime in her head. Part of her refused to accept it could be true, but all the facts fit.

She heard her car tires humming along the road. Point by point, she reconsidered each fact. She had to be sure. Before she accused her friend of murder, she would give her a chance to turn herself in to the authorities. This was someone she loved and trusted. She had to consider the family members involved.

Perhaps she should speak with Keisha first. There were extenuating circumstances to consider. *Would a court understand?* As she exited the freeway, she vowed to stand by her friend. Candace stole from her, betrayed her. Myaisha didn't condone murder, but she couldn't stop loving someone so easily. What bothered her most was the lying.

Wipers flew across the windshield. The gray sky darkened as night fell. Glare from the street lights onto the wet pavement made for poor visibility.

She exited the freeway and entered a neighborhood which contrasted her own. Here the homes were older and the yards smaller. Landscaping lacked necessary attention, a testament to the income inequality of the residents. Because there were no sidewalks, she parked on the street adjacent to the mailbox. Rain sprinkled on her hat as she walked up the cracked asphalt driveway.

She steeled herself. Each step brought her closer to a killer. A friend she suspected of killing Candace—and Adán. She kept forgetting about Adán.

Knowing she approached the home of a murderer gave the neighborhood a sinister character. Stormy weather did not improve the atmosphere. Weeds covered the pathway. Rain dripped from the trees like a ticking clock. *Time's up.* A brief walk brought her to the front door. She knocked soundly on the wooden frame.

Whatever she expected, hadn't been what she found. Dressed in clothing from a fast-food restaurant, Lottie frowned at her. In an instant, she realized the office job had been a lie. *Too many lies.* The heart of these murders involved a lie. Both women stood there evaluating the other. Neither spoke.

She regained her composure first. She asked, "May I come in?"

A scowl spread across Lottie's face. "This isn't a good time, Myaisha. Come back—"

Bypassing Lottie, she made her way inside. "It can't wait. It's important." In the foyer, she held her position.

The door shut. Lottie said, "I just came back from work and I'm pretty tired. What can I do for you?"

Removing the book from her purse, Myaisha handed it to her. "I figured it out."

As her head shook, Lottie regarded the book as if touching it would befoul her. She walked away. On the left side of the hall, she pushed aside glass French doors, entering the study.

Myaisha followed.

After shutting the drapes, Lottie strode behind a large oak desk beside the floor length windows. Using a pencil from the desk, she scratched her scalp. "I don't know what you mean, but I'm really tired. Please, just leave."

This room held so many memories. Myaisha gazed at the warm tan walls housing shelves of books and knick-knacks. Family photos were prominently arrayed around the room. She had been in the study many times. Their writing group met here before Candace arranged for the conference room at Green Pastures café.

In that very room, she, Lottie and Mary discussed their manuscripts. Sometimes when no one had any writing to share they would discuss a new book they discovered. Lottie read her poems and short stories, expounding on her dreams of becoming published. Mary shared her poetry. They were the original members of the GWCWG. Now, one stood charged with murder, another committed the murder, and the third proceeded to mete out justice—not exactly the group's aspiration.

She watched Lottie retreat behind the desk where they wrote together, developed anthologies, and dreamed of what their group could accomplish. Myaisha asked, "Lottie, how could you? Candace was your cousin."

Unbuttoning her server's jacket, Lottie dropped it onto the desk. She collapsed into the chair, scratching her scalp with abandon. Large flakes cascaded onto the desk.

Hovered over the desk, Myaisha said, "Your psoriasis. That's how I figured it out."

Under knitted brows, Lottie frowned up at her. Squinted. "My psoriasis. This damned skin has been driving me crazy all my life." Her hands slammed down onto the wood desk top. One of the drawers popped open. She glared at the book.

Again, Myaisha offered it to her.

A snarl curled on her face. Lottie refused to accept the book, but viewed the cover. "That book—my book. I worked on it for so long, years. I thought it would be my entry into publishing—my break out novel. It would solve all our financial problems."

"Why did you lie to me about the job?" She placed the book on the desk, glancing at Lottie's work uniform.

Her hands scratching at her scalp, Lottie removed one of her hair extensions and tossed it into the trash can beside the desk. "Candace, that heifer, she's screwed me all my life." She plucked the book up from the desk and flipped through the pages. Her eyes landed on Candace's autograph. Snapping the book shut, she dumped it into the garbage can.

Myaisha touched her hand. "Why?"

Snatching her hand away, Lottie's eyes brimmed with tears. "Because we needed the money, that's why. Do you know how long I tried to get my book published? I queried agents and publishers for years. I asked Candace if she knew people, if she could reach out to her contacts, but she declined. Said she didn't know anything about publishing." Shouting, Lottie said, "She didn't know anything about how to get *my* manuscript published, but after I sold her the book rights all of a sudden she's published overnight."

Rain dripped off the gutters. A silence descended upon them. The room felt hollow.

Her voice soft, Myaisha said, "Your story is poetic. From the moment I started reading it, I knew it didn't sound like Candace, even her emails were painful to read. Poor grammar, coarse language. I thought I misunderstood her, and I was right. I never knew Candace. But the story..." Her eyes turned toward the book, sticking out the trash can. "Your story is good, Lottie. You should be proud of yourself."

"I would be if I hadn't given up." Lottie wiped her nose.

Myaisha sat on the opposite side of the desk. She asked, "Why did you let Candace publish the book under her name?"

Jumping up from her seat, Lottie plucked another extension from her head and discarded it into the trash. She peeled at the plaques on her scalp. "I didn't let her. Herman needed special treatments. The medical bills were horrendous. We borrowed against the house. Candace helped us with a line of credit. I knew we shouldn't trust her but the medical bills destroyed my credit, and Herman... He couldn't work."

Myaisha's hand reached out to touch Lottie. "You should have asked for help. I would have—"

Smacking her hand away, Lottie asked, "You would have what? What could you do? You were too busy with your own grief. And Josiah. I couldn't take money out of your baby's mouth." A tear dropped from her eyes as Lottie glanced at the book. "I sold the manuscript to Candace. All rights and ownership. She gave me twenty thousand dollars. Can you believe that? At the time it seemed like a blessing."

Blood oozed from the plaques on Lottie's hand where she scratched.

"When Mary and I started the writing group we thought we'd be published in a year—maybe two. But no—nothing. Suddenly Candace is interested in writing. She offered us a meeting place at the café. I spoke with Harriet the day after the group met. Candace planned to make money off our group. Everything she touched she ruined."

Myaisha helped with the story. "When Candace announced her book at our meeting you were surprised."

"I was flabbergasted. How did she get published? When she told me she used my book, published with her name. I felt like she stole my voice. Ripped it right outta my throat."

The night their writing group met came back to Myaisha's mind. She remembered the argument between Lottie and Candace she had witnessed. "You spoke to her that evening," she said.

"I only asked for a percentage of the royalties. She laughed. I asked to share recognition, receive some public acknowledgement.

Nothing. She refused every request I made." Tears splashed on the desk. Lottie clung to the desk with both hands as she leaned over it.

"But murder? What did it solve?" Myaisha asked.

Head lifted, a crooked grin crossed Lottie's face. Her face pivoted slowly from side to side. "I didn't kill her. I wanted to. I thought about it day and night, but I didn't do it. I didn't."

On reflex, Myaisha's body retreated from the disturbing expression on her friend's face. Glancing down at the desk, she viewed blood on Lottie's hands.

A lone, limp braid lay her hand as Lottie scowled. "You never understood how vicious Candace could be—absolutely ruthless. She said she couldn't help me without revealing she committed a fraud, which she would never do. She got a taste of the legal system when Philip had her arrested for forging his name on those business documents. She wasn't going to put herself in that situation again."

Coming from behind the desk, Lottie took a step toward Myaisha. "I begged, told her I had to work part-time at some stupid takeout joint in addition to my full-time job to support Herman. You know what she said?"

Myaisha clenched her fist to keep her fingers from shaking. "No. What did she say?"

"Candace said I married a loser. That's what she called my husband. Said I married an old man and a loser." Rearing her head back, Lottie laughed. Loud, maniacal, uncontrolled. Her laughter petered off into silence.

Rain tingling off the window panes became the only sound in the room

The heavy beating of Myaisha's heart almost drowned out the rain. Lottie's behavior worried her. Her friend was experiencing a mental breakdown. With her left hand, Myaisha searched for her cell phone in her purse. All the time, her eyes never abandoned Lottie's face.

Eyes bloodshot, Lottie cried soft sobs. Another braid fell to the ground. Head tilted to the side, Lottie walked around the desk and approached her. "She called my husband a loser."

Myaisha's intention had been to convince her friend to go to the police and confess her guilt. She wanted to secure legal representation for Lottie in order to obtain the lightest sentence possible. Given the present circumstances, she recognized her friend required professional help—medical assistance. She had to try. Her voice low, she spoke as if to a child. "So you shot her?"

A slow grin crept up Lottie's cheeks, it reached her ears, pulling her eyes farther apart. Her head tilted awkwardly to the opposite side. Tears streamed down her face. "She called my Herman a loser. I couldn't let her do that. I begged her. She called him a loser. I wanted to kill her. It would have been like putting down a rabid dog. Candace needed killing. But I didn't do it. I told you. I didn't do it. I didn't."

Had she ever really known any of her friends? These people she had trusted with her life, her son's life. In the span of two weeks, she discovered Candace swindled her clients, Mary purchased an unregistered handgun, and Lottie suffered a mental breakdown—oh, and she murdered two people.

She tried not to look down at Lottie's hand. When the drawer flew open, her friend removed the weapon now pointed in her direction. If she focused on the gun, she wouldn't be able to convince her friend to turn herself in. Peeking out the corner of her eye, she detected blood dripping down the back of Lottie's other hand.

Her hair a jumbled mess, Lottie removed another braid.

Braids. The extensions could be produced from Asian hair. Myaisha's mind focused on everything—anything—but the weapon in her friend's trembling hand. As she spoke, her voice seemed to come from somewhere outside of herself. She said, "Lottie, we have to call the police."

A grin hung on her face and Lottie's head swiveled in a half circle. "I can't. I told you. I didn't do it."

"Then where did the gun come from?" Myaisha asked.

Craning her head downward to view her hand, Lottie appeared not to recognize it, not to understand. Then she smiled and thrust the gun at her. "Oh. I'm showing you our gun so you can check it. See, it's not been fired."

She recoiled as Lottie leveled the gun at her chest. "Okay, Lottie. Give me the gun. I'll have it tested. Prove you had nothing to do with the murder." Managing to take one step toward her, Myaisha stopped when a voice spoke from the door.

"I don't think so. Don't move, Myaisha." Herman rolled his wheelchair inside the French doors at the entrance to the study.

From the corner of her eye, Myaisha glimpsed him. Hesitating, she refused to take her vision off Lottie. "It's okay. Lottie's going to give me the gun."

Ignoring her, he spoke to his wife. "Lottie girl, give me the gun."

Her attention ping-ponging between Myaisha and Herman, spasms racked Lottie's body. One hand held the gun while the other scratched her scalp.

With her head facing Lottie, Myaisha viewed him from the corner of her eye. "Herman, you have to help me convince her to go to the authorities."

Using the automatic controls on his wheelchair, Herman maneuvered further into the study.

In concert with his movements, Myaisha inched closer toward the exit. Hoping Lottie would focus on her husband, she planned to escape and send for help. However, when she moved, Herman stopped.

He angled his chair in her path. The wheelchair blocked her exit. With a stern glare, he raised his voice. "Lottie, bring me the gun."

In front of the desk, Lottie trembled. Her brows bent in confusion, she cried.

With the gun still pointed at her, Myaisha knew she had to alert the police. She tried to unlock her phone—surreptitiously dial 911—from inside her pocket. *Stall.* She said, "Herman, we have to contact the police. Lottie isn't responsible for what she did. We can hire a lawyer, get her off on diminished mental capacity."

Confusion crisscrossed his forehead. He grimaced. "You think I'd let them take my Lottie to jail for something she didn't do."

Myaisha's face fell, her head turned toward him. She regarded him, seated in his wheelchair. Piecemeal, her eyes enlarged.

Returning her gaze, he nodded. "Candace deserved to die. Do you know how many lives she destroyed?" He tried to roll further into the room, but when he wheeled forward, she inched closer to the French doors.

"No, you don't," he said, pointing his chair in her direction. "You should've stayed out of it, Myaisha. I didn't want to hurt you. I've always liked you."

"You don't have to hurt me, Herman. We can go to the police. Explain—"

"No, we can't!"

His shout stopped Lottie's crying, but her shaking increased. He held out his hand toward his wife and apologized. Raising both hands toward her. "I'm sorry, baby. I didn't mean to upset you. I did this for you—all for you. I love you. I didn't mean for you to have to struggle taking care of me."

His chair inched forward, closer to Lottie.

Myaisha's feet pivoted toward the exit.

He faced her. Leered. "Candace didn't suspect a thing. I asked her if I could stop by the office—told her it would only take a moment. She agreed. Never figured a man in a wheelchair could be a threat. No one did. No one ever does."

Ignoring her dire circumstances, she thought back on the crime scene. She realized the tires on Herman's wheelchair transferred the hairs to the office linoleum floor.

"I don't know how many people saw me enter her office," he said. "It didn't matter. I noticed a long time ago people don't look closely at people in wheelchairs. It makes them uncomfortable."

Her brows furrowed. Stuck for the present, she might as well get her questions answered. "Why Adán?"

"He knew too much—got greedy and demanded money. He called Lottie after the funeral. Told her he knew about the manuscript. She told me, and I sent him a text from her phone, arranged to meet up. When he saw me, he got a surprise. The fool was no better than Candace. A user."

Advancing toward his wife, he paused when Myaisha gained upon the door. She knew he would have to choose between going for the gun or her. Unsure of what Lottie would do, she intended to run for the door at the first chance. She had squeezed all over her phone, but hadn't managed to connect with 911 yet.

"How did you kill Adán?" she asked.

"Easy. I barely had to get out the car."

"You can't kill me." She spoke with more confidence than she had. "I'm your friend, your doctor. We've known each other for years. You've taken care of Josiah, taught him how to fish, to build a birdhouse."

"It's your fault. You should have minded your own business. I can't let anything happen to Lottie. I'm all she's got. Right, babe." He smiled, trying to get Lottie's attention.

Pulling another braid from her head, she stared at the gun. Her eyes glossy with tears.

Holding out his hands, he said, "Lottie, give me the gun. Bring it here, baby."

The gun pointed in various directions as she trembled. "Herman, I—I'm scared."

Encouraged by her response, Myaisha tried to reason. "Candace and Adán are dead, Lottie. They were murdered. Are you going to let me become victim number three?"

When his turned toward her, with a strange glint in his eye, Myaisha understood she wouldn't be victim number three. *Kelley.* "Why? What did Kelley do? She was no threat to you."

He smirked. Gripping the arms of his wheelchair, he started to rise out of his chair, "She stole the manuscript from Candace's safe. I had no choice. I didn't know how much she knew. She became a liability, and now you are too."

Those last words escaped from his mouth as he leaped forward and jumped on her. They wrestled. She kicked his legs out from underneath him. He grabbed onto her as he fell toward the ground. She squirmed loose from his grasp and sprinted for the door. As she rounded the corner out of the room, she saw him hobbling toward Lottie. In the foyer, she reached the front door, her hand encircled the knob.

A shot rang out and then a cry. Lottie screamed for help.

One more step and she would be outside. Free.

Lottie cried out. "Myaisha, help me. Please! Herman needs help."

Her doctor instincts overrode her sense of self-preservation. When she returned inside the study she spotted him on the ground. Arthritic hands clutched his chest, he became dyspneic. In an instant, she ran to his side. Kneeling down, she assessed his vitals. *ABCs.* A second later he lay flaccid, body limp. Before she could direct Lottie to call 911, she heard police sirens in the distance.

She had managed to dial 911. *Good job, girl.* All her attention and energy was now directed at saving Herman's life. Placing his head in a neutral position, she delivered two rescue breaths and started chest percussions.

A weeping Lottie knelt beside her praying. Between tears, she said, "Please save him. I know he tried to kill you, but he's all I got. Please."

Chapter 29

Curled up on a plastic chair in the corner of the police department, Myaisha watched the officers performing their work as they moved around the station. Wondering how they could function as if nothing tragic happened, she realized it was similar to how doctors operated in the midst of tragedy—life prevails.

The water bottle in her hand remained unopened. She wasn't thirsty, not even hungry. She felt spent. Images of the evening flashed through her mind, transporting her back to Lottie's house.

An ambulance had arrived while she performed CPR. Police soon followed. She had explained what occurred to the paramedics, and gave them a synopsis of Herman's medical history. Lottie accompanied him in the ambulance, and EMS sped away.

Myaisha's shoulders ached from the chest compressions. Transferred to the police station by the detectives, she spent hours regurgitating the events of the evening. She explained how she reached the conclusion Lottie murdered Candace, only to discover her error when Herman confessed his guilt. The police permitted her to call

Deniece and Josiah, but three hours passed in the dumpy chair before Todd returned.

His soulful eyes regarded her. She watched him approach, braced for more questions. Her eyes fell on the fedora in his hand.

"You dropped this in the house," he said. "I thought you might want it back."

Her hand trembled as she reached for it. Examining it, she wondered whether to put in on her head, or leave it behind. No more Easy Rawlings for a while.

He crouched down beside her chair. "Sorry we kept you this late. I can take you home."

She unwrapped herself from the chair, stretched her body free. "I'll be fine. I need to pick up my car. It's at Lottie's house."

"Come on, I'll take you. I have to return to the crime scene anyway."

No argument from her. She wanted to go home, hug Boomer, and take a long hot shower. Maybe have a drink somewhere in between—or two.

As they exited the police station, she walked behind him. Caught sight of herself in the glass double doors. She looked frightful. Placing the fedora on her head, she felt a little better.

Bleary eyed, she climbed into the front seat and leaned back against the head rest. They traveled in silence. For the first half of the trip, she zoned out. A blur of large trees whizzed by her window. It would take her a while to process everything. Her eyes started to close.

Stopped at the street light, he asked, "You gonna be okay?"

Wiping sleep from her face, she sat up and regarded his profile. He didn't appear disturbed by what transpired—of course these people weren't his friends. He was a police officer doing his job. Her gaze drifted out the window again. "I'll be fine. Thank you."

"I tried to return your call."

"Sorry I missed it." From her periphery, she noticed his chin tense. She sensed he prepared to deliver bad news. She asked, "What is it?"

He frowned. "How did you know I was about to say something?"

"I noticed your jaw."

"I thought you might like to know we found Mrs. Wayne."

"Where?"

"The woods behind her school. A jogger found her, actually the dog did—must have picked up on the scent."

Her nose wrinkled. "How did she die? Did he shoot her too?"

"No. He struck her on the back of the head."

She wrapped her arms around her chest, rubbed her arms. "I don't understand about Kelley."

"Mrs. Wayne had copies of the manuscript. Her husband found them squirreled away in their apartment after we notified him about her death. Even if she hadn't understood what they meant, she posed a threat. Also, I believe he planned to frame her for the other murders. We found both Rolex's on her body and a phone that appears to have belonged to Mr. Knight. The missing laptop was under the passenger seat of her car."

"But he struck her on the back of the head?"

"I guess something went wrong with his plan. When he couldn't frame her for the murders, I guess he went ahead and killed her."

"Thank you for telling me. I wish I had figured it out sooner. I had it all wrong."

He turned the corner onto Lottie's street. "That's why I called you. After we discovered Mrs. Wayne murdered, I worried about you. When I listened to your message, I called you back. I put out an alert on your car when you didn't answer."

She acknowledged his comments with a silent nod.

He steered the vehicle down the road. People lined the street or sat on their porches, ogling for a view of the crime scene.

"Mrs. Williams had been at work during Mrs. Knight's murder. We confirmed her alibi with her employer at the burger joint, cleared her of the homicide from the start. Tomorrow morning we'll return to the Bradley Building. Search for anyone who remembers seeing Mr. Williams in his wheelchair."

"Hmm. It's like *The Purloined Letter* by Edgar Allen Poe. Hidden in plain sight."

"I'm not a Poe fan, but I can tell you Mr. Williams had never been a suspect. Because he wasn't a business associate of Mrs. Knight, he never made our list." He pulled up behind her car and parked. He eyed her. "You should have called us."

"I didn't expect things to end this way. It was foolish, but I wanted to give her a chance to obtain legal representation before she surrendered to the authorities." She heard the weariness in her voice as she spoke.

He turned to face her. "A whiff of oil led you to a murderer?"

She nodded. "The smell reminded me of Lottie because of her psoriasis. She uses a coal tar shampoo. It smells horrible. If you ever smelled it, you wouldn't forget the scent. Candace's book lay on the passenger seat of my car. Oil, Lottie, and the book—I re-evaluated everything I knew. Candace's appointment and the unlocked doors."

"It would explain why Mrs. Knight didn't have her gun out. She wasn't afraid of a man in a wheelchair."

"Poor, Lottie. A trial will be devastating for her family." She noticed Todd's jaw tighten again. She sighed— more bad news.

He said, "Mr. Williams died at the hospital. Heart attack. He never regained consciousness."

A tear escaped her fatigued eyes. Her mouth refused to open. She wanted to thank him for informing her about Herman, but couldn't find her voice. After a minute, she cleared her throat. "I should go to be with Lottie."

"They admitted her to the psychiatric floor. She had a complete breakdown, beat her head on the floor, pulled out her hair. It was horrible. She had to be sedated." After his statement, he exited the vehicle.

She got out and walked toward her car.

Several police cars and a forensic van occupied the driveway.

He watched as she settled into her vehicle. Motioned for her to roll down her window. "Thanks doc-Myaisha. I appreciate your help."

Tears welled up in her eyes. "What did I do? I accused my friend of murder. I made a mistake."

"You helped. Go home. Get some rest." He took a step away, and turned back. "Oh, and don't do it again."

Steering away from the curb, from the rearview mirror Myaisha viewed him standing in the street. By the time she reached the corner, he had entered Lottie's house. She signaled and turned onto the main street.

Chapter 30

One more patient chart. Myaisha typed faster. She had plans for the afternoon and she wanted to leave as soon as possible. Gazing down at the floor where Boomer lay on his back, legs spread wide, she said, "I'm almost done."

He whined.

"I mean it this time."

A short bark, he rolled over and curled up beside her desk.

Two knocks sounded on her door. Dina stuck her head in the doorway wearing a shielded face mask.

She sighed. "Dina—"

"Doctor, there's a woman here to see you. Your lawyer."

She withdrew her reprimand and stood. Candace's estate lawyer entered. Myaisha offered her a seat.

Setting her briefcase on the chair, the lawyer remained standing. "I can't stay," she said. "I wanted to let you know we discovered a bank account Mrs. Knight had in High Point. Only a small amount of money remained in the account, but she had a safety deposit box, which contained a large envelope." The lawyer removed said envelope from her briefcase.

In silence, Myaisha accepted the package.

"We inventoried the contents, but I felt—well, when you read the letter inside, you'll understand why I brought them over to you."

She thanked the lawyer.

After the attorney left, she finished her charts and closed down her browser. "See, Boomer. Mommy told you she would finish on time."

One bark and he jumped to his feet. Whining, he circled in front of the door.

Before she made her exit from the back door, she said good night to her staff. It had been a long, difficult week. She was looking forward to the weekend. As she walked toward her Honda, a familiar car came around the corner and cruised up beside her vehicle.

Opening her car door, she allowed Boomer to hop inside. She scrolled down the windows and waited.

Grace sauntered over. "I'm glad I caught you before you left. I'll email my bill, but I wanted to check in on you. I heard about Monday night. How you doing?"

"Fine, I guess. Thanks for coming by."

"No problem. Right now, you're my best client." Grace laughed. "Anyway, I wanted to ask you about the Greensboro Alliance. What do you want me to do with the information?"

"Are you done?"

"I collected a lot, but I can dig further."

"No, just give me what you have right now. It might come in handy when I have to sort out the estate."

After she shared more information about her research, Grace departed.

Turning over the ignition, Myaisha settled in the car.

Boomer barked.

"Okay. We're going this time. I promise." They headed for the park.

The setting sun glistened off the murky pond in the center of the park. Ducks waded in the water. Squirrels played hide and seek up the willowy limbs of the bamboo colored crepe myrtle trees. Tiny pink flowers littered the earth. Myaisha wore a light sweater as wind stirred the air.

Seated on a bench, she tethered Boomer where he could sniff around the grass while she reviewed the contents of the envelope from Candace's estate lawyer. Several sentimental items were inside, a banana slug key ring, a picture of her and Candace on the Santa Cruz boardwalk, and a letter. It didn't take long for her to identify Candace's distinctive handwriting on the scented colored paper.

In an instant, she'd been transported back to coastal California. Memories of her and Candace lying on the field at the base of Cowell college overlooking the Pacific Ocean flashed across her mind. She smiled, remembering how they would braid each other's hair, while discussing their classes, and planning their futures. Tears pooled in her eyes, she read the letter.

Mya, if you're reading this I'm dead. Charles Marshall or one of the administrators from the Alliance killed me. I'm not going to say more except stay away from them. They're ruthless. Believe me. Those bastards would kill you and not think twice. I made you my executor because I trust you, and I love you. I've always loved you. I'm sorry about the investment business. I didn't mean to cheat you. People called me a bitch and I was. I worked my ass off. They expected to invest and become rich with no work and no risk. If they had listened to me, they would've been. No short cut is honest. I don't regret anything I did, except you. I'm glad you backed out, but you put me in a difficult spot. I had to hustle to get the money somewhere else, but you were right.

I envied you. Your family, your marriage. Never change. When you think of me, picture Santa Cruz. Remember what we shared. I would tell you to keep the money and retire early, but I know you'll give it all away. Don't get mad about what people say about me. I said worse about them. The only opinion I ever cared about was yours. Love, C

Myaisha's tears dotted the paper. Drying her eyes, she returned the letter to the envelope and then into her purse. She waited in the park with Boomer. Dogs barked. Children laughed. Seated near the pond, she restrained him on his leash.

Minutes passed before a gray double wide truck parked next to her Honda. She smiled. Seconds later, AJ hopped out the truck and placed a baseball cap on his head. He opened the back door of the cab and a brown labrador leaped out. The key fob beeped and he and his dog headed in her direction.

Wagging his tail against the table leg, Boomer sat up. He tugged at the leash and whined. Patting his head, she directed him to sit. With a bark of discontent, he obeyed. He whimpered and waited for this unexpected arrival.

Stopping a few feet away from her and Boomer, AJ said, "This is Zoey. Does Boomer play nice?"

"Yes. He's great with dogs." She relinquished the lead a little.

AJ allowed Zoey to sniff Boomer. Accepting the intrusion, Boomer waited for his turn. As the dogs conducted their introductions, AJ took advantage of Boomer's distraction to give her a kiss.

Acquainted with each other, the dogs fell into step together. Myaisha and AJ led them through the park. Tugging on their respective leashes, the labs tried to get at other animals.

With a watchful eye on their fur babies, she and AJ strolled casually. She felt his arm occasionally brush up against hers.

"How's it going with the estate?" he asked.

With her floppy sun hat shielding her eyes, she stopped to let Boomer relief himself against a tree. "It's going to take time. Because of Candace's illicit businesses, we have to wait until the authorities complete their investigations into the real estate fraud in Charlotte. Then there's the business with the Greensboro Alliance."

Holding Zoe's leash, AJ said, "I read something in the *Greensboro Times* about Charles Marshall. The police located him in Florida trying to catch a flight out of the country."

"I know. I heard about it on the radio. The estate lawyer hired an accountant to go over Candace's finances, separate the fraudulent businesses from the legitimate stuff."

"Can you sell the house?"

"Yes. It should sell quickly."

"Good. I'll be glad when this is over for you."

"Once the accountants determine which monies are legal, I hope to financially assist Candace's former clients—help people like Mary and Harriet, who were deceived."

Glancing over at her, AJ said, "When I heard what you did—You could've been hurt, Myaisha. Or worse."

"I didn't think about it. I only worried about Mary going to prison. That's all that mattered."

"You matter." He held her hand.

We matter. Few people received a second opportunity at happiness. She had one. Fingers entwined, together they watched Zoey and Boomer trot along the trail, barking at squirrels.

As the sun descended over the trees, she appreciated the cerulean sky. Breathed in the woody air and let it out slow and long. Glancing up at AJ, she admired his distinctive sculpted features. Different from Sammy, but the same. Both strong black men—good men. Two in one lifetime. Squeezing AJ's hand, she cuddled against his muscled arm.

He kissed her forehead as they sauntered along the trail.

She reflected upon second chances and considered a trip to Santa Cruz.

If you enjoyed *Murder Is Revealing*, please leave a review. They are extremely valuable for self-published authors.

Please check out my website, , and discover other books in the series, *Murder In Gemini* and *Murder Between Neighbors*, and experience more adventures of the Greensboro Women of Color Writing Group.

Prefer paranormal urban fantasies? Learn about *Dark Blood Awakens* and *Dark Blood Curse*. Thriller readers will appreciate *Hollow Voices*, a psychological thriller.

www.ingramcontent.com/pod-product-compliance
Lightning Source LLC
Chambersburg PA
CBHW011206190726
48288CB00013B/3340